The Inevitable Past

The Inevitable Past

CARRIE JANE KNOWLES

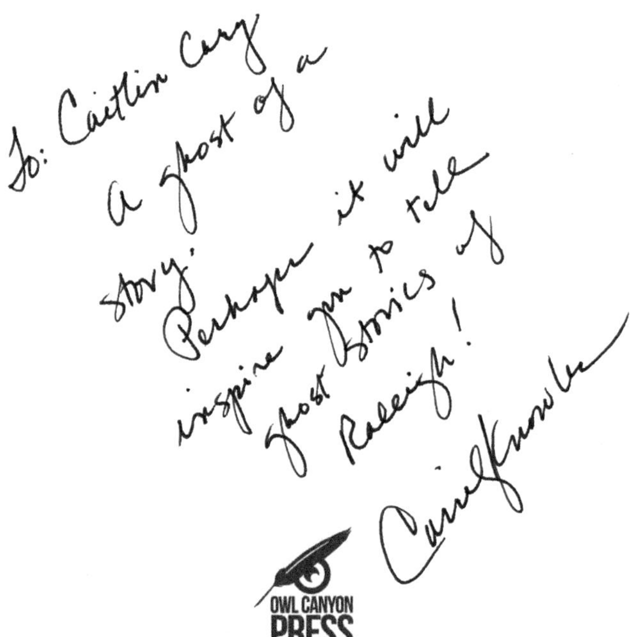

First Edition, 2020

Library of Congress Cataloging-in-Publication Data

Knowles, Carrie Jane.
The Inevitable Past —1st ed.
p. cm.
ISBN: 978-1-952085-01-7

Owl Canyon Press
Boulder, Colorado

OTHER BOOKS BY
CARRIE JANE KNOWLES

The Last Childhood:
A Family Story of Alzheimer's

Lillian's Garden

Ashoan's Rug

A Garden Wall in Provence

Black Tie Optional:
17 Stories

A Self-guided Workbook
and Gentle Tour on How to Write
Stories From Start to Finish

☜☜☜

COLUMNIST
Psychology Today: Shifting Forward
psychologytoday.com/shifting-forward

☜☜☜

2014 NORTH CAROLINA
PIEDMONT LAUREATE IN SHORT FICTION

☜☜☜

CJANEWORK.COM

I am the grandmother you never knew. The one who vanished. The unsolved crime.

I never held your father in my arms. Only in my heart. But I was with him every step of his life.

As I am with you.

I am your blue eyes and your fair skin: a flutter, a thought, a whisper. I use dreams to guide you over the rough spots my life has created for you.

My dreams are your dreams. I am part of you. What happened to me the night your father was born has shaped your life. I rest deep in your DNA.

I cannot change that. I wish I could. My experiences have made you slow to trust. Shadows make your heart race. I know.

But, the good of me is in you as well. You are strong because I was strong. You fight back. You speak your mind. You have courage and are curious. You are smart like your father. You are the best of me.

It is time for you to know who I was and who you are because of all that happened. And why I have come to you.

I need your help.

1893

ONE

I was twenty-two and restless when my life changed. Twenty-two and dreaming of living in the bright city of Chicago, by a lake so big it was impossible to see what was on the other side. Back then I wanted nothing more than to be living in a world that was anything but flat farmland filled with rutted rows of corn and beans, and mud when it rained. I was not ready for what would happen.

There was nothing on the farm for me. By the fall of 1893, after I had turned twenty-two and it was clear I had no prospects for marriage, I knew, just as I knew the sun would come up, then go back down again, that when my parents died my older brother and his wife would inherit the farm. And, that when my younger brother took a wife, he would be given a few adjoining acres of land where he could build a house and begin a new life.

But, as the unmarried daughter, tottering on the edge of becoming a spinster, I would not inherit anything and would eventually become a burden to one or both of my brothers if I did not leave.

Unmarried, I was without prospects of either land or support. My mother worried about me. My father and brothers didn't speak of it, as if by speaking, they would stir a troubling wind that might threaten to unsettle the comfort of our predetermined lives.

At nineteen, twenty, then twenty-one, and finally twenty-two, I was long past old enough to be married and starting a family of my own.

Those awkward barren years after high school were a strange and unsettling time for me.

Not that my attitude, as my mother used to say, helped at all. To be clear, I never once knelt by my bed at night and prayed for God to send me a husband. I had spent a lifetime watching my mother plant, harvest, cook, clean, and wait patiently at the end of each day for those few moments of evening light when she could at last sit quietly in her chair by the living room window and work on her mending or, if she was lucky, stitch together another square for a quilt. I loved my mother, but I did not want what she had. I wanted something more. I ached for a different life that was my life. I don't think my mother understood why I had to go away.

You've never seen pictures of me. In fact, there was only one: the picture that was taken when I graduated from high school. In that picture, I was wearing a long, gathered skirt and blouse I'd made from a bolt of soft grey linen. I wasn't the most skilled seamstress, so I concentrated more on making something that was simple and serviceable rather than layered with ruffles and finery. I gathered a third of the skirt material in the front, then bunched the rest of it in the back as though I had thought about making a bustle, but decided against it once the fabric had been cut. I wasn't much for fashion. I didn't want anything fussy. I wanted something comfortable. I didn't care for the large leg of mutton sleeves everyone in my class adored, so, instead, I cut long thin sleeves for the blouse and created a small standup collar that neatly circled my neck. No lace.

Although not much of a seamstress, I was good with embroidery, and, in my one flight of fancy, I sewed fifteen tiny pearl buttons down the front of the blouse and finished each buttonhole in silky, deep grey floss using a pretty French satin stitch. I was particularly proud of the buttonholes I'd made. No one could or would see them but me, and I guess that was the point. They were my secret pleasure, hidden beneath the fifteen mother-of-pearl buttons I sewed on. I had a bit of dark blue fabric left over from the Sunday dress I had made the year before and used it to create a sash that I wrapped around my waist and tied in the back.

While I chose a serviceable, all-season weight, grey linen, some of the girls in my class made fancier graduation dresses out of delicate pale pink or creamy white voile, trimmed in hand crocheted lace. My fellow classmates made no secret that their fancy graduation dresses would also be their wedding dresses. When you grew up on a farm, you learned the value of living a practical life.

The ensemble I created was clearly not meant to be a wedding gown. It was, however, the outfit I would wear to church on Sundays and to my brother's wedding the following December. There was to be no wedding in my future. But, I did not know that then.

As was the style of the day, I wore my hair pulled back, twisted neatly in a bun and secured with thin metal hairpins. I carried myself well. I wasn't ugly like you might think someone in a small town who was twenty-two and unmarried might be. Most, including my mother, described me as nice looking, but plain. I read a lot.

I didn't have a high school sweetheart. That was not meant to be. When I turned twenty, a widowed neighbor, ten years my senior, came calling. To his and everyone else's surprise, I refused his modest proposal of a chance to step into the worn slippers of his dead wife in order to raise his three young children and help tend his farm.

That's when everything shifted. Sensing that some unchanging life course had now been put into motion, my mother gave me the wedding quilt that she and the ladies of the church had pieced for my dowry.

Whether you marry or not, she said, you are going to need something to keep you warm at night.

It was a beautiful blanket of tiny-patched gold, green and brown squares. I was happy to have it. The nights on the farm were cold, but not nearly cold enough for me to hang my future on a loveless life of housework and raising another woman's children just to keep warm.

You're not getting any younger, my father warned me.

Or any prettier, my brothers added.

My best friend in that entire flat world of endless farmland was Georgette. She was two years older than I. What we had in common was that we both liked to read. When we were growing up she'd come over to our house after church for Sunday supper nearly every week, or I'd go to her home. When the table was cleared and things washed and put away, we'd take our books outside and sit on a blanket under a tree and read. We'd read and sometimes draw pictures. Georgette was a better artist than I was, but I was better in math. We knew each other well through the books we read and didn't have to talk much.

Georgette had graduated from high school two years before I did. Back then, if you had finished high school and could pass the state teacher's exam, you could teach. I was sixteen and a half and Georgette was just three months shy of turning nineteen when she became Miss Georgette and I became her student.

I had read everything she had read and knew all my tables and could calculate a whole mess of big numbers in my head much better than she could, but I never gave her any trouble in the classroom. No one did. Miss Georgette was tall, stood straight, and had survived the torments of her four older brothers. She was not someone to mess with.

Once she started teaching, Georgette moved away from her family's farm as soon as she had saved enough money to buy a small house in town on Main Street. The house had a big front porch and a garden out back. The living room was the biggest room in the house. It went from the front door to the back with her two small bedrooms off to the left side and the kitchen and dining area on the right. An imposing, wood-burning pot bellied stove was situated in the middle of the living room so it could heat the whole house. There were two windows in front and two in the back, and together they brought in enough light to make it possible to open the curtains and read until the sun went down without ever having to light a lamp.

Like me, Georgette was not going to inherit the family farm and, if she didn't marry, was most likely going to be some kind of burden on her brothers in her old age unless she could find a way to support herself. Unlike me, Georgette knew what she wanted and was happy staying put. She liked teaching. She liked the rhythm of it. She said it was a lot like planting a garden: you put in seeds, watched them grow, then, after the harvest, you rested until another year of planting came around.

Year after year, the flatness of the land and the constant rustling of the wind as it whipped across the long straight rows of sugar beets, turnips, potatoes and sweet corn made me crazy. It was different for Georgette. Even in the coldest weather, she slept with her windows open so she could hear the sound of the wind as it blew clean and fast across the flat farmland around us, whistling its promise of changing seasons through the corn rows.

Farm work felt like a burden and held no mystery for me. Georgette, however, liked working with a shovel, digging, weeding and pounding in wooden stakes so she could tie up pole beans and trailing cucumber vines. She rejoiced in anything she could watch grow whether they were children or corn stalks.

As soon as she bought her house, she dug up two bright pink hollyhocks from her mother's garden and planted them on either side of her porch steps. Down the side of her fence she planted a long row of old fashioned tea roses that she'd started from cuttings. When Georgette wasn't curled up in a chair reading a book, she was sitting on her porch turning the pages of the Burpee seed catalogue to decide what she'd order next.

With her father's help, she plowed up half of her backyard for a vegetable garden and a wide flowerbed across the front of her porch three feet deep so there would be plenty of room for whatever flowers she wanted to plant each year.

Georgette kept her flower orders a secret, even from me. Her gardens were legendary. As spring moved on into full blooming summer, everyone who came to town made sure to walk by her house in order to see what was growing in her front yard. One year, she planted an explosion of multi-colored anemones bordered in crisp white candytuft. Another, she ordered and planted every kind of yellow flower you could imagine. There were tall yellow snapdragons, delicate yellow buttercups, bright yellow marigolds and exotic yellow day lilies.

Every fall after the first frost, she'd carefully harvest the seeds from her flowers and put them in tiny paper envelopes that she'd label with the common as well as the scientific name of each plant. If you were one of her students and did well on a test, or did something else spectacular like recite your tables, correctly rattle off the seven wonders of the world, or name the major rivers in the United States and what states they crossed, she'd give you one of her flower seed envelopes to take home. Students, as well as parents, treasured those seeds. Like a flowering report card, the success of her students bloomed across every garden in the county.

Miss Georgette never planted the same flower garden twice. So you could tell, by what flowers bloomed where, how each child had done in what year. If you didn't have a child in school, you could usually get one of her precious seed packets if you invited Miss Georgette for dinner. She had a fondness for stewed chicken and dumplings.

The Burpee catalogue was Georgette's favorite thing and when she'd made her choices and sent away for her spring seeds, she would cut off the cover of the catalogue and tack it up on her living room wall. Although it wasn't the kind of thing most people would do, it was pure Miss Georgette, and I agreed with her that the covers were genuine works of art.

Georgette's gallery of seed catalogue covers hanging on her living room walls awakened a sense of wonder and fired in me a desire to go to a fancy big city museum to see what real art looked like.

Georgette didn't ever seem to care if she got married. Four brothers had been enough men in her life. As long as she made sufficient money teaching school to put food on her table and buy seeds for her garden every spring, she was happy.

She was the one, however, who put the idea of Chicago in my head. After I graduated from high school and we could go back to just being friends again, Georgette and I continued to spend Sundays together after church reading and dreaming. She dreamed about what she was going to plant in her garden, and I dreamed about what I might do and where I could go that would be better than staying on the farm.

To her credit, Georgette didn't take any offense that I wanted to leave. She understood that sitting still wasn't for everyone. She was the best kind of friend.

You've got wings, she said. You need to fly! I've got dirt on my shoes and need to stay put. Which doesn't mean we can't be friends. Just means one of us is going to stay here and the other one is going to go away. Besides, you're too restless to teach school, and the farming life doesn't suit you one lick.

Mother said she wouldn't let me leave the farm and go to Chicago unless I had a place to sleep when I got there. To sleep, as if she believed I was merely going for an overnight and when the morning came, I would come to my senses and be back for Sunday supper. I had my own ideas as to how my life should spin out and they had nothing to do with coming back home.

Georgette had an aunt, her mother's older sister, a widow, who ran a boarding house on the west side of Chicago. Her name was Mrs. Levy. When mother said I couldn't go unless I had a place to sleep, Georgette wrote to her aunt and asked if she might possibly have a room for me.

Her aunt wrote back within a week saying she would most likely have a room available in April and any friend of Georgette's was welcome to become a boarder. Board was a single room with two meals a day: breakfast and supper. The cost for boarding was $4 a week.

At first I was elated, then later quite overwhelmed by the thought of spending another dreary grey winter trapped on the farm. The situation felt beyond my capacity and my good spirits. Sensing my growing anxiety, when my birthday came on October 8th, the anniversary of the Great Chicago Fire, my mother gave me a gift of some wool she'd spun from the past spring's shearing.

If you're going to Chicago, she said, you'll need to knit a warm shawl for yourself so you'll have something proper to wear when you're out for an evening stroll.

Wanting something more sophisticated than a plain white shawl to wear, I dyed the wool in a bath of boiled red onions, turning it a golden shade of brown. The color felt bold and grown up. Knitting the shawl kept my hands busy over those six long months of waiting, and also kept me dreaming.

For someone who had never been anywhere before and knew so little about the world, I had big dreams of walking on real sidewalks, seeing real art, working in a clean office rather than in the dirt. Georgette had been to Chicago once to stay with her aunt and said it was marvelous. Whenever my spirits lagged, she would tell me stories of fancy restaurants and ladies clothing stores where the dresses were already made and all you had to do was pic out one, put it on and walk out the door. I could hardly believe there was a dress anywhere in the world that was already made for me.

Georgette also told me there were gaslights that lined the walkways in Chicago that were lit every evening, turning night to day. I could hardly believe it.

It's the most beautiful light, she said. Simply marvelous! Like moonlight, only brighter. And there are streetcars. Everyone calls them grip cars because of the way they travel down the street being gripped by the great gears built right into the street.

We'd sit on her front porch for hours, watching the day fade from the sky, talking about Chicago and what kind of work I might do in an office there. At Georgette's request her aunt sent the want ads every week from the newspaper, and we would pour over the opportunities posted there.

There were plenty of jobs for young unmarried women in domestic service or scrubbing shirts in the laundry, neither of which I wanted to do. There were also bookkeeping jobs and jobs as a typewriter.

I had a good head for figures, but had no training as a bookkeeper, so I crossed that option off my list. I was, however, fascinated by the idea of learning to be a typewriter.

Neither Georgette nor I had ever seen a typewriter except in a magazine. We studied the pictures carefully, but puzzled over just how the words managed to go from the machine to the paper. Much about the workings of the typewriter was a mystery. We could clearly see that there was a whole alphabet strung out on the keys, but not in the order we had learned the letters. Plus, we couldn't figure out from the pictures if we needed to relearn the alphabet going from QWERTY across to the right and down the keyboard, or start from the bottom row and learn ZXCVB on up to the top row. We'd quiz each other and no matter how much we studied it, it just didn't seem right. The whole thing was baffling. At least the numbers across the top row were in an order we understood.

When we tired of trying to memorize the strange typewriter keyboard, Georgette would fold the magazine we had been studying and push it aside. Then she'd rock back in her chair and whisper one word: Marvelous!

When Georgette talked about it, Chicago was simply marvelous. A wonder! There were bound to be typewriter jobs a plenty! The city was a marvel of tall buildings, gaslights and grip cars, bustle and noise. Exciting things were happening everywhere you looked. It was a city teeming with a new world of opportunities for a young woman like me with no husband or child to hold them back.

One Sunday afternoon, after I finished putting away the things from supper and washing the dishes, I walked to town to see Georgette.

The week before, Georgette had told me that she knew someone who wanted to buy some of her flower seeds, and she was going to ride over to the next town to visit them on Saturday. Georgette always saved a dozen or so little envelopes filled with flower seeds each year and kept them in a metal spice tin on her kitchen shelf. She called those packets of seed her secret fund.

When I got to her house, she was sitting in the dining room with a big black Remington typewriter perched on her kitchen table. It was something! So black and shiny, the keys polished to a high gloss, the letters nestled inside each key bright white and commanding.

Georgette had the study book that came with the Remington opened on the table beside the machine.

It says here, she said, pointing to the book, that you put your left little finger on the A, your ring finger on the S, middle one on the D and your pointer on the F. Then you put your right pointer on the J, middle finger on the K, ring finger on the L and pinky on the semi-colon.

Georgette made room for me to sit down. I wiped my hands down the front of my dress and gently placed my fingers on the keys just as she instructed me to. It felt oddly comfortable.

What about the G and H? I asked.

You press the G with your left pointer, the H with your right. It says here to keep your pinky on their base keys to help your hands stay oriented on the keyboard. Here, Georgette said, pushing the book my way. Roll in the paper and practice the first line.

The quick brown fox jumped over the lazy dog's back.

I searched the keys looking for each of the letters as I worked my way cautiously through the sentence. I could hear the sharp clack and crack as the keys struck against the hard rubber roller, but didn't take my eyes off the keyboard. I was afraid my fingers would get lost.

When I came to the end of the sentence, I took a deep breath and looked at what I had done.

The quick brown fox jumped over the lazy dog's back.

Georgette flipped through the study book.

Shift key, she said. The shift key makes the capital. You push down the shift key with either your right or your left pinky then type the letter you want capitalized.

My hands were strong from working on my parent's farm, but my fingers were weak and unaccustomed to pushing keys. I held the shift key and struck the T.

Do it again, Georgette said, opening the book to the practice piece. The sentence has all the letters of the alphabet in it. If you keep doing it over and over like the book says, your fingers will eventually know where to find the keys. The book says that if you're going to be a typewriter, you have to practice every day, like practicing the piano, until you can find the keys without looking.

I took a deep breath and pressed down hard on the shift key. My fingers slowly worked their way through the sentence and the unfamiliar alphabet of the Remington. I closed my eyes and tried to visualize the keyboard Georgette and I had been trying to memorize. If I concentrated, I could see the keys in my mind and reach for a letter as I saw it, careful to keep my little fingers perched on their home bases: A for the left, and the semi-colon for the right.

I kept at it until the light was nearly gone from the sky and my fingers ached. I learned how to use both my left and my right little fingers to push down on the shift key in order to engage the capital letters. I also learned how to lift my right hand off the keys and click the silver lever when the roller on the carriage reached the end of a line of type and it was time to advance the paper to start a new line. Once the paper was advanced and the carriage was in place, I'd take a deep breath, look down at the keys, and once again place my fingers properly on the keyboard: A S D F on the left, J K L, on the right. My little fingers, the ones I'd just about ignored most of my life, anchored my next attack.

Even though I could find all of the letters on the rows fairly quickly, with only an occasional look at the keyboard, the letters that I struck on the page were uneven: some like S and L, so faint you could hardly see them, others, like the G, H, T and U so bold and strongly struck they nearly cut a hole through the thin paper. Two or three times, when my fingers got ahead of the mechanics of the machine, there was a wreck of crossed keys and I had to stop and gently untangle them.

Georgette struck a match and lit her hurricane lamp.

Getting dark, she said. Before you got here I drew a picture of the keyboard for you so you can practice at home.

When I got home, I cut my nails short so they wouldn't catch on the keys as my fingers jumped from row to row, slowing my progress and sometimes causing the keys to jam.

From Monday through Saturday, I helped my brothers with chores around the farm and put up vegetables for the winter with my mother. On Sunday afternoons after church and supper, I walked to Georgette's home to practice on her typewriter. Little by little, my fingers got stronger and became accustomed to knowing where to go on the keyboard.

Eventually, I could type my name without looking, and could even close my eyes and type whatever Georgette told me to type while she was talking. Taking dictation, is what she called it, and as long as she spoke slowly and evenly, one word no faster than the next, I could keep up and type what she said with some accuracy.

There was something full of wonder about it all. I loved the sound the machine made as the keys jumped up and hit the paper, and the crisp ring of the bell signaling it was time to advance the carriage.

I practiced every evening on my silent paper keyboard, in the same way I thought a pianist must practice, making sure each finger struck equally, so the letters would come out round and black on the page.

By March, I had enough money saved from selling vegetables and eggs in town to buy a one-way train ride to Chicago and at least a month's room and board. Being able to type and type well would be my meal ticket to start a new life of my own.

I just knew if I could get a job as a typewriter in one of the fancy high rising offices on Michigan Avenue Georgette had told me about, I could discover real art to see, find sidewalks to stroll on, grip cars to ride with ease from one place to another, a room of my own, and realize whatever other dreams I hadn't even dared to think about in the shadows of those magical gaslights.

TWO

When I wasn't practicing typing, I worked on knitting my shawl. I chose a traditional triangular shape with long tapered ends and used a tiny seed stitch to give the wool some thickness. To finish it off, I crocheted a wide scalloped edge around the border. I finished knitting it a few weeks before Christmas and pressed the tight rows of stitches with a warm iron, making it smooth so it draped softly over my shoulders.

The shawl was big enough to cover my back from my neck to my waist. I could crisscross the long tapered ends in the front and knot them together in warmer weather, or cinch the ends tight around my waist and tie them in back creating a kind of cocoon to keep me warm when it was cold.

Even my mother thought it was beautiful.

Wear it, she said, for Christmas Eve services.

I wore my grey linen dress and wrapped my beautiful shawl around my shoulders. I didn't sit with my family that evening, but rather, in the last pew as though I was only dropping in for the songs and might have to leave before services were over. My father wasn't happy with me, but my mother understood. It was my silent shout of independence. It was a coming out of sorts: proof that I was not trapped in this small town or beholden to the farm, but getting ready to leave for bigger things. Georgette sat next to me and linked her arm proudly in mine.

When spring came and it was time for me to leave, I didn't have many goodbyes to declare. Most of the girls I knew from school were married by then and had at least one child. I had nothing to say to them, and they had nothing to say to me. Our lives had taken different turns, and I didn't need them to remind me what I might be missing by not having the stability of a husband and a farm. Likewise, they didn't need me to remind them that they had settled for less than what I thought was desirable.

I couldn't sleep the night before I left. I stood by the window, watching the setting sun cause the night sky to blacken with sleep, and listened one last time to the wind tease the budding tree branches to let go of their dead winter limbs. When morning came, I washed my face and watched the sun break through the darkness and become a soft line of light against the edge of the newly plowed fields beyond my window.

From the hallway outside of my room I could hear my two brothers waking up and getting dressed. I heard the crackle of thick bacon slices sizzling in my mother's biggest black skillet. Heard her counting under her breath as she cracked two-dozen eggs from the basket full she'd just collected. Listened as she rummaged in the drawer looking for the long handled fork with the broken tine that she always used to whip the eggs. Smelled the coffee boiling.

I had no appetite but was hungry for the comfort of warm food. It would be the last meal I ate with my family. The last time I sat at our long kitchen table. The last time I heard my father say grace. Saw my brothers reach in silence for another biscuit. Helped my mother clear the table. Washed the dishes or hung the damp tea towel on the back porch railing to dry.

There was an order and easiness to it all. It was just another day for them. It was life, as I had always known it, as natural and predictable as the sun coming up or going down. I knew that as soon as my brothers finished eating breakfast, they would pull on their boots and go out to milk the cows. Once the breakfast dishes were washed, my mother would skim the cream off yesterday's milk to churn butter before she busied herself with making lunch. After lunch, my brothers would hitch up the plow and clear another acre for planting. My father would mend a fence, feed the pigs.

But, today wasn't a usual day. It was awkward and different. My brothers didn't take seconds on biscuits. Instead, they looked longingly at what would normally be theirs as though my mother had warned them the extra biscuits were for me to take on the train.

When my brothers got up from the table, there were still three biscuits on the large china platter along with some scraps of bacon. While they stood to the side and watched in silence, my mother picked up the biscuits, broke them open with her fingers and stuffed them with the bacon. She then wrapped the biscuits in a clean tea towel and dropped the warm bundle into my satchel.

You might get hungry, she said. Never been to Chicago myself, but I imagine it's a far piece and who knows if there's anything to eat on the train. Is someone going to meet you?

My father turned away from me as if he were ashamed of my leaving, the foolishness of all of my big city dreams. He pulled on his work boots and took his coat from the hook by the door.

If you're going to leave us, we need to get going, he said.

He took his hat out of his coat pocket and slapped it against his leg as if it were covered with dust and disgust.

You going? He asked my mother.

My mother took off her apron and smoothed a wisp of hair behind her ear before putting on her coat.

Told you last night I was going, she said.

My brothers shifted their collective weight as if they were one person, not two. Neither one of them spoke. I fastened my satchel and drew my shawl around my shoulders. I kissed each of them on the cheek. The cows bellowed from the barn. My oldest brother picked up the milking pails stacked by the backdoor. My younger brother walked behind him to the barn.

I guess it's time to go, my mother said.

My father pushed the door open and walked out. My mother and I followed.

THREE

My father carried my bag to the train station platform.

You can come back, he said.

Before I could thank him or say goodbye, he had turned and walked to the buggy. My mother stayed on the platform until the train came. We talked about the weather and about the plans she had for her kitchen garden. She asked me again if someone was going to meet me when I got off of the train. When it was time to board, I gave her a hug. Her back was stiff, her eyes closed as if she were fighting not to cry.

Once in my seat, I watched as she waved me off. I pressed my hand against the window until the train had pulled away from the station and she was gone from sight.

I realized, as I watched her standing on the platform waving, that the only time I ever saw her without an apron on was when we went to church or town. I knew so little about her, other than the biscuits she made, the eggs she counted as she cracked them or the butter she churned. It made me sad to watch her disappear from my life. I didn't know what she dreamed of or even what she liked or didn't like about anything. As far as I knew, she was happy with her life. I had never heard her wish for another. I had no idea how old she was, just that she was old and not likely to ever go any further away than town for the rest of her life.

As the train lumbered down the tracks gaining speed, I sat by the window hoping to see my father's buggy trot by. But, the train drifted down the track faster than my mother was able to walk back to join my father. I never saw them again.

For the first couple of hours, I tried my best to memorize the way the flat farmland stretched across the horizon. I wondered, as we passed each small white farmhouse, if there were biscuits left from breakfast on the various kitchen tables and fresh butter being churned.

Georgette had not come to the train station to say goodbye. It was a Tuesday and she had children to teach. We had said our goodbyes the Sunday before and made promises to write. I told her I hoped she would come visit. She said she'd try. I thanked her again for buying that Remington typewriter so I could learn a trade and find a job.

A trade. I was, indeed, trading a life like my mother's for a job typewriting. As farm after farm went flying by, I closed my eyes and prayed that my mother was happy. If there was something I hadn't noticed, hadn't understood about some quiet joy to be found in the endless rhythmic slap of the paddles churning cream to butter, some secret pleasure gained from the mystery of turning flour to dough, or a sense of wellbeing hidden in the gentle movement of the seasons from planting to harvest, I hoped she felt it. I wanted to believe that in the short daylight hours of winter there was time for her to read a book or work on her sewing in order to make the sameness of all the mornings in her life worth it.

I knew from searching the papers, looking for a typewriting job, that my days working in an office would be long and there would be no seasons. But, there would be a world of difference, of new things, new places, and new people for me to meet.

Although my father had told me I could, I was certain I would never go back to the farm.

FOUR

We were all farm girls who came to the big city to find a different life in the tall steel buildings. Chicago was the biggest thing any of us had ever seen. Most of us came from downstate or from farms up in Wisconsin like I had. We were prairie girls. Our every day dresses were not made of black and white yard goods like the uniforms we were expected to wear in our jobs, but sewn from feed sacks strewn with faded flowers, or gingham check and plain grey linen.

Chicago was unlike anything we had ever seen or known. Chicago was not like the towns we came from. The towns from our pasts were made of one wide street lined with a feed and dry goods store, a church at one end of the street and a school at the other. For most of us, town was a long buggy ride from the farms where we lived.

We all had several things in common: we had brothers who would inherit the farm; we didn't have husbands; and we didn't want to teach school.

We also all needed jobs. Some of the girls took housekeeping jobs or childcare positions with families and lived with them. For the most part, the rest of us chose to live in boarding houses, because that's what was available for a young single woman, and all any of us could afford.

The prettiest girls among us managed to get sales jobs at the fancy department stores or were hired as receptionists at one of the businesses downtown. The best paying jobs went to those of us who could type. We weren't called typists, but typewriters, as if we were the machines. We were expected to dress like the typewriters as well: long black skirts and clean white blouses buttoned up tight all the way to our throats. I had known, from the ads in the newspapers, what I would be required to wear, so I got fabric and made one black skirt and two white blouses before I left home. That one black skirt, two white blouses, a couple of everyday gingham dresses, along with my good grey linen outfit, were all the clothing I carried with me in my suitcase to Chicago.

I also had a pretty good winter coat and the thick woolen shawl I had knitted before I left home. If I wore my coat and pulled my arms and hands under the shawl, I was able to withstand the worst winter weather. There was plenty of cold to be had in Chicago and so much wind. So very much wind.

I had carried the paper keyboard that Georgette had created for me in my purse and practiced on the train. The first thing I did when I arrived in Chicago, after checking into Mrs. Levy's home and depositing my things, was to buy a newspaper. I circled the typewriter jobs available and the next morning went by the grip car into downtown to begin applying for jobs.

My hands were shaking so hard during my first interview, I couldn't type as fast as I needed to or as accurately. By the third interview, I was doing better. By Thursday the next week, I was lucky enough to get a job with the Studebaker Company in the billing department typing up orders and taking dictation. Georgette had prepared me well.

Most of the girls at Mrs. Levy's boarding house worked in the big department stores downtown. One of the girls, who wasn't as pretty as the rest and who didn't have nice clothes to wear, worked in a laundry. Her hands were always chapped and raw from the harsh soap and boiling water she had to use in order to get the gravy stains out of the shirts she washed. I was the only one among us who was a typewriter.

No matter where we worked or what we did, Mrs. Levy would greet us when we came down for breakfast every morning and wish us a good day. In the evening, while we ate supper together, she would ask each of us what we had done that day. She always listened to what we had to say, her head cocked slightly to the left side as though one ear heard more clearly than her other. She made everyone feel welcome as if we had a right to be there and she was glad we had come to be with her.

The billing office at Studebaker consisted of only three people: Mr. Bristal, the boss, Mrs. Anders, who was the bookkeeper, and myself.

When Mr. Bristal hired me, he inspected my hands and told me that I was expected to keep my nails trimmed and neat. No cheap nail polish. No wedding bands or promise rings announcing I was thinking of having children. He said he preferred single girls as his typewriters and if I was thinking of getting married I needed to give my two weeks' notice.

Mrs. Anders and I shared the big office in the front. She didn't seem as old as her name implied. She was thirty and like me, wore her hair pulled back in a bun at the nape of her neck. Like me, she didn't wear any makeup. Not even lipstick. She had a beautiful cameo broach that she always wore pinned at the throat of her clean white blouse. She said it had been her mother's.

We weren't allowed to talk much beyond good morning, but we managed, when Mr. Bristal was downstairs checking on the production of our various orders, to whisper to each other. We were afraid to speak out loud, both because he might hear us and also because, if we were talking or laughing, we wouldn't be able to hear Mr. Bristal approaching as he walked down the hallway. Neither of us could afford to lose her job.

Mrs. Anders said she had gone to night school to learn bookkeeping and that she liked it. It was quiet work, and for the most part Mr. Bristal didn't bother her because he wasn't much for numbers. She told me that she was lucky she was good with figures because bookkeepers were scarce, so no one cared if you were married as long as you were honest and could balance the books. She said typewriters didn't have it so easy.

There were lots of girls who knew how to type, so it would be best if I didn't cause trouble of any kind.

She also whispered that most of the typewriters in my position hadn't lasted much more than six months or so and she hoped I would manage to keep my job because she liked talking with me. We made a promise to have dinner together some night after work. I told her I had never been to a restaurant and that I wouldn't know what to do or how to order. She said her husband would join us for dinner. He was a grip driver and got off about the same time we did. She said she'd told him all about me, or at least as much as she knew, and he wanted to meet me. With him along, we wouldn't have to worry about being two women eating alone.

We never got a chance to have that dinner.

Despite the silent confines of my job as a typewriter, I had come to Chicago looking for a kind of salvation from a rutted life on the farm. Every morning, as my cold hands fumbled to push the fancy mother-of-pearl buttons of my blouse through the tiny buttonholes I had made, I closed my eyes and prayed a kind of prayer to myself: This is what I wanted. This is why I came here.

Being a typewriter was supposed to be just the beginning of my new life in the city. I did not know what my next steps would be or how I would find my way into a bigger world of art and ideas or where my new life would ultimately take me.

When I boarded the train to come to Chicago, it was the first time I'd been anywhere. By the time I tired of looking out of the train window, watching one plowed field after another drift by, I realized I wanted more than anything in the world to get as far away from cornfields and dark dreamless nights as those rails would go. Eventually, I fell asleep in my seat, and when I woke, what I saw were more cornfields and tiny houses caught in a windbreak of trees on a barren expanse of farmland. I also saw roads going somewhere and horses pulling carts and children waving at the train as it rolled by through town as if they too dreamed of going, going, going somewhere else.

I tell you all of this, my beloved granddaughter, so you will understand what has shaped your life and what I am going to ask you to do. That train window, those long stretches of cornfields and tight little houses braced in a clutch of trees against the wind are the ones I saw as I ran away and they are the same ones you now see in your own dreams. I know.

Have you also seen that little room in Mrs. Levy's boarding house? The dark grey wallpaper studded with pink roses? The quilt my mother made for me that I took along with me to keep me warm? Do you dream of me taking off my black skirt every night and hanging it on the back of the closet door so it won't drag in the dust and need brushing? When you walk down Michigan Avenue, do you feel the thin leather soles of my shoes, my only pair of city shoes, scuffing against the sidewalk? Do you dream of the thick black cotton stockings I washed out every other night hoping they would last a few more months before I had enough money saved up to buy some others?

Did you ever wonder where these strange thoughts come from? They are the bits and pieces of my life that have traveled through to yours. Puzzle pieces. So many things you will need to sort through in your own life to make sense of your own feelings and fears.

The shop girls who lived in the boarding house also wore long black skirts and white blouses to work, but they were able to wear lipstick.

Even if I could wear lipstick to my typewriter job, I couldn't afford it. I had never worn lipstick. Neither had my mother or my friend Georgette. Farm wives and teachers didn't wear lipstick.

Lipstick was one of the things I dreamed of.

My hair was a dark brown like yours. My eyes slate blue just like your eyes. What I dreamed of was a tube of deep ruby lipstick that I could touch to my lips and use to rouge my cheeks. The women on Michigan Avenue, the ones who wore silk dresses and carried satin-lined fur muffs in winter and delicate silk parasols in summer, all rouged their cheeks and stained their lips crimson.

You once told someone that wearing bright red lipstick and blue jeans was your way of declaring to the world that you were not bound by others' expectations.

My dreams are your dreams.

There is more to my story that you need to know.

FIVE

It was the waning edge of winter, 1893. Spring was coming soon, and people were anticipating the opening of the World's Columbian Exposition. Everyone in the city felt the excitement, but they also felt a rising sense of fear.

The Exposition signaled a sense of hope despite the dark cloud that hung in the air. There were rumors of a financial crisis. Fears that the banks might close. Nothing felt sure or steady.

Banks were for rich people. Once I paid for my room and board every week, I took what little money I had left, tied it in a handkerchief and slipped it under my mattress. I always locked my bedroom door.

I didn't think what was happening in the rest of the world might have anything to do with me. I was wrong.

One rich man killed himself by jumping out a window just a block from where I worked. Another locked his office door and shot himself. People didn't talk about the looming financial troubles; they whispered, huddled and worried.

In addition to the possibility that the banks might shut their doors, there were also rumors of strikes by the union men who were working day and night to build the Exposition. A possible strike, however, brought a thin bit of hope for the thousands of people who were unemployed. Every day, long lines of men stood in the mud and the morning cold waiting by the locked Exposition gates in the hopes of finding work. They weren't union and didn't want to join. They didn't care how long their workday would be or even what their working conditions would be. They just wanted to work and be paid so they could feed their families.

There were no unions for women. We didn't have anyone out there demanding an eight-hour day for us, or time off for lunch, decent wages or protection from being fired for no good reason. Every woman who had a job was vulnerable.

I soon discovered that I wasn't any different.

As the weeks of rumors turned to headlines and locked bank doors, women who had jobs began to worry about keeping them. Like the men waiting at the gates of the Exposition hoping to get work, women whose husbands or fathers were now unemployed started applying for jobs. These women lined up each morning outside office doors, wearing their best Sunday dresses and their only pair of shoes.

I passed them on the way to work, and turned my head the other way when I saw the women waiting outside on the sidewalk for the office doors to be unlocked and flung open to the possibility of employment. The faces of these women were weary, their shoulders poised for disappointment.

As the weeks of rumors rolled on without stopping, the number of women standing in line in front of the Studebaker Company hoping for a chance to work grew. Every morning, Mr. Bristal would invite one or two of the youngest and prettiest women into his office to talk. Sometimes, if a girl was young and pretty, he'd bring her to my desk and ask if I would get up so she could take a typing test.

Obediently, I would stand aside watching as the woman's nervous fingers darted here and there pecking and hunting for the next letter. Invariably, keys would jam or the strokes would be uneven and the resulting typing unacceptable. When the clatter of wrongly struck keys grew, I would turn away and hold my breath as if I couldn't bear to watch.

When each woman who was lucky enough to be asked to take the test pulled the paper from the roller and gave it to Mr. Bristal, he would put his hand on her shoulder and shake his head, then let his had slide down her body and press against the small of her back as he escorted her out of the office. Relieved that I was not the one being escorted out, I would take my seat again and resume working. After a few minutes passed, Mr. Bristal would walk back to my desk and let the typing test drop from his hands just far enough away for it to touch the edge of my table before it tumbled to the floor. He'd stand there looking at me, hands shoved deep into his pockets until I pushed my chair away and reached down to pick up the paper and throw it away.

I guess I always knew one day someone prettier than I was, who could type faster than I could, would be standing in the hall hoping to have my job. It was only time before someone who wouldn't make any mistakes when she took her test on my typewriter, someone who wouldn't mind at all when Mr. Bristal put his hand on her shoulder or the small of her back, would come along and I would lose my job.

A small mirror hung over the washbasin in my room at Mrs. Levy's house. Every time I washed my face I looked into that mirror. Was I pretty? Pretty enough? My eyes were a soft grayish blue, just like yours. My hair was thick and an unruly shade of brown. I tied back my hair and twisted it as best I could into a tight bun at the nape of my neck, securing it with thin metal pins. Makeup was a luxury I couldn't afford. But, even if I had enough money to buy makeup, I couldn't have worn it to work and wouldn't have worn it anyway. I had come to Chicago to find myself, not to find someone else.

Before I left the farm, my mother came into my room one night to warn me that city men were different from the ones on the farm. She said a farm boy wanted a good woman who would cook hot meals, keep the house clean, and raise strong children who could work in the fields. City men only wanted one thing.

When my mother began to talk about what city men were looking for, she got quiet and looked over her shoulder, as if she were afraid someone might be listening. The air in the room stilled. There was a terrible silence. My heart raced. Eventually, my mother shook her head and refused to go further. I knew by the way she stopped talking and sat close to me stroking my arm that what city men wanted was dirty.

She didn't ever tell me anything about sex and I didn't ask. All I knew about that sort of thing was what I had witnessed with the animals on our farm.

When my parents took me to the train station the afternoon I left, my father carried my bag to the platform and said his goodbyes then went back to the buggy. My mother waited with me on the platform. When the train whistle blew to indicate it was time to board, she put her hand on my arm and squeezed it as tightly as she could.

Remember, she whispered, what I said about city men.

When I got to Chicago I was able to see for myself how city men were different from the men I had known before. For one, they wore suits not overalls to go to work. They talked loud and walked fast. Sometimes when you passed a man on the street, they would look at you. Sometimes they wouldn't. Often, they would stop on the streets to talk with other men. When a pretty woman passed by they would tip their hats in greeting then go back to talking while they watched the woman walk down the street.

From what I overheard on the grip cars or from the men on the streets or in the offices, the city men didn't talk about a cow that was off its feed or that the crops needed rain. They talked mostly about money and sometimes about the news.

There was always news in this new world of Chicago. News about anything and everything you could imagine. On occasion, someone would leave a newspaper on the seat of the grip car or on a park bench and I would pick it up and read as much as I dared. The world was bigger and more dangerous than I ever thought possible.

There were so many places I wanted to see, things I wanted to do. The newspapers told stories of what was happening in New York and how it was possible to take a boat to London. I wanted to go and do and see everything in the world. I was excited about having a day off and riding the grip car to the very end of the line just to get out, walk around and discover what was there.

I couldn't wait to sit down in a restaurant and be able to choose what I was going to eat for supper.

I was young and so naïve about the ways of the world. I believed it was all mine to have…until it wasn't anymore.

The day it happened was a Saturday. We were supposed to get off by six, but there had been more work than usual that week and Mr. Bristal said we couldn't leave until it was all done. As daylight began to fade, I could see the gaslights below our building being lit one after another down the long street in front of our office. Six-thirty, seven, dusk turned to dark. My shoulders and fingers began to ache. My legs got restless from sitting so long.

A little before eight, Mr. Bristal came out of his office and dropped more work on my desk. He told Mrs. Anders she could leave.

Mrs. Anders closed her ledger and put on her coat. She took her time, waiting for Mr. Bristal to step away from my desk and walk to the door to let her out. She touched my arm as she passed. I looked up. She paused.

Be careful, she whispered.

He locked the door.

I picked up the work orders he'd put on my desk. Brashly, I called out to him. They were the same ones, I said, that I had finished in the morning. I stood up so I could show him the reports.

You must be mistaken, he said, walking towards me.

He put out his hand as though he was planning on examining the papers himself.

No, I said. Look.

Instead of taking the papers, he knocked them out of my hand onto the floor and grabbed my wrist, twisting my arm behind my back. I struggled. He pushed me against the wall and covered my mouth with his other hand.

That girl, he whispered in my ear, the one this morning, so pretty. Didn't you think? She wanted your job. And I told her what I tell all of them. You never know. That's what I say. You never know what's going to happen. Do you?

He jerked my arm that was behind my back while at the same time pulling up my skirt with his other hand to my thighs.

If you scream, no one will hear you. No one will help you. I'll say you wanted it. You want it, don't you? You girls always say you don't, but I know you always want it.

He let go of my arm, grabbed my shoulders and banged my head against the wall when I tried to push away and run.

One of the metal pins I had used to secure my hair that morning dug into my scalp.

My ears started ringing.

Do you hear me? I'm only doing this because you want me to. If you scream, I'll hurt you.

He let go of my shoulders and pushed his left hand against my mouth.

I could taste the salt and dirt on his skin. The hairpin tore deeper into my flesh. Blood started dripping through my hair down my neck.

Did you hear what I said about that pretty girl? If you scream, she'll have your job tomorrow morning and you'll be out in the street where you belong. If you tell anyone, they won't believe you. Why would they? You're nothing to look at. What man would want you?

I held my breath, hoping I'd faint. He took his hand from my mouth and tore at my underwear until he had made a clear passageway in order to begin pushing himself inside. It was like he had become an animal, thrusting his body into mine, over and over and over again like I'd seen the bulls do.

Cows always arched their necks and bellowed when the bull would mount. Their bodies would tense. They wouldn't move, instead, they'd dig their hooves deep into the ground like they were frozen in time. Unable to move. Trapped in the weight of what was happening.

The cows instinctively knew there was no way to fight what was happening. They also knew that when the bulls finished their business, they would roll off and stumble away blindly as if they had been spent and weren't good anymore that day for anything else.

Was this what my mother wanted to tell me, but couldn't? Were the men in the city just like the animals on our farm?

I waited for that moment when Mr. Bristal was spent, then raised my knee up fast and hard into his crotch. I felt a surge of strength that comes from raw anger. He let go of me and shot back a step, his head jerked high with pain. I spit in his face. I didn't have a plan. Just knew this was my only chance to make right for what he had said and done to me. I lunged forward with every intention of scratching out his eyes. I wanted to hurt him. Blind him if possible.

He grabbed for my arm but instead caught the last two fingers of my left hand. I struggled to get free, kicking at his legs and ankles. That's when he twisted with all his remaining strength until my fingers snapped. The sound was like a freshly picked green bean being broken in two.

I wanted to fall out of my skin, onto the floor. There was so much pain, there wasn't anything I could call pain anymore, just a wave of nausea that forced its way up my throat. In a flash, his suit jacket and shirt were covered in vomit. My vomit. My anger. His penis tainted with my blood.

I broke your fingers, he said, pushing himself away. Just to be sure you'll never work here or anywhere else again.

Then he stumbled to the door and unlocked it.

That pretty girl? He said, buttoning his pants. The Irish one with the soft blue eyes and auburn hair? I told her to come back on Monday. That you had business you needed to finish here before you left.

I grabbed my things and ran.

My hand began to swell as I walked home. I was afraid to get on the grip car. My clothes reeked of sweat, semen and blood. My stockings and underwear were torn and bloodied. There was blood in my hair from where my hairpins had torn my flesh. I was shaking. People I passed on the street looked away as if minding their own business was the most important thing they might do that day.

Fear is a horrible thing. It can crush you if you let it.

When I got to the rooming house, I went straight to my room. I didn't have dinner or speak to anyone. I locked my bedroom door. I filled my washbasin with water and took off all my clothes. I washed my face and dabbed the blood from my neck and legs. I rinsed out my ripped underpants as best as I could and I tore them into strips. I held my throbbing hand under the dirty water. All the tears I had within me ran down my face. When I couldn't cry anymore, I wrapped those strips of cloth around my broken fingers, tying them together. Ever so slowly, the aching drained from my heart to my hand, I struggled into my nightgown, got into my bed and fell into an exhausted sleep.

My past is your present. We are one.

SIX

I slept all Saturday night and into Sunday. I heard Mrs. Levy knock on my door once or twice that first evening and into the next. I pretended I was sick and needed to sleep. She said she would bring me something to eat. I told her I wasn't hungry.

It's okay, she said. I am here to help you.

My arms and hands were bruised and sore. My vagina was torn and bleeding. When I at last got up from bed, I took the knotted handkerchief from beneath the mattress and counted my money. I had managed to save enough for two weeks board. Three weeks, maybe, if I walked everywhere, rather than taking the grip car. I had to find a new job.

When Monday morning came, my broken fingers were badly swollen and useless. They didn't hurt as badly as they had at first. Instead, they throbbed like a nagging toothache. I knew I couldn't get a job in the laundry with a bad hand. I also knew I couldn't ever be a typewriter again. I had planned to pretend I still had a job so I could stay with Mrs. Levy until I found something else.

I forced myself to get up that Monday morning in time to have breakfast with the other boarders. I couldn't wash my face or brush my hair and could barely manage the buttons on my blouse, but I got dressed as best I could. Once I sat down at the dining table, I kept my left hand on my lap, out of sight, while I ate.

When the big clock in the hall chimed seven, signaling it was time for the boarders to leave for work, Mrs. Levy asked if I could help her clear the table. The others got up and left without saying anything as if they knew.

I started to push my chair away from the table.

Sit, Mrs. Levy said, pouring me another cup of tea and buttering the last slice of toast, cutting it in half from corner to corner, and putting it on my plate. Let me see your hand.

I lifted my left hand from my lap and placed it gingerly on the table. I picked up one triangle of toast with my right hand and began to eat. I couldn't speak.

Mrs. Levy got up from the table and went to the sideboard. She pulled out a bottle and a crystal tumbler. She poured a generous bit of brandy in the glass and waited until I had eaten the second piece of toast before she handed it to me.

Sip this slowly, she said, but drink it all. Let me get you something else to eat.

I took a sip of the brandy. I had never had alcohol before and the first taste shot through my body like a wave hitting a rock. The second sip burned my throat. I tried not to choke.

Mrs. Levy returned with a pile of buttered and sliced toast and a cold chicken leg. I picked up the toast and stared at the chicken. I was hungry and wanted the chicken but knew I couldn't cut it with a knife and fork.

This is no time to worry about manners, she said. Pick it up with your good hand. Eat, but eat slowly. You're going to need something nourishing to get the healing started. This is going to hurt and I don't want you to faint.

I picked up the chicken with my right hand and began eating.

She went into the kitchen and brought back two basins, one filled with water, the other empty. Next to the basins, she laid out two linen tea towels, a silver soupspoon and her embroidery scissors.

Take another sip of the brandy, she said. I've got to cut off your bandages. If you need to cry out, you do that. But don't move. Last thing in this world I want to do is hurt you more than you've already been hurt.

She slipped her hand gently under mine and began to wedge the thin tips of her scissors into the tight bandage I'd made from my underwear.

I took another sip of the brandy and closed my eyes. I could hear the blades of her scissors. Snip. Could feel as the pressure of the bandages let go. Snip. Feel the blood release and pulse through the bruised and broken bits of my twisted fingers. Snip. Feel the pain shoot up my arm. Snip. Feel the room spin and the heat of the alcohol rush to my head.

Mrs. Levy dropped her scissors and pushed aside my plate of food in order to clear the space in front of me.

Put your head on the table, she said, her voice calm but commanding. I'll hold your hand. I won't let it drop. Just let it rest in mine. Put your head down. And breathe. Slowly. Stay with me. Don't faint.

I fought back. I kicked him. I did what I could to stop him. I told Mrs. Levy.

Shhh, she said, stroking my tangled hair. You're not the first bit of broken I've had to fix. You let me know if you're going to be sick.

She pulled the empty basin close to my head so I could reach it if I needed to.

I'm going to keep cutting. When I have everything off and your head quits spinning I'm going put your hand in this other basin, the one full of water. The water is cold and it's going to hurt at first, but in a minute or so it will begin to feel better. You okay?

I nodded my head.

She snipped three more times then pulled the last few bits of bandage away from my hand. My head was still on the table. The room around me was twisting and spinning with alcohol and pain.

Do you think you can sit up? It'll be easier for me to fix your fingers and I'll be less likely to hurt you.

I used my good hand to push myself upright. I could see, now that the bandages were gone, that both fingers were black with blood and the palm of my hand badly swollen.

I'm guessing he did more than just break your fingers, she said.

I turned my head away.

She touched my chin and tipped my head up so I had to look at her face.

I'm going to say this once, she said quietly, and I want you to remember this forever. You didn't do anything to make this happen. And, whatever he said to you, you forget it. What happened was wrong but there's nothing wrong with you. I'm proud that you fought back. Proud of you. You hear? I don't care what happened. You fought back and you're here and you don't ever have to go back there.

He broke my fingers so I would never be a typewriter again, I said.

You're smarter and the world is bigger than being a typewriter. That's for sure. Now, let's get that hand soaking in the cool water while I tear some fresh bandages.

While my hand was soaking, she wrapped the silver spoon with a strip of cloth she had torn from one of the tea towels then lifted my hand from the water and patted it dry with the other towel.

Drink that last bit of my best brandy, she said, and turn your head that way, towards the clock in the hall. I find if you don't close your eyes, but look out straight at something solid like that clock, the room won't spin so badly. I'm going to put the bowl of this spoon in the palm of your hand then try my best to straighten your fingers along the handle. It's going to hurt. Know any songs you can sing? Singing keeps the mind off of hurting sometime. Sing as loud as you can. If you want, I can sing with you.

I started singing the Battle Hymn of the Republic. My grandfather used to sing it when he was chopping wood and I knew all the words by heart. Mrs. Levy joined in. I turned my head and stared at the clock. She pressed the back of the bowl of the spoon into the palm of my hand. When we got to the line about He hath loosed his fateful lighting, she gave a quick pull and snap of my broken fingers, and laid them out stiff along the length of the spoon handle. I kept singing with her as loudly as I could. By the time we got to the second verse, she had finished tying my two broken fingers to the spoon handle. Then she tore another wide strip of linen and started wrapping the bowl of the spoon against my hand until it nestled snugly into my swollen palm and my fingers were secure.

Wiggle those other fingers a bit and see how that feels. Let me know if it's too tight.

Everything about me ached. I couldn't speak. The room spun like a child's top. I wanted to say thank you, but I couldn't. I let my forehead rest against the table again.

You let me know when you think you can move. I'm going to hold onto you. Help you up the stairs back to your room and put you to bed. You've got some more resting to do. We need to get that hand elevated so it has a chance to let the swelling go down. I'll get some extra pillows so we can get it propped up. You'll feel a whole lot better once the swelling goes away and you've had some sleep.

The air is a bit fresh this morning, like maybe it might be spring. Fresh air heals. I'll get your window open and bring you another quilt. Bring you some clean nightclothes too.

I'm going to need the clothes you've got on so I can get them washed and hung out to dry before dinner. I hope you don't mind, but when I knew for sure you were sleeping that first night, I unlocked your door and came in to check on you. I had to be sure you were okay. That's when I noticed that your petticoat and your skirt were soiled and torn. A little cold water and lye soap will get out most of that blood. I'll do my best to repair where things are torn, if I can't fix what's wrong, I've got a petticoat and a dress or two that might fit you. I saw your hand was wrapped in what looked to be strips of cloth I'm guessing you made from your torn underwear. I'll buy some new ones for you today.

I can't pay you for the underwear. I only have enough money for another couple weeks, I said.

Like you need to pay for what that man did to you? Lord, I'd be the first in line to Hell if I took your money, that's for sure! Right now, you need a warm bed, a little time, some fresh clothes and a way to start over.

SEVEN

Shame is a strange kind of denial. And, denial is just another form of lying. Like all lies, by the time you've denied something happened five or six times, or let yourself think that nothing happened, You begin to believe it.

It's amazing how quickly the discomfort of denial evaporates, and in its place a comfortable truth that's really a lie evolves.

True to her word, Mrs. Levy let me stay with her as long as I needed to until my hand healed. I didn't have enough money to pay her for her kindness. She told me not to worry, that I could repay her by helping around the house. I wasn't much help, but I did the best I could. I set and cleared the table, hung clothes on the line, dusted, helped to serve meals and got up early to gather eggs from the chicken coop out back.

In truth, I tried my best to busy myself when the other boarders were around, but once they left and my few chores were done, I rested.

I had never been so tired in all my life.

You're healing, Mrs. Levy said. Your body is trying to forget, to get up again and go on. Rest. You need to rest.

When I wrote to Georgette, I didn't, I couldn't, tell her I'd lost my job. I didn't even have the words to let her know I'd been raped or my fingers broken so I would never be able to be a typewriter again. Instead, I talked about how wonderful her aunt, Mrs. Levy, was and that she had hired me to help around the boarding house so I could make a little extra money.

I wrote about riding the grip cars and the beautiful shadows that crisscrossed the wide sidewalks all along Michigan Avenue when dusk fell and the gaslights were lit.

When I wrote to my mother, I told her about the weather.

A lie can be so many things: What you say; what you don't say, or even what you deny happening. I had never lied in my life, so it shocked me to discover how easily one lie came after another as I pieced together a new world for myself that I could live in without shame.

About six weeks after my fingers were broken, I went out to the chicken coop to gather the dozen eggs we needed for breakfast. When I came back in, Mrs. Levy asked if she could look at my hand.

I stood by the window in the early morning light while Mrs. Levy unwound the bandages from my hand and her silver spoon. Once she lifted the bowl of the spoon from the palm of my hand, she gently placed two fingers into my hand and pressed.

Squeeze my fingers, she said.

My hand felt awkward and weak as I attempted to curl my own fingers around hers. My little finger was stiff and still oddly twisted.

Squeeze as hard as you can!

A shock of pain shot up my arm.

Try again. Your fingers are stiff and it's going to hurt, but try.

I tried again, this time more slowly. Little by little, the broken fingers curled and squeezed.

Now, open your hand and try again, but this time faster and harder.

I closed my eyes and thought about all those nights when I practiced on my silent paper keyboard. Tried to remember how I pushed to make my pinky fingers hit the keys hard, then held those weak small fingers down, pretending I was holding the shift key, striking capital letters neatly across the page.

Good, she said. Really good. Open and close your hand, let your arm swing a little from side to side to get the blood moving down your arm. Good. Now, let me look at your hand.

I held out my hand. She scooped up a small dab of butter from the bowl she kept in the kitchen and gently massaged my fingers, helping to stretch them back to normal. Then she took her other hand and forced my fingers to curl around hers, tighter than I had been able to do without her help.

They'll be stiff for a while. Maybe forever. It's not perfect, but, then, there's not much in this world that's perfect, is there?

I had never thought about perfect before.

Want to try cooking the eggs this morning? She said, guiding me to the basin in the sink where she washed the butter from my hands and hers.

It was a Thursday. Poached eggs and toast. Mrs. Levy had already filled and lifted her biggest pot onto the stovetop and lit the fire. The water was beginning to boil and swirl. She measured out a big tablespoon of vinegar and stirred it into the pot.

Once the first egg you crack into the water begins to whiten, you keep stirring and crack the next, drop it in, and so on, until they are all in, swirling around, she said, but not touching.

I carried my basket of fresh eggs over to the stove and cracked the first one into a teacup, making sure the yolk was whole. The heat from the stove and boiling water, the acrid smell of the vinegar, and the slight tinge of blood at the edge of the yolk made my head spin. My stomach heaved.

I grabbed for the edge of the counter, tipping the basket of eggs onto the floor. I began to throw up. Mrs. Levy grabbed me. Held me. Tears stung my face. I gagged and threw up again.

It's okay, she whispered. It's only eggs.

When my body calmed, Mrs. Levy wiped my face with her apron and sat me down in her kitchen chair. She handed me a glass of water.

I was afraid this might happen. You to need to drink some water. Little sips. And eat a cracker. I'll bring some upstairs for you when I finish with breakfast. You eat these crackers when you start feeling nauseated again. Eat as many as you like. I've got plenty. And drink all the water. You'll feel better once you eat a little something and drink. Think you can make it up the stairs while I clean up?

Once the room quit spinning and there was nothing left in my stomach to bother me, I went up to my room and shut the door. It was nearly light outside and the other boarders were starting to stir. I could hear them getting dressed, lacing their shoes, chatting to each other as they gathered in the hallway and walked downstairs to the dining room.

I untied my shoes, slipped off my skirt and blouse and lay down on the bed in my underclothes. I pulled my mother's quilt up over my shoulders. I didn't want to eat anything. All I wanted to do was sleep.

I don't know how long I slept before Mrs. Levy came upstairs and knocked on my door. The knocking startled me awake. I grabbed the quilt and wrapped it around my shoulders before opening the door.

You must be starving, she said.

I shook my head and stumbled back to the side of my bed. The room tipped slightly. I needed to sit down. I told her I was sorry about the eggs, that I didn't know what had happened or what was wrong.

You need to untie your corset, she said, gently moving the quilt away from my shoulders so she could untie the ribbons that were binding my tender stomach and chest.

I took a deep breath. The warm air filled me and calmed my head.

Does Georgette know?

I shook my head.

Your parents?

I closed my eyes. I couldn't answer. I hadn't allowed myself to think about that night, to consider what might have happened. All the shame I'd been hiding deep inside of me came back in a shudder of tears. Mrs. Levy pulled the quilt up around my shoulders and held me.

What happened doesn't matter. It's yours to tell or not. More than likely, you've got a baby growing inside of you. Nothing matters but that. You can't think about that night. Got to help this baby forget about it too. This baby is innocent. You got hurt, but some good has come from it. That's what you've got to think about. I never had a chance to carry a child. Oh, I wanted to, but I couldn't, but I kept going. That's what God wanted for me. But, God wanted something else for you and you've got to keep going too.

I don't see a reason to tell Georgette or anyone else, but I've got some responsibility to help you since you've come this way into my world. But, I can't let you stay here once you start to show. People will talk. I can't stop them. But, I will help you. I promise. I'll find a way for you and this baby to be safe.

EIGHT

I slept all that day and into the evening. As daylight begin to dim and the long shadows of moonlight and night crept across my bedroom floor, I heard the other boarders coming home from work. Heard them hang up their coats, walk up the wooden staircase to wash their faces, and begin getting ready to go down to the dining room to eat.

I didn't want to get dressed and go downstairs for supper. I wasn't ready to meet anyone yet, and I wasn't hungry. Mrs. Levy came into my room during the day while I was sleeping and left me a piece of buttered bread and some cold sliced meatloaf. She made wonderful meatloaf, and I nibbled at it a bit at a time over the long day of sleeping, hoping to keep it down. I'd had enough of being sick.

Funny, how knowing something changes everything. I hadn't known before that morning that I was pregnant. All I had done the weeks before was worry about my hand and getting a job. All I could think about then was if I couldn't find a job, I would have to move back to the farm.

What a dark cloud all that simple worry had created! How quickly that farm cloud blew out of my life and another formed when I knew I had another life to care for.

My hand was no longer important. I had a baby growing inside of me. A baby that came from something terrible. The option of going back home was now wiped clean from my life. I couldn't go back. My family wouldn't want me. They would call my child a bastard. They would shame me even more than I had already shamed myself.

Shame had diminished my life. Shame had put me to bed and made me want to hide. I felt small and fragile.

Mrs. Levy knocked on my door. I didn't answer. She lifted the latch and stepped into my room. She was carrying my blouse and a fresh pitcher of water.

I'm going to wait to ring the dinner bell until you come down. You need to get dressed and carry on. You'll help me serve just like you did yesterday. None of that has changed and none of the other boarders will ever know differently unless you tell them. I've washed your blouse and pressed it. I'll help you get up and get washed. You can't hide from what happened. You've got to show this baby that you are strong enough to carry him or her safely into this world.

I can't, I said.

Mrs. Levy poured the fresh water into my washbasin, rinsed out a cloth and brought it over to me.

You will do this and everything else from this moment on for that baby. That baby doesn't know any shame, and you're never going to let your baby feel shame. You are going to be strong. I'm going to brush your hair and tie your corset for you. Not tight, but loose and comfortable. Got to give that baby room to grow. And you room to breathe.

I washed my face and let her brush my hair. She tied my corset loosely and helped me put on my blouse. She took my skirt from the closet and slipped it over my head.

This feels hard now, she said. But, if you don't get up today and put a fresh face on your life, you will struggle even harder to get up tomorrow. Today is the day. Are you ready?

I did as Mrs. Levy said and served dinner. I wasn't one to talk much with the other girls during meals, so it didn't feel strange that I kept silent. Mashed potatoes were passed from hand to hand, snap beans eaten, chicken bones stacked neatly on the bone plates. Cake cut, tea drunk. It was just like any other meal I had shared with the other boarders. Margaret, who was a clerk at the big department store near my office, asked about my hand. Others noted that the bandage was gone. I told them it was healed. Better. I was better.

But I wasn't. My mind was charged with shame and regret. I tried my best not to let anger flood through me. I dreamed of fighting back, of killing the man who had hurt me. I wanted to hate.

The next morning, when Mrs. Levy knocked on my door, I got up, dressed and went down to help with breakfast. I gathered the eggs, but couldn't cook them. There was something about the smell of cooking eggs that caused my stomach to heave.

Instead, I set the table, cut the bread, put out the jam and butter and made the tea. I rang the bell when it was time to eat. And, when everyone finished, I cleared the table and gingerly washed the dishes in the big kitchen sink.

My hand was healed, but stiff and awkward. I was afraid I might chip Mrs. Levy's pretty china, so I worked slowly, taking my time, letting my hands rest in the warm dishwater.

When I finished cleaning up and was hanging the dishrags on the back porch to dry, Mrs. Levy poked her head outside.

Get your shawl, Mrs. Levy said. You're coming to town with me this morning. You need to get ready.

Get ready. I was tired, but I didn't have anywhere else to go or anything else to do, so I went up to my room and got my shawl as commanded. The anger I had felt all night began to fester. I didn't want to be told what to do. I wanted to run from the baby inside me, but I had nowhere to go. I felt trapped.

I wrapped the shawl around my shoulders and tied the long ends tight around my body then walked downstairs. Mrs. Levy was standing there waiting for me.

She looked deep into my eyes. I knew she could see the thick wall of hatred I was building there.

You need to have the right words to talk about what happened. You were violated. Raped. That's what happened. Rape. It's a terrible word and a terrible thing and you can't make it go away. Things are happening inside of you. You've got a baby growing inside of you, and sooner than you can be ready for it, it will be here.

I wrestled with all my strength to hold everything in. Mrs. Levy took one step toward me and held out her hand. I stepped back then started to talk. It came out in a whisper at first then after the words started, they came in a torrent of hot tears.

I hate him, I said.

Of course you do, she said. But you've got to let that hate go.

The hate I felt burned inside of me. It sickened me. It made me hate myself.

I want to go to the police, I said. I need to tell them what happened. I couldn't then, but I'm stronger now. They should arrest him. Put him in jail. Hurt him like he hurt me.

You can't, she whispered.

He raped me. You've said so yourself. He broke my fingers so I couldn't be a typewriter anymore. He could do this to someone else. I have to tell them.

If you go to the police, they won't believe you.

Mrs. Anders, the bookkeeper in the office, she must know. She told me to be careful when Mr. Bristal asked me to stay and work late that night. She can tell them I'm telling the truth. He did this to me. He probably did it to the others before me, as well.

He'll say he didn't do it. He'll say you are lying about what happened. The police will say even worse things, like you wanted to have sex with him. That you tried to trick him. Mr. Bristal will say that you are a vixen, a whore, and you wanted money for sex and when he wouldn't give it to you, there was a tussle and you ran out of the room and broke your fingers because you fell. Mrs. Anders knows the truth, but she won't help you because she will be afraid she'll lose her job if she tells.

I don't believe you, I shouted. That isn't right. Mrs. Anders will speak up for me. I know she will.

She won't. And, the police won't either.

How do you know? I screamed.

I know, because I was raped before I was married. I went to the police. I asked for help. Instead of the man getting arrested, I was the one accused. I was the one threatened. I was the one on trial. No one helped me and when, like you, I discovered I was pregnant, I didn't have anywhere to turn. I had left home to be in the city and didn't know anyone and I couldn't go home. I was only nineteen. Alone. Scared. I sold my jewelry and everything else of any value I had and found a doctor, a butcher, who said he could help me.

Mrs. Levy stepped back. It was as though whatever shame she had felt then came blowing back and she had to move away from me for fear that she would be judged again.

Remember when I told you I didn't, couldn't have babies of my own? That I never carried another life inside myself? I was asleep when the doctor operated. Chloroformed. And when I woke, bleeding, hurting, crying, the doctor told me that it was a good thing I had come to him because I was unfit to be a mother and he had made sure I would never have the chance to be a mother again. He said I was impure. That it was obvious to him from the first moment he met me that I had let the Devil drive my actions and I got pregnant out of holy wedlock because I was sinful and unfit to be loved. It was worse than what happened to me at the hands of the man who raped me.

That is my secret. You can keep it or not. I have never told anyone else. Not even my husband. He wanted children and cried with me because we couldn't have them. He never knew why. I was afraid if he knew he wouldn't marry me and if he ever found out, he would leave me.

I will keep it, I told her. I stepped forward. I wanted to touch her, to thank her for not judging me the way she had been judged.

I can't let you go to a butcher. I can't let what happened to me happen to you. Tell me every detail and nightmare, she said. Let those thoughts and words escape. I will catch them and carry them for you so you can let them go. I will wait until the moon is full and I will write them down and burn them, turn them to ashes. Smoke and ashes. Done and gone so you can go on.

I started to talk.

All I could think about while it was happening, I said, was how the bull on our farm would mount the cows and the cows would dig in their heels and lower their heads as if they were resolved but shamed by what was happening. They just stood there stiff legged, feet dug deep, while the bull had them. When the bull finished, he'd stumble off the backs of the cows like all the power he once had was drained from his body. Most times, the cows would bellow loudly afterwards, as if they were screaming out to warn the others, while peeing a long hot stream as if to say they wanted nothing from the bull and he was best to get out of their way.

I thought about those defiant cows and that weakened bull and I lifted my knee and jammed it as hard as I could into his crotch. That's when he grabbed my hand and broke my fingers.

He broke my fingers, I said. I started to sob.

And your heart, Mrs. Levy said, wrapping her soft, thick arms around me. He broke your heart, but you can't let him break your spirit. What's done is done. You can't go back, and you can't carry what happened with you. If you do, it will weigh you down. It will change you. You can't let him change you.

I leaned into her arms and wept. She held me for as long as I cried. When I finished, she took a clean handkerchief out of her pocket and wiped the tears from my face.

Just as quickly as Mrs. Levy had opened her own heart and released her secret, it vanished like smoke, receded and was lost again in a tangle of painful memories she, like so many women, needed to keep hidden. In that moment, I knew the memory of my rape and other sharp things that had cut through my life would rest within me for the remainder of my days. Occasionally, like a sudden storm, my horrors would burst forth in declaration like hers had, then evaporate into the mist of the everyday.

You've done what you could. You've cried it out, and now I know your story and will write it down and burn it. Someone needed to know so you wouldn't be alone in this world. Your hand is healed. We're going to town and we're going to buy some wool. Something soft and pretty. Maybe yellow. Do you like yellow? Or, maybe a soft green. I think green could be nice for a baby hat and sweater. I've got some needles for you. Do you know how to knit?

I made my shawl, I said.

It's beautiful, she replied, running her fingers over the frilly crocheted edge. The stitches are fine and even, like you. Knitting can heal you inside. Can give you time to sort through your troubles. I've got a pretty pattern for a baby blanket that uses a tiny seed stitch like the one you used in your shawl. Makes a nice tight blanket. It'll keep your baby warm. You can use that same stitch for the hat and sweater. You've got work to do. Best you get started. Shall we go?

When I walked out the door with Mrs. Levy, I realized it was the first time I had been outside other than to go to the chicken coop to collect eggs since Mr. Bristal had broken my fingers. Being outside the protective walls of Mrs. Levy's home was at once strange and scary. Passing by men on the street chilled me. My shoulders pulled in, my hands tightened to fists as though I had to fight my way past the stares of the men in order to survive. I avoided making eye contact with anyone. I fussed with my shawl, pulling it up around my shoulders and tying it tighter whenever a man walked by.

Mrs. Levy linked her arm in mine and pulled me closer. She chatted about this and that, keeping up a soft banter in order to calm me.

Take a deep breath, she said, leaning her head against my shoulder. Rain is coming. Can you smell it? We could use some rain. I was thinking about putting in the garden next week. Thought I'd ask if you'd help. Onion sets and potatoes. Maybe snap beans and peppers the week after. Do you like snap beans? What about tomatoes?

I took a deep breath and smelled the rain in the air. I knew that smell from the farm. I wasn't much of a gardener, but had loved how every turned spade of rain-soaked earth was so rich with the mysteries of rotted leaves and winter you could taste it in the back of your throat.

My mother cooked snap beans with fat back, I said.

I kept walking, trying to let go of the tension in my body. I tried imagining the fresh picked beans simmering in my mother's big cast iron pot on the slow front burner of our kitchen stove. She would send me out to the garden right after breakfast to pick a basketful of beans, and we'd sit at the kitchen table snapping the ends off and pulling the tough strings. Once the beans were washed and settled in the bottom of the pot, Mother would top the mess of beans with a chunk of fatback then cover them with water, add a generous pinch of salt and start them cooking.

They'd simmer on that front burner all day until the one piece of fatback she'd placed in the middle of the beans had all but melted into the mound of greens below. By suppertime, the beans would be so soft and salty you could smear them across a piece of cornbread with the back of your fork.

I like snap beans, Mrs. Levy said.

The air was fresh. I swallowed a deep breath of it. I was suddenly glad Mrs. Levy had loosened the strings on my corset so there was room for the baby to grow. I wondered if the baby could smell the rain, could imagine that same pot of simmering beans that I had just imagined. Could the baby read my thoughts? I was pretty sure it could feel the movement of my body as I took each step. I tried to walk in a smooth rocking rhythm, being careful not to trip or step into a pothole.

It's been almost seven weeks since I was raped, I said. How big is my baby? Can it hear us talking?

Oh, Lord, Mrs. Levy said, pulling me closer. Let's see. I think it's not so big, maybe the size of a fat black-eyed pea or a blueberry. Don't know if it can hear us, but I think it can. It's like your heart. If someone says something nice, your heart can hear it, and it feels good. If someone says something awful, the opposite happens. It's like that, I think. It's like your heart. Just like you need to listen to your heart, your heart listens to you. It knows what you're thinking. I think that's the way it works with babies. They're deep inside you, like part of your soul.

Mrs. Levy bought two skeins of pale yellow wool and two of a soft mossy green. When we got back to the house, she gave me a pair of knitting needles and helped me count as I cast on the eighty tiny stitches to start work on my blanket.

When breakfast is over and the other girls have gone, you come sit in the parlor and knit with me. I've got a sweater I need to work on and it helps me to have company. We'll do our knitting after breakfast and get it put away before the others come home for supper. Best if we keep our knitting a secret.

I didn't know how much time I had to knit my blanket and baby things before I'd have to pack up and leave. I hadn't forgotten what she said about having to leave her boarding house once I started to show.

I had no idea where I'd go.

NINE

May came and I was still living at Mrs. Levy's boarding house helping her prepare a garden, serve meals and clean up. My stomach was growing but the lose dress Mrs. Levy had given me hid what was happening. I was beginning to feel a little better and Mrs. Levy decided it would be a good thing if I learned how to cook. I had never cooked that much at home. My mother had her ways and those ways didn't include having me in the kitchen. Except for helping her with fall canning, my mother preferred the solitude of cooking alone. The kitchen was her world, and I wasn't welcome.

Mrs. Levy said she liked the company. Sometimes I'd just watch what she was doing. Other times, she'd hand me a knife or a recipe and tell me to ask if I didn't know what to do next. My left hand was still stiff and there were more than one or two broken eggs in many of my cooking attempts, along with an occasional dropped piece of china. Mrs. Levy didn't seem to care.

Over time I became pretty good at making piecrusts and Mrs. Levy turned me loose on every kind of pie from chicken to chocolate. I had a little trouble working the dough with Mrs. Levy's long wooden rolling pin, but I learned through trial and error to use the palms of my hands to guide the pin smoothly over the lump of chilled dough from side to side, rather than my fingers.

My mother didn't care for pies, so we never had them. She said they were fussy and that the boys wouldn't eat them. The only pie I'd ever had before learning how to make them with Mrs. Levy were the pies that Georgette made when the rhubarb along the back of her house grew so big she had to do something to tame it.

Learning how to turn shortening, flour and water into something as fine and beautiful as a lattice top on a plump fruit pie was akin to magic. Every time I wove those delicate strips of dough across a mound of apples and cinnamon I wondered if I would have made a good wife for someone.

But, that chance was gone.

One day, I was feeling low and started crying for no clear reason. I was rolling out a piecrust when it happened. There was nothing wrong, just a hard sad feeling, as though my life had been lost and I had no way to gather it up in my arms again. Mrs. Levy stopped chopping onions and carrots for the beef stew she was making.

That baby, she said. The lucky one growing inside of you is going to be the happiest baby in the world. It's never going to cry because it's going to have potato and onion pie for lunch, chicken pie for dinner, strawberry rhubarb pie in the spring, sweet potato pie in the fall, and chocolate pie every Sunday.

Your baby is going to love pie!

My baby was going to have a mother but no father. When the house was quiet late in the evening and I could feel the shift in the air outside my window from sunshine to moonlight, I would lay in bed with my hands on the soft mound of my stomach. Each little flutter of the baby moving shot through my hands like lightning. The baby was now more than something awful that had happened to me. It was my future. A future I had never dreamed of. Never imagined for myself. Didn't know how to prepare for other than by knitting a blanket, a hat and a small pair of booties.

I began to fret that I wouldn't know what to do, that I wouldn't have the money to buy what the baby needed. Mrs. Levy told me there was nothing to worry about. She said that a baby could sleep in a bureau drawer lined with a blanket: that I didn't need a fancy bed, just a safe place for it to sleep.

One day, after the other boarders left for work, she gave me an old linen sheet and showed me how to tear it into wide strips then fold the strips into diapers. She told me that once the baby was born my milk would come in and I'd be able to feed my baby as long as I took care to feed myself.

She told me all this, then she got quiet and put her arm around me.

Your baby will be fine and you will know what to do. But first, you have to take care of yourself. You can't be angry, and you can't be sad anymore.

Your baby will now and forever be a part of you. You must make room in your heart for laughter.

When my baby started moving, fluttering in my womb like a small, trapped bird, I no longer remembered what my body felt like just to be mine. There was no before.

Before I was raped. Before my fingers were broken. Before I was going to be a mother.

TEN

Everyone in the house was excited. The long awaited World's Columbian Exposition was at last open. One of the boarders, who worked as a receptionist in the top floor of a tall office building on Michigan Avenue near Grant Park, said that before the gates opened in the morning, people were lined up down the street for as far as she could see.

All the boarders wanted to go. But the only day any of them had off was Sunday. The Sabbatarians, however, had fought hard and succeeded in keeping the Exposition closed on Sundays. The idea of taking a day off from work to see the Exposition was a dangerous one. One that most of the girls at Mrs. Levy's couldn't afford because missing a day of work could mean losing a job.

The Exposition was open at night, but even with the hundreds of bright lights illuminating the buildings and lining the walkways, everyone agreed that it wasn't safe for a young woman to stroll alone either through the streets of the Exposition or down the midway with its games, booths and the magical Ferris Wheel that spun its bright cars high above the whole of Chicago and Lake Michigan. However, it was exciting to read about in the papers and to hear from others who had been there. It was thrilling just to be so close and to imagine such a magnificent thing existing in the heart of the city where we lived.

There was talk about a special Chicago Day to be held in October, when offices would be closed and the people of Chicago would be able to attend for free. But, October was a long way away from May.

By the middle of May I could no longer lace my corset tight enough to be able to fasten the top two buttons of my skirt and the lose dress Mrs. Levy had given me was beginning to be tight around my middle. The other boarders whispered behind my back. The baby was beginning to show.

One afternoon while we were cooking dinner, Mrs. Levy asked if I wanted to go to the Exposition.

Oh, yes, I said, my face flushing with excitement.

I thought we could go on Thursday. There's someone I want you to meet. Her name is Jane Addams. She runs the Hull House, a settlement house for women not far from here. It's a nice place. About twenty women live there and she's built a school there for women to learn life skills and a program for young children. I've talked with Miss Addams. She said she might have a place for you to live if you're willing to teach the women how to knit. I also told her you made pies. Wonderful pies.

Georgette was a teacher, not me. I was a student. I'd been taught a lot of things, but had never taught anyone how to do anything.

I'm not a teacher, I said.

I think you could be. You have things the women need to know how to do if they are going to be able to raise their children and take care of themselves. You said you used to help your mother with canning and you know how to make a dozen different wonderful pies. All the girls love them!

I didn't say anything. I took the piecrust I had made that morning, and floured the counter so I could start rolling it out in order to make an apple pie for dinner. I didn't want to leave Mrs. Levy. I felt safe in her house. I knew my baby was safe there too.

I have another dress I thought might fit you. I let the seams out on the sides. It has a soft sash that ties in the back. Should be good for months to come. It's time, she said.

Do I need to pack? I asked.

No, she said. Not today. Before we go to the Exposition, we'll go to the World Congress Auxiliary Building for one of the Women's Congresses. Jane Addams will be there. She will be introducing Susan B. Anthony. Do you know about the work of the Suffragettes? They have organized women across the country in order to get the right to vote. The right to have some control over our lives.

Miss Anthony was arrested for voting in her hometown of Rochester, New York. She was tried and convicted but refused to pay her fine for breaking the law. The officials didn't know what to do, so they just let her go. But that didn't stop her. She says she won't quit fighting until all women have the right to vote.

My father used to say that women had men to take care of them so they didn't need to be able to vote. Georgette said she dreamed about having the right to vote. I wasn't sure what I believed or what I thought was right. I knew I didn't want a man to take care of me, but I never thought much about not having a man and needing to take care of myself. I never quite understood what having the right to vote would do for me.

Do you think women should have the right to vote? I asked.

Mrs. Levy laughed.

Mr. Levy was the one who introduced me to Jane Addams. He said I needed to get out of the house and learn about the world from her and how we could work together to make it better. My husband was a businessman and said that smart women were good for business. He said that women had better heads for knowing what was right then men did and that if he had his way, it would be men who didn't have the right to vote and women that did.

I helped out at the Hull House when it first opened four years ago. Mr. Levy was alive then, and he encouraged me to go there to help Jane and her friends. He said what they were doing was the right thing to do. That we should have more places in our world where people who needed a little help to get up on their feet could go. It's a good place. A place I wish I would have had when I was your age. Lord knows I needed someone to teach me how to take care of myself. I was young when I was raped and didn't know much about anything in the world. Maybe if I would have had Hull House, I might have been able to keep my baby. Might have been able to take care of both of us. But, then, I managed. When I got over what happened with my baby I took what little money I had left and went to night school like your Mrs. Anders. I had always been good with figures and eventually got a job keeping records for Mr. Levy's company. That's how we met. It was the luckiest thing that ever happened in my life. He was a fine man. I miss him every day.

But, he's gone now and the day is long and this house is too big for just me, so I keep my hands busy cooking and taking care of the girls who come to Chicago looking for work. Got my own little Hull House in a way.

How much will it cost? I asked.

Nothing. You just need to do your part by teaching other women how to knit blankets and booties for their children. If you get the chance, maybe teach those young mothers how to make a pie. I do believe that a woman can do most anything in the kitchen if she knows how to make a decent pie. And, you make the finest piecrust ever! You'll be safe at Hull House. I can come visit if you like.

When do I have to go? I asked.

Jane said they'd have a room ready for you on Monday.

The next day was Wednesday, and Mrs. Levy had a plan. When we finished with breakfast that morning, she said we needed to get started cooking. Her plan was to make two suppers: one hot to serve that night, and another cold one the girls could serve themselves on Thursday. Mrs. Levy said we'd get up early on Thursday and serve a good hearty breakfast of biscuits and eggs, then leave right after everyone had gone to work and the dishes were done and the dining room reset for dinner. She didn't know how long the Congress where Miss Anthony was going to speak would last, and she wanted to be sure we would have plenty of time to take in the sights of the Exposition in the afternoon before it got dark and we headed home. She thought it would be best if we readied the table for the evening meal before we left, put out what wouldn't spoil and cover it with a cloth. The rest we'd put in the icebox but have it ready in serving bowls. She'd let the girls know tomorrow morning that more than likely, we'd be getting home late and they'd have to serve themselves and clean up.

Mrs. Levy got a big pot of beef stew going for Wednesday's supper and I cut up the chicken, tossed it in flour and seasonings, and got it ready for Mrs. Levy to fry. After I finished with the chicken I started boiling potatoes and eggs to make potato salad.

Cold fried chicken is the best, Mrs. Levy said. It was Mr. Levy's favorite. He'd eat it hot from the skillet, but always had me cook up twice as much as the two of us could possibly eat so we could have it cold the next day with potato salad.

I'm thinking you should make a pie for dessert. Would you mind? There's some rhubarb in the garden ready for picking. Doesn't seem right that everyone else has to go to work and we get to have a day off strolling through the Exposition. A nice slice of your rhubarb pie might make the day easier for them. They'll get their chance to go to the Exposition. I'll make sure of it.

When I got up the next morning to make breakfast, I put on the dress Mrs. Levy had remade for me. It was a pretty dress: beautiful soft sky blue material with fine white stripes. It had a high white collar and cuffs, and the sash was satin and a deeper shade of blue. It was probably the prettiest dress I had ever owned. I loved the way the wide blue sash softened the waistline and tied neatly in the back, gathering up the folds of the skirt. The sash also did a good job of hiding my growing stomach, making it possible for me to go without my corset. It felt so good to be able to take a deep breath I was tempted to throw my corset away.

When the last boarder had left for work and the breakfast dishes were washed and put away, I swept the breakfast crumbs from the tablecloth and began laying out the plates and silverware for dinner. I put out bread, a fresh jar of tomato jam and a large bowl of applesauce to have with the potato salad and cold chicken. I threw a small cloth over the food in the center of the table and put the rhubarb pie on the sideboard along with a stack of plates and forks. Mrs. Levy had told everyone at breakfast that there was fried chicken in the icebox along with potato salad.

Ready? Mrs. Levy asked, grabbing her purse and her shawl.

For a minute I froze. I looked at Mrs. Levy's beautiful bone china and her lace tablecloth. I saw my rhubarb pie sitting on the sideboard next to a stack of her cut glass dessert plates. Saw the teapot poised next to a half dozen flowered teacups and saucers, forks and spoons stacked neatly on the side by the silver sugar bowl I had just filled. I closed my eyes and could imagine hearing the soft chatter of the other boarders coming down for dinner. The table was all set and ready, but I wondered if I was truly ready to leave this place that had so quickly become my home.

ELEVEN

The room was crowded with hundreds of women. Many of them were wearing white dresses with wide satin sashes, indicating they were Suffragettes. These women in white had pushed to the front of the auditorium in order to take up seats surrounding the stage. Other women were clustered together in their various groups wearing either badges or sashes declaring the state or organization they were representing. When Susan B. Anthony, dressed in a somber black dress with a starched white collar, was introduced and stepped up to the podium, the whole crowd waved white handkerchiefs in the air and cheered.

Miss Anthony stood tall and erect. The way she walked and stood made her feel like someone filled with experience and resolve. It was clear she had things to say and was not afraid to say them. Everyone leaned forward in anticipation of her speech. She was older than I expected.

She held everyone's attention.

I looked around the room and was taken by the sheer number of women and the energy they brought to the walls, the lights, the promise of it all. It was unlike anything I had ever experienced.

My heart nearly burst with anticipation at what she was going to say and what was to come next in my life. This building is why I was drawn to Chicago, I thought. I could feel the smooth banister of the polished marble staircase and the high arching ceiling above, calling to me, beckoning me to stay. I wanted to rest there forever. Everything about this magnificent structure was bigger than a cornfield. Bigger than any dreams I'd ever dared dream.

What is this place? I asked Mrs. Levy.

Mrs. Levy pulled me close to her and whispered in my ear.

This is going to be the Chicago Art Institute, where all the great artworks of the world are going to be exhibited once the Exposition is completed. Can you imagine?

I couldn't. All I had ever known about art were the covers of the seed catalogues that Georgette had torn off and tacked up on her walls.

This, I whispered to the baby growing inside of me, this is where I want to be. This is why I came here. I want to see everything. Know everything. Be here. Be here. Be here with you.

The meeting was called to order.

One by one Miss Anthony recognized the various groups of women represented in the crowd. As she mentioned each one, there was a polite round of applause. When she got to the end of her list, she stopped for a moment before going on.

Mrs. Levy squeezed my hand.

Miss Anthony continued speaking:

...women have been taught always to work for something else than their own personal freedom; and the hardest thing in the world is to organize women for the one purpose of securing their political liberty and political equality. It is easy to congregate thousands and hundreds of thousands of women to try to stay the tide of intemperance; to try to elevate the morals of a community; to try to educate the masses of people; to try to relieve the poverty of the miserable; but it is a very difficult thing to make the masses of women, any more than the masses of men, congregate in great numbers to study the cause of all the ills of which they complain, and to organize for the removal of that cause; to organize for the establishment of great principles that will be sure to bring about the results which they so much desire.

Political liberty. Political equality. These were all words I had never thought about before. I wished hard that Georgette could be there with me. I knew these were things she dreamed about.

Why hadn't I dreamed them as well? I had dreamed only of leaving the farm, coming to Chicago to make a life that was my own, not knowing what that life would be. Never imagining the life that was now before me.

I leaned in close to Mrs. Levy.

What does this mean for my baby? I asked.

Mrs. Levy linked her arm in mine and pulled me closer.

If women get the right to vote, we could change the world. Equality is a powerful thing. Can you feel the excitement? If we had the right to vote, we'd have a voice and could say what we think, and do what we know is right. Work decent hours and make the same wages as men. Have the same privileges. With the right to vote, we could fix things that are wrong. Women could join unions and have their jobs protected. Women like you could stand up for themselves.

And my baby? I asked again.

Would grow up in a kinder world.

After listening to Miss Anthony talk, we left and walked over to the footbridge arching over one of the large lagoons on the Exposition campus.

See that big building over there? Mrs. Levy said, pointing. That big beautiful building, The Woman's Building, was designed by Sophia Hayden. She's only twenty-one years old and is the first woman to ever graduate with a degree in architecture. Can you imagine? She dreamed this building. Drew this building. Breathed air into this building! Mrs. Levy said, spreading her arms to indicate the full width of the magnificent edifice.

A woman built that building all by herself? I asked.

No, Mrs. Levy said. She designed it. Drew up the plans and told the carpenters and stonemasons how to put it together. She drew a picture of the plans then told the men what to do and how to build it! Isn't that marvelous…

I had never heard of such a thing. My father and his friends built our home and the three barns on our farm, along with every other building and home in our small town. My mother might have told my father where she wanted him to put her kitchen or that she wanted a long wooden porch stretched out across the back where she could hang laundry and make soap if the weather was bad, but other than that, I can't imagine that she wrote anything down or drew any pictures. I had never known her to draw a picture of anything. I was pretty sure that an architect didn't dream any of the buildings in our town. But, of course, not one of those buildings looked like any of the buildings along Michigan Avenue.

A woman dreamed this building and told some men how to build it? I asked Mrs. Levy. She told them where to put the windows and the doors, and what to do to keep that big roof from falling in? She knew all that?

Amazing that someone, a woman, could do all that. The whole Exposition is a wonder. This bridge, this little lake filled with boats and those streets bordered with flowers! Have you ever seen so many beautiful flowers? There wasn't anything here a year ago but a big field filled with mud. I can't believe how beautiful it is now.

When we reached the highest peak of the bridge I stopped walking and just stared. What if I could go to college? Learn something I didn't know before? What if having that knowledge, could make it possible for me to have a life just like a man's? If that could happen, maybe I could do something as big as dream a building, paint a picture, or write a book.

I let my eyes sweep from side to side, taking in the full expanse of Sophia Hayden's eloquent building: the slender columns, broad staircase, the imposing balcony above the three arched doors and the amazing sculpture of women marching, women carrying babies, women standing proud and strong, nestled right under the peak of the roof high above the entrance. I opened my hands and pressed them gently along the sides of my stomach. See that, Little Baby, I whispered. That's your world. It's just waiting for you to come. Look how big it is!

Mrs. Levy took my hand and led me over the bridge.

It is wonderful, isn't. They're saying that it's the future. That this Exhibition is the future! That's what Susan Anthony was talking about this morning. The future. What can be. What should be. If Sophia can be an architect and have a building built here, then you can be something too. Having the right to vote is about being and doing whatever you can dream of. What do you think?

I think I want to be able to vote.

I could hardly sleep that night. Whenever I closed my eyes, my mind was flooded with all I had seen. The people, the buildings, the beautiful art everywhere. Since the only art I had ever seen before going to the Exposition had been the covers from the Burpee Catalogue that Georgette had cut out and hung on her walls, I was not prepared for the heart-softened mural of Mary Cassatt's that graced the walls of Sophia's building.

I had never heard of Mary Cassatt but decided right then and there that I would find out more about her. I couldn't quit looking at her painting, couldn't quit thinking about how she had made the women seem so real, so like someone you'd like to meet or wished you could be.

The Women's Building was filled with artwork, all done by women, even the sculpture on the outside of the building was created by two women, Enid Yandell and Alice Rideout, both 19. Nineteen! I was twenty-two and had done nothing but learn how to type.

I wanted my baby to see the artwork I saw, to know that there was softness and beauty in the world. I wanted my child to know that there were ideas bigger to be had and worlds to see that were much bigger than cornfields.

TWELVE

When Monday came, I helped with breakfast then went up to my room to finish packing my bag. Mrs. Levy had fixed another dress for me, this one was bigger than the last and she said she thought it would carry me through to the end. It was a pretty dress, dark blue with a white pique collar and cuffs. Like the other one, it had a wide soft sash I could tie loosely around the back as my baby and my waist grew. She had also washed and starched my black skirt and my two white blouses, along with the grey linen suit I'd sewn for myself when I graduated from high school.

You'll need these again, she said. Not right away, but soon afterwards. Give yourself time.

I tried to pay for the dresses she had given me.

You've been a great help, she said. It was the least I could do. Don't know how I managed all this time without you. Made me wish you could stay. I'll miss you.

Georgette had said she would miss me when I left the farm. She was the only one. My brothers didn't say much of anything when I left, and all my mother and father could do was look away when they said their goodbyes.

Thank you, I said. I can't thank you enough for all you've done for me.

It's time, she said. We'll have to take two different grip cars to get to Hull House. I'll travel with you all the way there and be there with you as you get settled. But I want you to know how to get there and back so you will know how to come back to visit. I've written it all down. You're welcome, you know, to come back to see me. I'd love to see you and that baby. It might have come from bad, but I just know it's going to be a beautiful baby.

I had never been anywhere before I came to Chicago. All I had known were large flat fields, wheat, corn, cows, pigs, church on Sundays, the one room school house with its small wall of books, Georgette's front porch and the pictures from the Burpee Catalogue. The sheer size of Chicago, along with the many gleaming white buildings of the World's Columbian Exposition stretching along the shore of Lake Michigan, and hearing Miss Susan B. Anthony's talk about women's right to vote, had been a potent tonic. It was intoxicating.

My broken fingers didn't matter anymore. Being a typewriter was no longer what I wanted or needed in order to make my life whole. The baby growing inside of me might have been born of ugliness, but I had divorced myself from what had happened and embraced the beauty of what was to come. My world was bigger than I had ever imagined it might be. I was on a journey, and my baby was coming with me.

That morning when I packed my suitcase and walked with Mrs. Levy to the grip car stop might have scared me a little because I didn't know what was going to happen next, but whatever fear I had didn't stop me from moving forward.

The trip that afternoon took me further than I had ever gone before on the grip cars. When we passed the Studebaker Company, I pressed my face against the window hoping to see Mrs. Anders standing by the window. I wished I could have gone back once to see her, to tell her what happened. To tell her I was going to be okay. She needed to know.

I had no desire to ever see Mr. Bristal again. The hate-filled fire in me had at last died down and I didn't think it would be any good for my baby to feel that anger boiling inside me again. What was past was gone. I turned my face away from the window, closed my eyes and held my breath hoping I wouldn't see him walking down the street. I didn't know what I'd do if I did see him, and I didn't want to find out.

You okay? Mrs. Levy asked.

Just a flutter, I lied. I put my hand on the small rising hump of my stomach.

When we get to Polk Street, we have to change cars. It's not far after that.

As we traveled over Polk toward Halsted, the tall brick and glass buildings of downtown began to dissolve into small wood framed houses. Houses similar to the one Georgette lived in. But these little houses didn't feel open and inviting like Georgette's, they felt crowded. Pushed beyond their capacity for neatness.

The small houses got meaner looking and grew shabbier the further west we traveled. Children ran barefoot in the dirty streets, wash hung from sagging lines strung out the windows and along the narrow alleyways between houses. Mothers and daughters sat on the once sturdy stoops holding babies as though they had been waiting a lifetime for the grip car to stop and take them somewhere else. There were no flower gardens.

There, Mrs. Levy said, pointing at the large red stone building that filled the corner. Hull House is over there.

She pulled on the cord, signaling our stop. The grip car slowed. I grabbed the handle of my satchel. The door to the grip car opened and we stepped down onto the street and began walking toward the entrance in the courtyard.

Everything around us was covered in dust. Although it was spring and the air was just beginning to warm, the street felt as hot as a sick child's breath.

I paused a moment and looked first at the imposing collection of red stone buildings, then down the long dirty streets on either side.

Hull House is a good place. A safe place. I wouldn't take you anywhere else. The baby, Mrs. Levy said. I couldn't let you stay. You know, because of the baby. There'd be talk. The other girls. It would not have been good for either one of us.

I shifted my weight and squeezed my hand tightly around the flimsy handle of my suitcase.

I know, I said. Let's go.

The resident director, Louisa, met us at the door. Jane Addams was at a meeting.

No need for Mrs. Levy to go any further with us, Louisa said. Hull House frowns on visitors walking the halls. Even poor people have the right to private lives.

Mrs. Levy put her arms around my shoulders and squeezed me as tightly as she could.

You know where to find me, Mrs. Levy said. I expect you to come visit.

She stepped back and pressed a fat envelop into my hand.

Traveling money, Mrs. Levy said. Enough to get you started somewhere new with a little extra to be sure you come see me first. Promise?

Afraid to speak, I shook my head yes.

You fought back. Never forget that. You fought back. You're strong. Stronger than I was or ever could be. I'm proud of you. You're good. There's nothing bad about you.

I dropped my suitcase, letting it tumble to the floor by my feet, and put my arms around her. The fear of what was going to happen to me, the terrifying nightmares of being lost and unable to care for my baby that I had been hiding from the daylight bubbled up and threatened to explode. I held tight for as long as I dared, then slowly let her go. I took a deep breath.

I knew then, just as I had known when I boarded the train to Chicago that I would never see my family again, that I might never see Mrs. Levy either.

I won't forget, I said. Won't ever forget what you've done for me. For my baby and me.

She kissed me on the cheek, turned and left.

Louisa picked up the suitcase I had dropped. I looked back over my shoulder in order to watch Mrs. Levy walk through the door.

Louisa began walking down the hallway toward the staircase without me. I rushed to catch up.

Do you speak Italian? Louisa asked. Polish?

No, I said.

We've got a lot of ladies who come here who don't speak English. Come straight off the boat from Italy and Poland. Young. So young. Married and scared. They come here because they don't have anywhere else to go to learn things. Miss Addams said you were going to teach knitting and do some cooking for us.

Pies, I answered. Both sweet and savory. Mrs. Levy said I make the nicest lattice piecrust she's ever eaten. And I know how to knit. I can teach people how to make shawls as well as bonnets, blankets, booties: things they are going to need for their babies.

Louisa looked over at my thickening waist.

Your husband hit you? She asked. Is that why you came here? People are going to wonder. Most are too polite to ask, but better if you just go ahead and tell them and be done with it so you can move on.

I used to be a typewriter, I said. But my boss raped me and broke my fingers.

My room was on the second floor in the main house. The kitchen was also in the main house as well as some classrooms. There were deep red Oriental carpets scattered throughout the various rooms and hallways, giving the building a sense of quiet. It wasn't the kind of place where you would talk loudly or run down the long hallways. All the residents were women. Except for the days Dr. John Dewey or some other man came to give a lecture, the place had the feeling of a convent.

I was fine with that. Although I was over my anger about what Mr. Bristal had done to me, I was far from over my fear of ever again being backed up against a wall by a man.

There was a grand sitting room on the first floor that was filled with clusters of comfortable chairs surrounding the biggest Oriental rug I had ever seen. At one end of the room there was a fireplace. I didn't have much time for sitting, but when I did, I wanted to sit as close to the fire as possible. There was something about the big open rooms and broad wooden floors that gave me a chill.

In exchange for my room and board, I taught knitting and worked in the kitchen. Once I cleared the dishes from breakfast, I turned my attention to pies. I made a dozen every day: six savories and six sweet. The savories changed from day to day depending on what meat was left over from the night before. If there was beef, I made dark gravy flavored with a bit of coffee for the meat and added potatoes and onions. If it was chicken, I used whatever vegetables we had with either rice or potatoes and a thick salt and pepper flavored sauce made from flour and milk. Leftover chicken was easy to work with and went with just about anything I could find to add with it: peas, green beans, carrots, potatoes, celery, onions, turnips, or whatever we had. I didn't like lamb much, because it had a sweet cloying taste, so whenever there was leftover lamb I made the gravy from the pan drippings and fat mixed with lots of carrots and onions in order to balance the sweetness of the meat.

The savory pies were popular in the coffeehouse at Hull House where neighborhood men would sometimes come by after work. The staff and the women preferred a good cup of tea and a slice of fruit pie in the afternoon. Apple was their favorite, but I wasn't always able to get apples so I made pies from whatever fruit came into the kitchen from the vendor. When I didn't have fruit, I made custard pies. No one complained.

I'd usually take the last pie out of the oven around four or four-thirty, have a cup of tea, then wash up to get ready to teach my knitting classes. By the time the pies were done, I didn't have much of a taste for food anymore so I'd wind up skipping dinner. I guess that's just what happens when you're pregnant.

I only had two women come for that first class at Hull House, one Polish, the other German, so there wasn't much talking and the class seemed awkward, long and the knitting difficult. All three of us left in frustration.

The language situation, or my lack of being able to make myself understood no matter how loudly or softly I gave the instructions, wasn't good. I began to get worried I was going to get kicked out of Hull House and onto the streets because I had failed to teach the two women how to cast on the proper number of stitches to make a baby blanket.

The next week, the Polish woman brought her daughter and things began to get better. Her daughter had learned English playing in the streets and had also picked up a few words of German, so things moved more easily.

The German woman brought her niece the next week. The girl was only five years old, spoke English as well as German and was happy to be doing something other than helping with her younger siblings at home. Before I could say she was too young to be in the class, the girl picked up a pair of needles from the basket in the middle of the table, asked for some yarn and stood up on a chair so she could see what we were doing.

There we were, the five of us crowding around the table, casting on stitches, talking in three different languages, learning how to knit baby blankets. If anyone noticed my growing stomach, no one was rude enough to say anything.

Over time, more women came, more blankets were made, and I felt as though I had found a place for myself.

Working in the kitchen and teaching knitting didn't leave me any time to pay much attention to the other things happening at Hull House. However, there was always something going on: the kindergarten and the camps, the coffeehouse, Shakespeare Club, sports events, lectures from

Dr. Dewey, classes in cooking and dressmaking and other domestic arts, as well as the many classes teaching English.

The place vibrated with the purposeful activity of coming and going and learning. On Tuesdays, there were checkups for pregnant women and a well baby clinic. Toddlers and older children usually accompanied their mothers on these visits, so I made a batch of cookies on checkup days in addition to my pies to serve to the children so they could have something to eat while they waited.

Whenever the Suffragettes gathered at Hull House, the place bustled with excitement. Dozens of women filled the halls and rooms, creating a palpable energy and the belief that things could change. There was talk of strikes, marches and organizing. New members got introduced, signs were created, and announcements made of who was coming to speak, where people were supposed to gather and what to do if anyone got arrested.

One afternoon, Miss Addams came into the kitchen and asked if I would make six additional pies. There was going to be an important meeting of the Suffragettes in the evening. The meeting would start early and go late. Many of the women would be coming straight from work and she wanted to be able to serve something.

Sweet or savory, I asked.

I'm thinking three of each. What do you think?

I've got plenty of chicken for three more pies and if I don't have enough apples, I'll make a couple custard pies.

If you're not too tired, I'd like you to come tonight. You're doing a wonderful job with the women in your knitting class. You're a natural leader. If you were a Suffragette, you could help your students understand not to be afraid of joining us. That we are all working together to get women the right to vote, protection at work, better working conditions, better lives, not only for them, but for their children as well.

I want to be a Suffragette, I said.

Do you have another dress? A white one? But, nothing with frills or flowers. We want our voices to be heard and our concerns to be taken seriously. We dress in white so people know we are Suffragettes, but we dress modestly so we can be taken seriously.

I have a black skirt and white blouse, and a grey suit I made for high school graduation, but neither outfit fits me anymore, I said, looking down at my rising belly. My baby is growing.

She put her hand on my shoulder.

Turn around. Hmmm, I might have something that will fit you. Come by my room when you finish with the pies. If you're going to stand with us as a Suffragette, you'll need a proper dress. I've got a hat for you too.

I wanted more than anything to be able to vote. To make a choice instead of being told what I could or could not do. I had snuck into one of their meetings the week before and was standing at the back of the room when I heard some women arguing about how in 1870 even emancipated male slaves were given the right to vote, but white women were not.

According to the law, one of the Suffragettes called out, a white woman is no better than a slave in this country!

The room rustled like a stiff satin dress.

Jane Addams stepped up to the podium to calm the crowd.

When you are a Suffragette, you are marching and protesting for the voting rights of all women: black, white, yellow or brown, she said.

We must never forget that each and every one of us is a slave if we don't have the same rights as the master who rules us. And if we don't fight to share those rights with those around us, then we are no better than that master with a whip in his hand.

Our success will not be measured by securing our own right to vote. It will be measured by guaranteeing that every woman in this country has the right to vote and be heard. We will stand together and speak for those who cannot speak for themselves for whatever reason. If we cannot do that, then we must sit down and be silent.

The room got quiet.

That evening was a revelation for me. The right to vote was something every man and woman should have. A right to vote would give us power to speak. I couldn't quit thinking about what Mrs. Levy had told me about going to the police, that if I told them what Mr. Bristal had done to me they wouldn't have believed me.

If I had the right to vote, would they believe me then?

THIRTEEN

We'll be gathering in front of City Hall Thursday morning. The Aldermen will be there for their monthly meeting with Mayor Harrison, so we will be there to make our wishes known. We aren't allowed to go into the chambers and disrupt their meeting, but we can be outside. So, we'll stand on the sidewalk and make the honorable men walk through us to get into the building, Jane Addams said.

I want everyone who is here tonight, to be there on Thursday morning. The meeting starts at ten, so we should be assembled, with signs, ready to greet the Aldermen and Mayor Harrison at nine.

Heads nodded.

Anybody know anyone married to one of the Aldermen? If we could get some of those wives standing with us, the Aldermen and the Mayor would have to listen to us. I'll ask Mrs. Harrison. Anyone else?

Mrs. Madden is a friend, someone shouted. I'll ask her to stand with me.

And, I know Mrs. Swift.

Jane Addams looked around the crowd.

Anyone else?

No one spoke.

That's a start. A good start. If we can get those three women to stand with us, we can get the others.

One by one, someone shouted from the back of the room.

One by one, echoed Miss Addams.

The white dress Miss Addams gave me was made of the softest cotton I had ever touched. It was cut on the bias and floated from my shoulders to my ankles like a soft cloud. My stomach was growing larger. The little kicks and ripples happened more frequently. Sometimes they made me catch my breath. Other times, they were a gentle reminder that life was growing inside of me and was about to change my life.

When Miss Addams gave me the dress, she also gave me a new white petticoat to wear with it. It was one she had asked her dressmaker to open up and expand with two wide cotton voile side panels. The slip was thin, filmy and full enough to allow room for my baby and my body to grow. The slip I had been wearing under the two dresses Mrs. Levy had given me had long ago begun to bind against my stomach and breasts.

When I pulled the billowy slip over my new body, I wanted to dance and twirl around the room just to feel the soft white fabric brush against my swollen body and my bare legs.

The seams had also been let out of the white dress, and it too was full and comfortable but very serious looking. The sleeves were long and plain. No lace or trim. The dress had a small rounded collar and buttoned cuffs at the wrist. The dress was neither flashy nor fancy. It was well tailored, grownup. There was nothing about it that said young girl.

The white dress Miss Addams gave me didn't feel like a graduation dress or a wedding dress. It felt powerful. I slipped my arms through the long thin sleeves and buttoned the cuffs. When I let the dress drop down the length of my body, I was pleased to discover, like the slip beneath it, there was an abundance of loose material flowing from my shoulders to my ankles.

The dress came with a long dark purple satin sash that was designed to fit around the waist and be tied in the back, gathering up and defining the shape of the loose dress. I had no waist by this time and was unsure what I could do with the sash to make what I was wearing look more like a dress than a nightgown. After a couple of tries, I settled on using the sash to define the space between the crest of my stomach and my breasts, creating an empire waist. Rather than tying the sash into a bow, thereby drawing attention to my breasts, I tied it into a knot and let the long ends of the satin tumble down the front of the dress, softening the edges of my new profile.

I stood before the mirror in my room and slowly swayed from side to side. I had never owned a white dress or any dress that was so finely made before and felt oddly beautiful in it. My changing shape did not make me want to hide behind the folds of the soft material. Rather, it made me feel like holding up my head a little higher. I felt a surge of pride. Arrogance? Maybe. I didn't care. I rubbed the two broken fingers on my hand. For the first time in a long time I wasn't afraid. I was no longer a typewriter in a black skirt and white blouse. I was a woman: a teacher, a baker, a Suffragette, and soon to be a mother.

I finished cleaning up from breakfast then ran up to my room to change. I put on the white slip and dress, pulled on a fresh pair of black cotton stockings and laced up my shoes.

Miss Addams had also given me a hat. Plain straw. Sensible: something to keep the sun off my face while we stood outside protesting.

I pinned up my hair and perched the hat on top, slipping the long jeweled hatpin she had given me through the back of the hat, securing it to my hair. I pulled my woolen shawl over my shoulders.

I was ready.

There was a quiet burbling of chitchat among the thirty or so women gathered in front of City Hall, but the conversation was not enough to drown out the noise from the passing carriages and grip cars. The air was tense and serious with our intention of being heard.

As the aldermen began to arrive, those women who had signs raised them. All of the women moved closer to each other, forming a silent barrier in front of the door. Jane Addams and others from the Hull House stood in the middle of the group. I took a place as close as I could to Miss Addams and the other Hull House employees.

We have a right to be heard, Jane Addams said as one of the Alderman stepped from his carriage.

I'm sure you do, Miss Addams, but I don't have time to listen.

Mrs. Harrison, the mayor's wife, stepped forward from the crowd.

And, why is that? Mrs. Harrison asked.

The alderman turned his attention to Mrs. Harrison.

Why, Mrs. Harrison, I'm surprised to see you here.

He turned around to see if he had an audience. He was not disappointed. In fact, he seemed quite emboldened by the gathering crowd. Men who had once been rushing down the street to their offices had now stopped in front of City Hall, waiting to see what was happening and what might happen next. Some of the women who were walking by on their way to work or shopping slowed then moved on. Others stopped and stood by the men, but some hurried by as if they were either ashamed or afraid of what might happen.

I'm surprised your wife isn't standing here with us. In fact, so surprised, I think I shall call on her tomorrow and ask her to join us the next time. Alderman Madden's wife is here, as well as Alderman Swift's, Mrs. Harrison replied.

Mrs. Madden and Mrs. Swift stepped forward and linked their arms with Mrs. Harrison's.

Now, now ladies, we cannot have this, the Alderman said.

Have what? Mrs. Harrison asked.

This…this ridiculous disruption of our society.

Disruption? Jane Addams asked. We are not here to disrupt anything, just to voice our opinion that it is time for women in our country to step up and have a voice, and the right to vote.

The crowd behind the Alderman was gathering members as other Aldermen arrived and people passing on the street joined them. The other Aldermen stood back behind the crowd, hoping not to be seen or forced to speak.

More carriages made their way down the street to the front of City Hall. One of them stopped and Mr. Madden stepped out.

Mrs. Madden waved to her husband.

Will you be home for supper? She called out.

The crowd erupted in soft laughter.

I'll see you at home, Mr. Madden said to his wife.

He adjusted his hat and coat, ducked his head and began pushing his way through the crowd to the front door. In order to go through the door, however, he had to break through the line of women blocking the entrance.

Will you stand with us? Jane Addams asked. Help us get the right to vote?

Sensing a fight, the crowd pushed forward.

Go home. All of you. You shouldn't be out here causing trouble. You need to be home taking care of your children. You don't have the right to vote because you don't need to vote. You have husbands to speak for you and to take care of you.

Emboldened by his declaration, I took one step forward. Then another.

What about me? I asked. I don't have a husband. Who is going to speak for me? For my baby?

Alderman Madden looked at me as though I was less than human, an animal.

You should have thought of that before you got pregnant. You're no virgin, no saint in that white dress. Truth be told, you and your child will be just one more burden on our society. Why should the likes of you have the right to vote? No one wants to hear what you have to say.

Someone in the crowd threw a rock.

Whore! Another shouted.

The crowd pressed forward. I covered my stomach with my hands and my shawl, trying to protect my baby. One of the Suffragettes put her arms around me and pulled me back away from the crowd. The others broke ranks from their barricade of the door and surrounded me. There were shouts and shoving.

A big man, with hands like a farmer, pushed through the crowd and grabbed my arm and shoved me to the ground.

I pulled up my knees and wrapped my body around my child. The man ripped the hat off my head and threw it to the ground.

Godless woman! Whore! He shouted.

I heard the shouts from the crowd and the sound of a police whistle. I closed my eyes and prayed I wouldn't be trampled.

Mrs. Harrison and Jane Addams linked arms and stepped in front of the big man. He kicked then spat at me before turning and running away. Mrs. Madden knelt beside me and helped me get to my feet. I heard a police whistle blow again, this time, closer, shrill and long like a warning. Then there was the clatter of horse's hoofs on the cobblestones. People scattered.

Before stepping into the now cleared doorway, Mr. Madden turned and looked at his wife.

Go home, he said again.

She turned her back on him and linked her arm in mine, helping me to get up and walk safely away.

My sides ached. My stomach cramped. While we rode the grip car back to Hull House, I could feel a thin warm trickle of blood make its way through my underclothes and down my thighs.

I felt sick. I didn't cry. All the tears I had ever held inside had fallen when I was raped. There were no more tears of shame or harm within me.

I was afraid. Not for myself, but for my child. I tried to steady my breath. Make my heart be calm so my baby would be calm. The only thing I could think about was that I needed to get back to my room.

Change my clothes. Wash away the blood.

When I got up to get off the tram, Mrs. Harrison stepped behind me and whispered in my ear.

You're hurt, Mrs. Harrison said.

Tired. I said. Just need to go to my room and rest.

You're bleeding. How far along? She whispered.

Seven, almost eight months, I said.

I'll walk behind you until we get to Hull House so no one will see. Help you to your room. Once you're settled, I'll go fetch the midwife. She needs to look at you. Check to see if the baby is okay.

The baby shifted. My heart caught a beat and held it. I couldn't breathe. I could feel the bile rise up my throat. I swallowed hard. The air around me spun. I closed my eyes and clutched at my stomach.

Sit down, Mrs. Harrison shouted.

She grabbed my shoulders and guided me to the ground.

Put your head between your knees. Breathe in slowly. Hold my hand. Squeeze it. Hard. Scream if you need to.

No, no, no…was all I could say.

It was too early. I began massaging my stomach, trying to calm my baby. My hands gently rubbing my stomach in larger and larger soothing circles until the baby stopped moving.

Stay with me, I whispered. Stay. I love you. Please stay.

My body ached. I forced a long slow clean breath into my lungs. I wanted my baby to feel a fresh rush of air. To know whatever bad had happened had passed.

Can you help me? I asked, offering my hand.

Mrs. Harrison pulled me up to my feet and wrapped her arm around my shoulders.

I need to get to my room, I said. My bed. To sleep. My baby is tired. We need to sleep.

Mrs. Harrison undressed me, slowly pulling my soiled clothing from my body. I washed my legs. She washed my back.

You're bruised, she said.

I think the bleeding has stopped, I said.

She found fresh underwear in my dresser. Took a clean hand towel from the washstand and tore it in two then folded half of it into a pad.

Just in case, she said.

She helped me into my nightgown.

Will you be okay by yourself? I'm going to get the midwife. Also, I need to tell Jane what has happened to you. Someone should know you're hurt.

No, I said. Please, don't tell Miss Addams. Don't tell anyone. I just need to rest.

I'm sending the midwife. She needs to check you, make sure…

I placed my hands on my stomach hoping to feel life. The baby didn't move.

Please, I said, tears streaming down my cheeks.

When I first found out I was pregnant, my mind and my body pulled apart from each other. It frightened me. I wanted to run away, as if by running away I could leave my soiled body, my baby behind and find my old self again. I couldn't imagine that anything good could come from a body being raped. Certainly not a baby.

Babies were supposed to be something you wanted. Something you hoped for and dreamed about with someone you loved. I had never had the chance to love or be loved by a man. My baby did not come from love. My baby came from some hateful place that had nothing to do with me. I felt detached from the life growing within me. It had more to do with Mr. Bristal's bull rutting than it had anything to do with me. But as I reluctantly caste on stitches to knit my baby's blanket, the soft wool Mrs. Levy had purchased for me passed through my fingers like a whispered prayer and I began to feel a change turning inside of me.

Every afternoon, after the breakfast dishes were done, Mrs. Levy had sat beside me in her parlor, knitting, chatting, while waiting patiently for me to find a place of peace with my baby. Through her steadfast patience, I had been able to knit a blanket that connected me with the child I was carrying. Knitting that soft yellow blanket had made me whole again.

You might say that love made me whole again. Love is powerful. I was there in spirit when you, my beautiful granddaughter, were born. I had waited so long for you to arrive, I prayed harder than I had ever prayed in my living life that you would safely draw your first breath. When I heard you scream, I closed my eyes and felt the rush of love rising up inside of me like a fire within my spirit. There is nothing like it. I had felt that love rush over me once before when your father was born and I couldn't wait to feel it again.

Love, however, is not what most people think it is. Love is not easy. Love changes you. It awakens things within you. It demands your response. It can be frightening if you are not ready to change.

I was not ready. But, with every passing day, change was happening within me and I couldn't stop it. As my waist thickened and I could no longer tie my corset, or wear the clothes I had carried with me to Chicago, the life growing inside of me began to take over whatever old life was still within me. When love strikes, you lose part of yourself.

From the moment I was raped, the young girl in me who was full of dreams of a new life in Chicago began to fade. Stitch by stitch, the new person I reluctantly became felt older. Not wiser. In fact, less sure of where I was going. My future was no longer the next job. Instead, it was the next day and whatever that day would bring.

One night when I was still living with Mrs. Levy, I awoke with a start when I felt the first flutter of my child moving within me. I pressed my hands against my stomach. I wanted to feel the movement again: to witness for certain that the baby I had once tried to run from had now become real. I was no longer one life. I was two.

I had never been much for praying. As a child, I had not been won over by the magical thinking of religion that God was sitting in heaven anxious to grant me my every wish.

While lying in my bed at the Hull House waiting for the midwife to come help me, I pressed my hands once again against the hardened mound of my stomach and began to pray.

Dear God, I prayed. I have never asked for anything much before except the next day. Please keep my baby safe within me. Let my baby live.

The midwife lifted my nightgown, placed her smooth hands along the firm crest of my belly and pressed her ear against my flesh to listen. She slid her hands down the sides of my stomach pushing a little here and there as she moved from my ribs to my pubic bone.

You've got more time, she said. The baby's head is already down but not engaged.

She turned her back so I could straighten my gown and cover myself.

How much more? I asked.

Maybe one month. Could be a week or two more, but not two months. The baby is still small. Has the cramping stopped?

I drew in a long slow breath, trying to reassure my unborn child that I was okay. That we were okay.

It's less, I said.

If you plan on keeping this baby, you cannot get out of bed until the cramping has stopped completely. Do you understand?

She raised her voice when she said this, as though I had suddenly gone deaf.

I understand, I said.

I came this time, because Mrs. Harrison begged me. I did what I said I would do. I made sure the baby was safe. My work with you is done.

What about when my baby comes? I asked.

I won't be there to help you, she said, turning away from me. This baby has come from no good. It is not my problem.

My heart began to race.

What will I do? I asked.

You should have thought about that before you got yourself pregnant. Enough babies in the world as it is without women like you doing what you've done. It's a good thing for your baby that you came to Hull House. They'll take the baby away from you for sure. That's what they do here with all the sinning babies like yours. They take them from the mothers soon as they're born and give them to decent Christian people who have good sense and good homes. Give that poor child of yours a life it deserves, not the one it would be headed for living with the likes of you.

Go away, I said, my voice cold and hard.

She left the room and closed the door.

The afternoon light was beginning to fade. I was hungry, but I was afraid to go downstairs. I wrapped my arms around my stomach, and rocked from side to side, gently cradling my baby to sleep. I pulled the covers over my head and let my hips sink deep into the mattress, trying to find a place for both of us to rest for the moment.

Before morning light filled my room, I knew, if I wanted to keep my baby, I was going to have to leave Hull House.

I wanted to sit on Georgette's big front porch and rock in one of her chairs. I wanted to, but I knew I could not go home. Home was gone for me the minute Mr. Bristal pushed me against the wall and tore my clothes. Georgette could never know what happened to me.

I could not go back to Mrs. Levy's. I knew a baby, one from sin, would cause problems for her and her boarders.

I had heard murmurs about babies birthed at Hull House that were given away. Had seen well dressed ladies come empty handed into the clinic then leave with a baby in their arms. The young girls who birthed them would stay a few weeks, healing, crying, scrubbing floors, washing windows, making beds until they could fit into their old clothes again and leave out the backdoor.

I still had the money Mrs. Levy had given me. Plus a little I had earned baking extra pies for various staff members at Hull House. I also had the baby blanket, bonnet, sweater and booties I had knitted when I was with Mrs. Levy, along with the diapers we'd made together that one afternoon. And, I had my mother's quilt.

I got up sometime between midnight and dawn and put the baby things I had made into the folds of the quilt, rolling it as tightly as I could so I could tie it to my larger suitcase. Before I tied on the quilt, I packed the dresses Mrs. Levy had given me, along with my black skirt, white blouse and grey suit. It was everything I owned.

I worked as quickly and as quietly as possible. When I had everything ready to go, I snuck out of my room in my nightgown and went out back to find the white dress I'd worn to the rally. True to her word, Mrs. Harrison had arranged for the slip and the dress to be washed. The bloodstains were gone. The dress was slightly damp from the evening air. I took it off the line and brought it back to my room. There wasn't room in my suitcase for my nightgown, so I pulled the slip and dress over what I was wearing and pulled on the last fresh pair of stockings I had.

Once I had washed my face and fixed my hair, I carried my suitcase and my shoes and tiptoed down the stairs to the kitchen. Just as I had hoped there would be, I found a plate of cold chicken, three roasted potatoes, some biscuits, and half of an apple pie I had made the day before. I took four pieces of chicken, the three roasted potatoes, and all of the biscuits; tied them into a bundle with a tea towel and stuffed them into my purse. I ate two slices of the pie then put on my shoes and walked out the backdoor, down the alleyway, to the train station.

FOURTEEN

The moon hovered low in the sky. The sun was just beginning to edge up on the horizon. It was dark. I hadn't been outside in the dark since the night I was raped.

I heard the rattle of a milk cart slowly making its way down the alley. A rat skittered in my path. The gas streetlights sputtered and hissed, casting long yellow shadows. I heard heavy footsteps coming up behind me. The man grunted as he took each step. I didn't turn to see him but could sense he was a big man, possibly drunk, going nowhere or maybe somewhere. As he got closer, his footsteps quickened until he was right up behind me.

I could smell garlic and beer on his breath. I kept walking.

I pulled my shawl around me, hiding my baby belly.

Kind of early for someone like you to be out walking the streets, ain't it?

The milk truck stopped, then rattled again as it moved forward. I could hear it coming closer.

God must laugh at us. We humans pray for the strangest things. Right then, what I prayed for was not for the man to turn and walk away, but for the milkman to come out of the alley and onto the street and see what was happening and save me. I wanted the driver to tell the drunk to leave me alone. I wanted him to jump from his wagon and fight for me. I wanted him to take my luggage, offer his arm so I could hop into his wagon and have him carry me safely to the train station.

I wanted proof there was a God.

How much can any of us ask of God? Was there a limit? A quota? Had I used up all I had been given when I asked Him to keep my baby safe?

If I scream, he'll hear me, I said, nodding in the direction of the approaching milk truck. I stopped walking and planted my feet wide apart, firmly on the ground in order to make it harder for him to knock me down. I drew in a deep breath, pushing the fear from my lungs and replacing it with anger.

No reason to be screaming anything. You ain't much older than my own daughter. Wouldn't want her out at this hour. Where you going? Why you carrying such a big tote? You running away or something?

I heard the rattle of the glass bottles as the slow moving horse pulled the milk wagon over the rough cobblestones and came into clear view in the distance.

I kept walking.

The milk cart came to the head of the alleyway and into view then stopped.

The drunk man turned and stumbled back into the shadows from where he had come.

I ran toward the milk truck. The horse whinnied, tossing its head over its shoulder. The man on the milk cart snapped the reins. The horse lurched forward. The bottles rattled. The gaslights sputtered. A thin edge of morning light moved slowly across the cold cobblestones.

The truck ambled on into the next alleyway.

I didn't stop running until I reached the grip car that had just stopped at the head of the street and got on.

The sun was up in the sky just enough to have chased whatever was left of the moon away when I arrived at the train station. The last days of summer were long gone. The air was damp and heavy with an early morning chill. My hands and feet were cold and the thin white cotton dress I was wearing felt strangely out of place.

Where are you going? The station clerk asked.

I hadn't had time to think about where I wanted to be.

Someplace warm, I said.

Florida? He asked.

Mrs. Levy and I had walked through the Florida pavilion when we went to the Exposition. It was a beautiful pavilion decorated with pictures of white sand beaches and rich green orchards ripe with hundreds of orange and grapefruit trees. We drank samples of fresh squeezed orange juice and ate marble-sized kumquats, peel and all. I had never heard of a kumquat before and most certainly had never tasted anything that was both tart and sweet and so tiny you couldn't really nibble on it but had to put the whole thing in your mouth at once.

Florida, I said.

Jacksonville, St. Augustine, Waldo, Gainesville, Ocala? He asked.

There was a big map hanging on the wall behind him. Jacksonville had a star by its name. It looked like it was close to the ocean. I had never seen the ocean before. I had been amazed at the beauty of Lake Michigan the first time I saw it. I know people had said the ocean was bigger, but I couldn't believe there could be anything in the world that was bigger than Lake Michigan, and I thought it would be good to see for myself.

Jacksonville, I said.

The ticket man looked up. I could tell he had some question about the baby I was carrying.

Train goes first to Pittsburgh. That's a big stop. One where you will have time to get off if you want and walk around to stretch your legs. The porter will let you know when it's time to get back on. The train makes some other stops along the way, but none of the stops are as long as the one in Pittsburgh. Once you get to Macon, you change trains and catch the one that goes to Florida. When all is going well and there's no cow on the tracks or some bad weather, it's a three-day trip, he said. Sometimes longer. Last week one of our trains ran into some fallen rocks on the tracks and they had to wait 'til things got cleared before they could go on. It took nearly five days from here to Jacksonville. We don't carry a doctor on the train. Your husband going to meet you?

I tucked my left hand under my shawl hiding the fact that I didn't wear a wedding band.

In Jacksonville, I said.

The ticket man nodded.

Like I said, there's no doctor on the train. Five days going to be okay with you and that baby you're carrying? One of the porters had to deliver a baby just last week on the train going to Florida. We don't really like it when things like that happen. Don't really have a proper place for a birthing on the train. The whole thing caused quite a fuss with the other passengers.

I've got time, I said. Five days, even ten will be fine.

Okay, then, he said. Ever since we had that baby come on the train last week, I've been told I need to ask. Got to let people know there's no doctor on the train and the porters don't care for delivering babies. They're not trained to be midwives. Just porters.

By the time I boarded the train, I was exhausted and took a seat by the window in my compartment so I could rest my head against it. I let the gentle rocking of the train lull me to sleep. Although I woke from time to time, I slept most of the day and through the night. I was hungry but too tired to eat and also knew that I didn't have enough food to carry me through to Florida and would need to ration it out over the three, possibly five days of the trip.

The porter woke me once we got to Pittsburgh and said we were stopping for a bit and I might want to get out with the rest of the passengers and stretch my legs. My feet were swollen from sitting so long and it felt good to walk around for a few minutes.

While I was walking around, a woman in a bright colored skirt and shawl approached. Her skirt shifted around her ankles as she swayed through the crowds, her hand outstretched for coins as she moved from person to person. I had never seen a gypsy before, but knew without asking, that she was one. Her dark hair fell down her back like brushed silk. She had gold coins sewn to her shawl and rings on every finger. Without saying a word, she sat down beside me, took my hand and gently uncurled my fingers. Her middle finger, the one with the large amber ring, traced the lines on my palm.

It's okay, she said. I know you have no husband to meet you. You are carrying a little boy. He will have a good life. His life will not be without heartbreak, but it will be good.

Where will we live? I asked.

She folded my fingers back against my palm and held my hand in both of hers.

I do not know everything. Just those things you might want to hear. What you don't want to know I do not tell.

She had a small leather bag that she wore like a purse hung from a long strap from her right shoulder to her left hip. The bag was old and worn and decorated with beads and bits of feathers and bone. She reached into her bag and drew out a small linen bundle that was tied with the kind of string butchers use to tie up packages of meat.

Rosemary and lavender, she said, holding the bag up close to my face so I could smell it. Do you have a nickel?

I didn't have much money left after buying my tickets, but felt compelled to buy what she was offering, as though she was an angel sent by God in answer to my prayer. I dug into my purse and brought out a nickel. She took it.

This will help you sleep. You and your baby are on a journey. You're going to need to stay calm for your baby no matter what happens.

I held out my hand. She put the small bundle in my palm and closed my fingers tightly around it, crushing the tiny bits of the herbs in the pouch as she did so. I could smell the rosemary and lavender come alive in my hand.

Hold it up to your face, she said. Breathe in as big as you can so your baby boy can smell it too.

How do you know it's a boy?

The woman pushed my hand near my face.

Breathe, she said. Sometimes you just know.

As my ribs expanded, making more room for my baby, he moved. I could feel he was part of me, but his own self as well, like he had a life and I was just there to carry him to it.

Then she spoke as if she could read my mind: *That's what women do, she said. We carry both the joy and the burden. We help. We hold on.*

When I thanked her for the herbs, she placed her hands upon my head. She closed her eyes and whispered a kind of prayer or incantation. I let my hands rest on the crest of my belly. I felt her energy pour through my body and into my womb.

When I looked up, she was gone.

When I got back on the train, there was a new woman in my compartment. When I sat down next to her, she pulled her skirt up tightly against her legs to make room for me to sit down. There was also a man in the seat across from us. He was big enough to nearly fill the whole bench. There was not room in the compartment for a fourth person.

We traveled in silence. I stared out the window watching the fields and houses drift by. When it was suppertime, the woman who was sitting next to me gathered up her skirts and her pocketbook and slipped out. I presumed she was going to the dining car and prayed she'd return soon. The big man remained.

He made no pretense of being polite. I was hoping he would also leave, but when he didn't, I opened my purse to retrieve and unwrap one of the chicken pieces I had taken from the kitchen. I was hungry and started to eat. He stared at me. Then he shifted in his seat, drew the curtains to our compartment closed, and leaned forward, his thick forearms resting on his broad thighs.

Where's your husband? he asked.

I took a bite of chicken hoping my full mouth would be an excuse not to answer.

Ain't got one, do you?

He inched forward until his hand brushed against my knee.

I moved my legs so his hand wasn't touching me. I swallowed and took another bite of chicken. I turned my face away from his. His words and his warm breath had turned the taste of the chicken sour in my mouth. I forced the food down my throat. I wrapped up the remaining bit of chicken and pushed it back into my purse. I had an urge to run. I looked out the train window.

While that other woman is in the dining car buttering her toast, why don't you hike up that fancy white skirt of yours so I can take a good look at what you've got in there? Hmm?

The fingers of his left hand flicked across my knees again. I instinctively kicked out. He grabbed at my ankle. I tried to scream. He leaned closer and pushed his other hand against my mouth. My stomach lurched.

The train whistle blew and the great iron wheels of the train screamed out. The porter walked through the car calling out the next stop. The train rocked forward then jerked back, unsettling the man.

I broke free and ran from the compartment.

I tried to catch up to the porter, but passengers with their bags were coming out of their compartments, blocking my way. Others filed in behind me.

I moved along with the crowd.

When I got to the exit, the porter held his hand out to help me down. I shook my head.

Where you going?

Florida, I said.

You got a ways to go. They should have told you when you bought your ticket that you need to change in Macon, not here.

He jerked his head to the side indicating I needed to get out of the way so others could get off.

Where's the dining car? I asked.

Four cars to the left. If you're hungry you need to hurry. They quit serving supper in half an hour.

I nodded and moved to the left in order to make my way down to the dining car. When I got there, I stood in the doorway waiting to be seated. I'd never eaten in a restaurant, much less a dining car, and wasn't sure what I was supposed to do. I didn't have any idea if I had enough money to eat anything, but was pretty sure they weren't going to let me eat the rest of my chicken in their fancy place. My stomach growled.

The dining car porter walked over to where I was standing.

You with someone? he asked.

I shook my head.

Follow me, he said, picking up a menu.

Halfway down the dining car, we passed the table where the woman who had been in my car was seated. She reached out and touched my arm.

Would you like to join me?

Yes, I said.

The porter put the menu down on the table opposite the woman and turned to walk away.

The woman waited until I was seated before she spoke.

The special tonight is sliced tomatoes and baked beans. Where are you going?

Florida, I said, studying the menu. The special, sliced tomatoes and baked beans, was fifty-five cents. Tea was five cents. I had at least two more days on the train, maybe more. I wondered if I could just order the tea.

My stomach growled.

I hear being pregnant makes you hungry, the woman said.

I nodded my head.

You have family in Florida?

Always wanted to go there, I said. "See the ocean. They say it's bigger than Lake Michigan."

The woman laughed.

Much bigger, she said. I love the way the sun plays off the waves of the ocean as they roll onto the shore. It's kind of like seeing music, if that makes any sense. First time I saw, and heard it, it I couldn't believe it! The constant movement and roar of the waves and the water, the sunlight playing on the water's surface, the wind, it's all very musical and magical. I could sit on the beach listening to it and watching it for hours. You're going to like it, I'm sure. You and your baby.

A waiter passed with a plate full of smoked haddock and boiled cabbage. The oily smell of the fish and cabbage made me feel faint. I reached into my purse and drew out the bag of lavender and rosemary. I squeezed it as tightly as I could and held it to my face. The train rocked a slow back and forth.

When is your baby due?

The waiter came to the table.

May I take your order?

The special for me, she said. Sliced tomatoes and baked beans.

And to drink? he asked

Water with my meal, and tea afterwards, she said, handing him the menu.

The waiter turned to me.

And for you, ma'am?

I'll have the sliced tomatoes and baked beans, I answered. And just water.

When the waiter left, the woman started talking again.

Traveling makes me hungry, she said.

It's a long way to Florida, I answered.

She studied my face for a moment. I looked out the window.

That man, in our compartment, she said. Do you know him?

I shook my head and breathed in the smell of the gypsy's herbs in the hopes of settling my stomach.

You're wearing a white dress. I assume you're a Suffragette. He didn't seem like the type who would want a woman to have the right to anything. You should be careful. He kept watching you while you slept. Kept inching his foot closer to yours, like he was trying to trip you up or touch you. I pulled in my skirts so he couldn't touch me. Men can be dangerous. I think he was drunk. He smelled bad.

Our food came.

So, are you? A Suffragette?

I heard Susan B. Anthony speak, I said. At the World Exposition in Chicago.

You're from Chicago?

I thought a minute before I answered.

Ever been there? I asked.

Is it true what they say that every building at the Exposition is white and that the whole city lights up at night with electric lights? That you can see every wonder of the world there?

I nodded my head then began talking.

There's this pavilion there about women, that was designed by a woman. A woman architect! The hall was the biggest building I had ever seen and it was filled with artwork, all by women. Did you know there was such a thing? Then I heard all these women speak about having the right to vote and to do whatever we want to do and it was thrilling. Like a dream come true.

What does your husband say?

I pushed the silver tines of my fork into the flesh of one of the thick slices of tomato and pushed some beans on top of it with my knife. I cut a small bite.

I don't have a husband. I had a job in one of those big buildings in

Chicago on Michigan Avenue. I was a typewriter. My boss asked me to work late one night, and after he locked the doors, he pushed me against a wall, I put the bite of tomato into my mouth.

The woman pushed the remaining beans on her plate off to the edge. She signaled the waiter to bring her some tea.

You don't have to tell me anything else about what happened, she whispered.

The waiter put a small silver tray on the table with a teapot, some sugar, cream and one china teacup and saucer.

Another cup please, the woman said, signaling the porter. And two slices of pie.

I waited until the waiter left.

I… I started to say.

You're almost finished with your meal and I really don't want to go back to our seats and be with that horrid man, so I thought we should just sit here, have a cup of tea together and enjoy a slice of pie. You would be doing me a favor to stay a while longer. Please let me treat you.

Thank you, I said.

I finished my meal. She poured me a cup of tea. The pie came. I told her all about going to Chicago and Mrs. Levy teaching me how to knit and make pies, and how, once I started to show I moved to the Hull House and worked in the kitchen.

She listened without interrupting. I hadn't talked so much since I left Mrs. Levy and as each of the words tumbled out onto the table and the train moved into the night, rocking back and forth like a cradle, I began to relax.

She motioned to the waiter for a fresh pot of tea. The dining car was nearly empty. The waiter brought the tea and placed our bills on the table.

Anything else?

She placed three dollars on the table before I could get the money out of my purse.

We'll be sitting here for a while longer, she told the porter. It's more comfortable than our compartment. Please keep the change.

Yes, ma'am" he said, picking up the money. Just let me know if you want anything else.

My face flushed. I was embarrassed I had told her so much of my circumstances that she knew I couldn't really afford to pay my bill. She reached across the table and put her hand over mine.

Does anyone know you're going to Florida?

I shook my head.

The train stops in Atlanta before going on to Macon. That's where I get off. You have to promise me that you will let someone know where you are once you get to Florida.

I promised her I would.

Don't worry, I said, taking the last sip of my cold tea. "I'll be fine. My baby and I will be fine. The gypsy even said so."

My dear, dear granddaughter…I was so young. Your age. Of course, I thought things would be fine. Why wouldn't they? I had survived being raped. I had done something worthwhile teaching women at Hull House how to knit. I had learned to bake pies. I was on a train going to a new life, a new place in the sun. Why couldn't I have a child on my own and raise him? Why couldn't or why shouldn't I go to Florida and start a new life. I had seen a building that was designed by a woman. Fallen in love with artwork made by other women. Had taken a stand for women to gain the right to vote. Why couldn't I be anything and do anything I wanted?

Before I left the farm and went to Chicago, all my dreams had been dreams that came from the books I had read. My world was the world in the dusty pages Georgette and I shared sitting together in the shade of my parent's big willow tree.

But, my life was changing and I was beginning to make different plans. Once I was in Florida, I would let Georgette know where I was. I would tell her all about everything that had happened to me. I would contact her, but not until my son was born and my new life was begun.

I was afraid to tell her before. She might come looking for me. Might try to get me to come back home. There would be no turning back for me after my son was born. Once my new life, whatever it was going to be, was begun, I would be safe.

Once.

Once upon a time.

Even though I had been raped, I really didn't know about how truly evil life could be. How unforgiving. How dangerous.

I hope you will never know what I have known.

This is why I must tell you what happened, and ask for your help to make it right.

FIFTEEN

After we finished with our tea and pie, we went back to the compartment together. The fat man was still there. We went to the porter to ask if we might switch compartments and was told that there were no other accommodations available and that we should be happy we had a seat.

The woman and I sat close to each other, arms linked, as though sitting close would protect us from him. I must have been exhausted by the travel and fell deeply asleep, with my head on her shoulder, not waking when the train stopped in Atlanta and the woman got off. When I woke, the fat man was sitting next to me and two other men, both rough looking with dirty boots, were sitting across from us on the opposite bench. The fat man's legs were spread wide so that his right thigh was pressing along the side of my left leg.

I moved closer to the window to get away from him, and when I did, he moved his leg, pinning me into the corner. I turned my head and looked out of the window. We traveled in silence.

The train swayed back and forth, making its slow way from Atlanta to Macon. It was dark outside, but the ground was bathed in shadows cast by a full moon that shone like a golden lantern above the jagged line of the trees.

As I gazed out the window, my baby became restless, as though he too saw the moon and the shimmering light beckoned him to come. I had heard the women at Hull House talk of the full moon, of how babies came quickly when the moon was full. A pain shot down the front of my body and I felt a hard ridge rise up the center of my stomach like the sharp edge of a mountain range. My heart raced. I put my hands on either side of my stomach hoping to calm my baby. I tried to take a deep breath, but a second wave of pain, like a hammer striking the thin bone of my pelvis, stopped me. I held my breath.

The man sitting directly across from me leaned forward.

How far you going, Miss? he said, rubbing his hands together out of habit.

The fat man's leg pressed harder against mine and he put his hand on my knee.

Little Miss says she has a husband and he's meeting her in Florida.

He threw back his head and laughed, while at the same time squeezing my knee. I squirmed, but couldn't move further away.

What kind of man would let her pregnant wife travel this railroad all the way from God knows where to Florida by herself? I'm willing to bet this here child she's carrying is someone's bastard and that she doesn't even know the father's name! Do you sweetheart?

The man who asked where I was going leaned back and slapped his knee laughing.

Well, let's hope that baby stays put until Florida 'cause I want no business of birthing any baby, bastard or not. Ought to be a law about pregnant women staying put so strangers don't get caught up in their mess. If you'll excuse me, I think I'll find somewhere else to sit.

With that, the man who had spoken to me got up and left. The second man followed him. When the two men had left and the door to our compartment was closed, the fat man pushed his hand between my knees. I tried to scream, but nothing came out. I pushed him away with all the strength I had and stood up and grabbed my purse and my satchel.

Where you think you're going? This ain't no tram where you can just ring a bell and get off. You're on a train. Next stop, Macon. It'll be late when we pull in. The station will be empty. In case you haven't noticed, we've been moving kind of slow ever since Atlanta. I'm pretty sure you're going to miss that train you're counting on to take you to Florida. The next train that goes to Florida won't leave until morning. Gonna be near midnight when we get to Macon. Where you gonna go? Who's gonna help you? One of them darkie porters? Like they gonna get all up in your mess and take your word against a white man? Anyway, who'd believe anything you've got to say with that big belly of yours? Who you running away from, anyways?

You don't know anything about me, I said, wrapping my fingers tightly around the handle of my satchel. I was pretty sure I could knock him down if I had to.

All I want to know is what's up under that skirt of yours. Ain't never had one as ripe as you. Ready to go. Must be something special. That's what I'm thinking. Think I might also want to get a taste of one of your big old titties. Whooeee, they big as melons and I bet just as sweet as some of that Tuppelo honey they got down there in Florida! You bet I want a taste of that.

The compartment was small. In fact, it was too small for me not to miss hitting him if I swung at his head with my bag. He could catch my arm, throw me off balance, and possibly hurt me. I took a deep breath, stood up and let my feet slide a little apart so I had a firm stance. I thought of how a bull, waiting to mount gets a little dazed, almost blind with drunk anticipation in the way they hunch their shoulders, duck their heads, then rush the cow.

I counted on that moment when that man would try to stand, to take me. That's when he would be his most vulnerable: head down, weight shifted forward in anticipation.

The weight of my growing baby had shifted my own sense of balance. I felt awkward sometimes just walking. I knew I didn't have a chance to kick out at him or try to jam a knee into his crotch like I had done with Mr. Bristol.

No, this would have to be a blow to the head. A hit so hard as to knock him off balance for just enough time for me to open the door of the compartment and step out.

I didn't think he'd try to follow me once I left.

Yes indeed, first thing, I'm going to get my two hands on one of those big titties of yours, squeeze it just a little to see if some of that sweet milk comes out. Take a little sip or two, just to get things started...

The train jerked through a curve in the track and the man pitched forward a bit as he tried to stand. I swung my arm back, then across my body and whipped it hard as I could at his head.

I caught him at his right temple, grazing his eye with enough force to draw blood. He dropped to one knee and covered his face with his hands, screaming. Blood dripped down his fingers onto the floor.

I reached behind me and opened the door, slipping out before he could catch his breath, get up off the floor and come after me.

I pulled the door shut and walked as fast as I could down the middle aisle to the ladies room in the next car. I stepped in and locked the door, dropping my suitcase on the floor.

There was a small window in the ladies room, I fiddled with the lock and pushed it open, letting the cool evening air fill the room. If I stood on tiptoe, I could watch the moon glide by, casting long tree shadows onto the railroad tracks.

I watched as the shadows flickered by and listened for footsteps. At some point, I leaned my back against the wall and slid to the floor, letting my legs jut out in front of me so I could comfortably roll to my side and rest my head on my satchel. The baby was still, but my stomach was growing harder and harder with each sharp contraction. It wasn't time. I lay as still as possible hoping to lull my body and my baby back to sleep.

Every time I heard the heavy steps of the fat man and saw the soles of his shoes under the crack of the closed door as he passed in the hallway, I held my breath. Once, he stopped in front of the door and rattled the door. The porter came by and told him the men's room was in the next car back. The fat man moved on and I waited until I couldn't hear his footsteps anymore before I took my next breath.

Shadows are like whispers: you are never quite sure what you see or what you hear. The sound of passengers walking through the car past my doorway was like a shadow. My heart tightened every time the footsteps approached. The moon played tricks with its incessant flashing of night shadows, frightening me as the train pushed on to Macon. I couldn't sleep.

I could hear people opening the doors of their compartments and gathering their suitcases. I guessed, as the train lurched forward, then rocked back and the air was filled with the screeching sound of steel on steel as the conductor put on the brakes, that we were coming close to the station. Someone put their hand on the door and rattled the knob. I held my breath.

The train whistle blasted, announcing that we were arriving. I heard a jumbled bubble of talk and shuffling feet. A child cried as though it had been awoken in the middle of a dream. The porter called out the stop and the announcement that Macon was the end of the line.

I waited. The footsteps and voices grew faint. I heard the porter walk down the aisle of the car, opening and closing doors, looking for luggage I guess, or stowaways. He knocked on the bathroom door.

Macon, last stop for the night. Everyone off.

Just a minute, I called out.

Even if you got a ticket, you can't sleep on the train. I don't make them, but that's the rules. I know you been in there a while. Had to run off that gentleman who was banging on the door more than once. You okay?

I straightened my dress and fixed my hair. I picked up my bag. I didn't say anything or make any excuses for what was taking me so long to get off the train, I just walked slowly down the center aisle of the train car, looking closely as I passed by each compartment, making sure there were no shadows.

The train station was big, but not as big as the one in Chicago. There were people in the station, some were milling about and others were standing outside waiting to be picked up and taken to one of the local hotels. My stomach growled.

I thought I was safe out in the open, so I found a seat at the end of one of the long wooden benches and opened my purse. I still had two chicken legs left and a couple of biscuits. I put the dish towel on my lap and started to eat.

I hadn't planned on eating everything, but I was still so hungry, I couldn't make myself stop. I ate slowly, wanting to make it last until my next meal. I hadn't drunk anything since the tea I had with my slice of pie and I was beginning to get thirsty.

By the time I finished eating and stood up to find a place to get a drink of water, the station was nearly empty. The stationmaster was closing up his office and turning off the lights.

You planning on spending the night here? He asked. We don't advise it, but we can't stop you. If you know what I mean. These benches can be hard, but if it's all you've got, it's better than nothing I guess. Plus, you'll be out of the rain, if there is rain, but it doesn't look like it tonight. We leave the door here unlocked, but I have to lock up the offices and everything else. I'll leave the ladies room unlocked for you. You've got a few hours to wait until the next train comes along. Where you going?

Jacksonville, I said.

Someone going to meet you in Jacksonville?

I nodded my head.

Well, then, goodnight. I'll be here five-thirty in the morning. I'll see you then.

I asked if there was some place for me to get a drink of water. He said there were drinking fountains outside: one marked colored, the other white.

I gathered up the chicken bones and took them to the trash. Afterwards, I walked around the waiting room, looking out the various windows, watching leaves blow down the street and listening to the gaslights sputter.

The clock in the hall chimed. It was eleven. I was tired, but not yet willing to lie down on one of the wooden benches and close my eyes. I wished the stationmaster had locked the doors so I would know I was safe.

The big moon outside cast a warm yellow glow through the windows. It was as if they almost forget to turn off the lights, but not quite.

I left my satchel on the bench I'd been sitting on and stepped outside to get a drink of water. The water was cool and fresh as if it came from a deep well. I hadn't tasted water that good since I'd left the farm. The water in Chicago, although good, was city water. It wasn't at all like the water from the farm. For one deep aching moment, I missed the farm and wondered what my mother had done that day. Had she had time to do some fancy work after supper was over and all the dishes washed and put away? I hoped so.

The fat man from the train came out of the shadows. His thick arm catching me under the chin, locking my head and jerking up so hard I thought my spine would snap. I couldn't breathe or cry out. His breath was hot with whiskey. He lifted me up so my feet were dangling off the ground. I tried to kick back at his legs and he tightened his arm around my neck. I tasted blood. I began to choke. My throat was raw and burning. My lungs inflamed with a desire for more air.

I closed my eyes and grabbed at his arms with my fingers, doing what I could to make him let go. He loosened his grip just long enough for me to get one shallow hot breath. Then he tightened his arm around my throat again and began to drag me back into the station.

Once inside, he took me to the darkest corner, spun me around and slammed my head hard against the wall. I could feel my eyes roll back into my head. Could taste the rush of blood as it pounded through my throat and head. My legs couldn't hold me. My arms fell heavy against my sides. He grabbed me by the shoulders and held me up like I was a ragdoll and shook me. My head bounced back and forth against the wall until the tight skin of my scalp split open and I heard my skull crack. A slow flow of blood, thick like porch paint, began to pool in the fold of skin at the back of my neck. I closed my eyes and felt myself slip a little away from my body. The pain I was feeling in my head turned warm and dull.

Never had one as gone as you, he said.

Then he slapped me hard as if he were trying to wake me from the dead.

I need you to wake up. Look at me! It's no good unless you look at me!

I could barely hear him over the whooshing sound of blood pounding through the veins in my head. It was like I no longer had a heartbeat, but just a rush of blood pouring through me trying to escape.

He let go of my shoulders and I slid to the floor. I felt him pull up my dress over my stomach, felt his rough fingers dig at the taut-stretched flesh of my womb.

Like some ripe melon just waiting for someone like me to come along and…

No, no, no, the words struggled to break free of my throat and fall like a dry whisper from my mouth. I wanted water. Air. Anything to soothe the frightening cramping feeling that was now tearing at my womb. I tried to visualize my arms, my hands, and my feet moving, taking my child and me away to a safer place. My mind struggled. I couldn't move my body.

He slapped me again. My head snapped from side to side and I bit my tongue. Blood pooled in my mouth. I choked on the blood, turned my head, and spit onto the floor.

He kicked at my legs. I pulled my feet up and managed to roll to my side, letting the length of my now burning belly rest against the cold floor.

When I felt the hard wooden heel of his boot crush my right hip. The pain was everything. I had nothing. I could hear the man grunting. Could feel his hands tearing at the soft places of my body. I closed my eyes. Let the thoughts of the new life I had just begun dreaming escape like butterflies in a storm. As I let go, the pain began to fade and my mind began to slip further away from my body. It startled me. The only way back was clear. I had to welcome the pain. I gritted my teeth and clinched my fists, digging my fingernails into the fleshy pads of the palms of my hands in the hopes of holding on for the life of my baby.

SIXTEEN

THE MATRON

From the moment the police brought her limp body to the Door of Hope and laid it on the bed in the back of the house, I knew she and I were made from the same cloth: she was silent in her secrets just as I was silent in mine. She was running from something, just as I was running.

I brushed her matted hair away from her young face and held her hand. It was burning from a kind of fever that happens when a mother struggles to hang on to her baby when something has gone wrong. The woman was still alive, but I felt certain she would not be for long. I pressed my ear against the hard crest of her pregnant belly and listened, praying I'd hear the galloping heartbeat of a baby about to be born. I told the police to go fetch the doctor.

While I waited for the doctor to come, I asked the cook, Miss Rae, to bring me a jug of cold water and a basin of hot water along with some rags. Together, we bathed the woman as best we could. She was heavy in our hands, the kind of dead weight that bodies claim when they are near the edge of leaving this world for the next, as if they have one last chance to be firmly on this earth. Her breathing was slow and heavy.

I told Miss Rae to sit on the front steps and wait for the doctor. I wanted to be alone with the woman so I could pray for her.

When I touched her, I could feel that she was carrying more than a baby. She was burdened with secrets and perhaps unspoken dreams. She didn't feel fallen, but more lost seeking both a new life and shelter just as I had sought a new life, a fresh start and a second chance when I had come to the Door of Hope.

I did my best to straighten her clothes and make her look decent. I wanted the doctor to see what I saw. That there was something more to save than just a body, there was a frightened soul. Which is not to say that the other girls were without souls or without need, but she was different. I felt as though she had not come to the Door of Hope, but that she had come to me. She needed me. And I needed her.

Even beaten and unconscious, I felt her body strain to hold onto her baby until it was safe to let go.

The police told me the stationmaster had found her in a puddle of blood in a corner of the train station lobby when he came to work in the morning. She was unconscious and had no satchel, no purse, and no identification. The stationmaster told the police he had remembered talking to her the night before when he turned off the lights. She had told him that she was on her way to Florida but didn't say where she'd come from. He hadn't asked to see her ticket.

I squeezed the woman's hand. She needed to stay with me until the doctor could get to the house to save her baby. The doctor never ran to help us but always took an easy time coming when I called because he believed there was nothing sacred about his duty to save my girls. He was a drunken sot of a man, but the only doctor in town who would come to our home to deliver the babies. I knew he believed the lives of the young women and their children were not worth his trouble. The first time I met him, he told me that I was wasting my time praying for the girls and that there was no one who came to the Door of Hope worth saving.

The young woman's eyes fluttered. She moaned but didn't speak. I knew she might die and wondered if she could hear me, if she might be the one to carry my own burden with her to the other side and free me to carry on the work I was now meant to do. My heart opened for just a moment and my confession began to pour out.

I am running too, I whispered as I brushed her hair and wet her dry lips again with a fresh rag dipped in the cool water. But I have found a home. And, now it is your home. You and your baby are safe here.

What is it about another person's silence that gives you permission to speak?

I had come to the Door of Hope a year ago over my own rough road of secrets and silence. My marriage was a bed of lies and deception. It was a bed that I had helped make because I allowed my husband's deceptions to be part of my story, so they became my deceptions as well. Shame made me hide from the truth. What I learned from my years of willingness to accept and embrace his deceptions was that we do what we need to do in order keep on living. No matter what the cost in the end.

I bent close to the dying woman's ear and whispered the truth: I had no high calling from God to do the work that needed to be done at the Door of Hope. All I had were years of experience that had taught me how to have compassion and a firm hand with which to guide my girls through the shame the world made them carry because of their mistakes.

Unfortunately, I knew more about the lives of the girls I cared for and what they came running from than most of the genteel churchwomen who built the Door of Hope would ever understand. And, quite frankly, there was no reason to try to explain it to them. But, I knew, oh yes, I knew, and that was part of my secret.

When I was forty-two, and a spinster with no prospects of marriage, the first and only man who ever looked my way waltzed into my life making promises of love. I was an easy mark. He was ten years older, tall and handsome with a smooth way about him. Before he asked me to marry him, I was bound to a rather unfulfilling life of church on Sundays, rolling bandages for missions, and knitting blankets for other people's babies. I had no other suitors and spent my evenings sitting through silent meals with my parents. I was an only child and a burden to both of them.

His sudden proposal of marriage was like a golden door swung open on a world full of promises. It was a dream, a wish come true. My parents didn't approve of him. I didn't expect them to. I was desperate to wear a wedding ring and be called Mrs., and I didn't care what anyone else thought. Someone wanted to marry me. That's all that mattered.

He came courting in a rented buggy one Sunday afternoon, and we rode straight to the courthouse in Randolph County. The Justice of the Peace married us. My husband said he was sorry he didn't have the money for a wedding ring, but some day he would and when he did, he'd buy me the prettiest ring in all of Georgia.

Once our marriage license was signed, my new husband drove the buggy back to Macon and we boarded the train for Alabama, without even stopping to say goodbye to my parents.

The home he took me to was a small rough-hewn, two-room cabin in the woods about a mile from town. Our closest neighbor, an old man who lived by himself and raised hogs, was a half-mile away.

After we had been together for three days, my husband got up from our marriage bed, packed a small satchel and announced he had to go back to work. He was a mechanic for the railroad. He worked on the engines and switching equipment and was sent where needed. When he left, it was the first time I had ever spent a night alone in an empty home.

I had lived my whole life in my parent's home in Macon and slept to the sound of trains coming and going through the night. I was not used to the silence of the country or the hoot of owls and the restless movement of deer and foxes walking through the woods by moonlight.

My husband's work for the railroad often took him away for days and weeks at a time. I tried not to think about the days he was gone, only those times when he was by my side. After a while, I became used to the long days alone. I took care of the chickens that roamed our yard and woods, tended the garden, took long walks, and kept myself busy waiting for him to come home again. At first, those few days a month when he slept by my side seemed to be enough to sustain me.

Then the children arrived. We had been married but a few short months when I discovered that I was not my husband's first wife.

One weekend when my husband came home, he carried two children with him: six-year-old Anne, and eight-year-old Joseph. After I fed the children supper and put them to sleep on a makeshift bed of blankets and rags piled up in the corner of our bedroom, he told me that their mother had died, that he was their father and I would now be the mother who raised them.

The next morning he got up early and left for work. As usual, I did not know when he might return. When the children got up, they didn't seem surprised that their father was gone. After I fed them breakfast, Joseph told me that they were not supposed to let me know that their mother had not died but, instead, had run away. That was how I became a mother.

Being an only child, I had not spent much time around children and did not know what to do with them, so when breakfast was done, I told them to come outside and help me in the garden. I kept a comfortable distance from them at first, fearing I don't know what. That they might run away? Or that they might tell their father I was unfit to raise them? They also kept their distance from me.

I stayed and they stayed and we learned to be good company for one another. Working in the garden, gathering eggs and raising chickens, cooking dinner, reading what few books I had brought with me and teaching them to read and write felt a lot like playing house or being a strict but loving school teacher.

Over time, I believed we grew to care for each other even though I knew instinctively that Joseph only stayed with me pretending I was his mother until the day came when he would be old and strong enough to walk away on his own. I did not begrudge him his desire to build his own life. After all, I had wanted and done the same. Anne, however, never grew a desire to leave. She became my shadow.

When I was alone with them, I was their mother. Whenever their father came home, their attention turned to him and I slid uncomfortably into the background and my role as wife.

Over the years, I had many reasons to suspect my husband of infidelities. And just as many to look the other way. I had nowhere else to go, no other life to live. I felt like I couldn't, as his first wife had, disappear and leave his children.

Eventually, I discovered there was yet another wife. I could never figure if she was his third wife, or his second, which would have made me his third. In any case, I found out she was younger than either I was, or his first wife, and living in Tampa, Florida near the train station. And, he, quite conveniently, was frequently called to work in Tampa. They had one son together who was born two years after we were married.

By then, I was past the years of bearing children and my husband seemed to lose interest in me as a wife. When he came home, it felt more like he showed up to see his children than to share a bed with me.

One morning, just nine years after we married, he got up before dawn and left, taking the few things he kept at our house with him. I knew he wasn't coming back and half suspected he was going to live with his wife in Florida. Anne was 15 at the time and still living with me, while Joseph, at 17, was long gone into a life of his own.

Truth can be an awful burden, even bigger than the burden of a lie.

I realized that morning that I had run away from my family to marry a man whom I wanted more than anything to believe loved me, and even if he didn't love me, he needed me to raise his children and I was grateful for that. It was a strange comfort.

If I had learned anything in those cold years of marriage it was that you had to be careful when you ran. You had to be sure you were running to somewhere, not just away.

That morning, with little money and a daughter with, as yet, no prospects of marriage, I had to find a safe place and a way to invent a new life for both of us.

I was fifty, heartsick and tired. After breakfast, I told Anne we should get on our knees and pray.

Together, we prayed for a lie, a fresh start. We told God we were willing to do His work for the rest of our lives in order to strike some kind of bargain that might deliver us into a better life. When we got up from our knees, we made another pot of tea and counted the money I had hidden away in the bottom of the flour bin.

I had just enough money to take Anne with me away from shame and Alabama to my family in Macon, Georgia, to the home I had once run from out of a desire to defy my parents and marry the only man who ever said he loved me. Perhaps he did love me in the solemn moment when I took his hand in marriage, but that love wore thin in a few short years, and I didn't know how to leave him without abandoning his children.

I had stayed in my hollow marriage because I felt a sense of duty to the children. They had already been abandoned once and to be abandoned a second time would forever change the course of their precious lives.

The stories we tell ourselves in order to survive. The ragged thread we weave together in order to stay grounded in this world. He loved me once, I told myself. I was a married woman. I had children to raise and a household to manage. I was someone. And when he left, I was no one and I was shamed.

The burden of what I did to change my life had become too heavy to carry anymore, so I confessed it all to the beaten woman who had been brought to me, as if she were a priest with the promise that she would carry my secrets to her grave. In exchange for what?

By the time the pot of tea had cooled the morning my husband left,

Anne and I had built the lie we planned to live on. We decided to say we were not abandoned, but he, the children's father, my husband, had died. We went out into the woods and dug a deep hole where we buried a few books and the pots and pans. We gathered a pile of rocks to cover his lie of a grave, created a tombstone from wood on which we wrote his name and the date of his departure from our lives, his death: September 13, 1892. When that was done, we wrote to Joseph, to tell him his father had died and that Anne and I were moving back to Macon to be with my family.

How does one weave a life that will let you escape the truth of where you came from? The only thing we knew to do was to leave our weaknesses behind in that secret grave we had dug in the woods.

I had taught Anne, just as I had taught Joseph, how to read and write. Anne was smart, as well as kind and compassionate. She had a soft touch with broken things. She also had a strong desire to get away, not run away, but go somewhere else in the world where her strengths could be built upon. She was still young and without full direction, so we prayed some more and hoped for a sign: a whisper in the night that would light her way to a safe place.

When we got to Macon, Georgia, we moved in with my brother and promptly joined the Vineville Methodist Church. Shortly after we arrived in Macon, the preacher announced in the Sunday service that the church was looking for young people to carry the gospel to other lands. Without hesitation, Anne stood and said she felt a calling, that God wanted her to take that bold step and become a missionary.

After many interviews and hours of prayer, she was eventually selected by the church council to go to the mission they had built in Korea. She was to work in the hospital assisting the doctor. It was a perfect situation for her. They would pay her passage as well as a small monthly stipend to cover her living expenses. The money was minimal since she would live at the hospital where she was to work, but it was a chance to build a life where no one knew her past.

I helped her sew two new dresses, one dark blue, the other a soft rose. I also knitted a warm shawl for her. I knew nothing about Korea, but suspected they must have cold nights, and some cold days in winter. The churchwomen gave her a sunbonnet, three white aprons, a new pair of sensible shoes and some medical supplies for the mission hospital.

When I put her on the train headed for Savannah, where she would catch a boat that would eventually take her to Korea, we held hands and prayed. We prayed our lie would never be uncovered. We said a prayer of gratitude that Anne had found a path to travel that would take her into a new life. We prayed that I might find my way as well, and we prayed for forgiveness and hoped that we would never have to lie again.

I held the woman's hand and told her everything. I clung as tightly to her as she was holding to the life of her child. I let the rhythm of my breath catch the rhythm of hers, hoping to bring the strength of my breath to her life. After my confession, I sat with her in silence, waiting, and breathing.

I was easily twice the age of the woman whose hand I now held as if by holding it I was holding on to her life. Fifty-one and a liar. Married for nine years and had probably slept with my husband less than twenty times in those long dark nine years, always waking to him being gone, knowing his lies were twisted into my dreams and sewn deep into the fabric of my life. Were his children born by his first wife? His second? Who knows?

After a while, I didn't think about whose children they were anymore, because they were my salvation. They taught me how to care. They filled my days with purpose and some loving. I say some loving because I had never known for sure what love was, but I knew I cared for his children. I taught them how to read and write, I told them about the world outside of their father's cabin in the woods. I prayed each night that they would find a better life than the one I had fashioned for myself. We cared for each other from sun up to sundown and when there were bad nights, storms, frightening dreams of loss and regret, we held each other.

They taught me to hold on.

It was my lie that cut them free. Cut all three of us free to find better. It was easy to fashion, even easier to say: their father, my husband had died. We buried the thought of him deep in the woods beside the sorry cabin he'd built for us.

We left with what few things we had, fed the chickens, closed the cabin door, and went in search of a new life.

What lie would this woman have to tell in order to cut herself free? What lie of hers would I have to carry with me to my grave if she woke and spoke to me?

From time to time the woman stirred. She tried to speak. I tried to listen. I struggled with some primal instinct to want to know her name. Not knowing, however, would make it possible for me to take her child, if she died, and raise it as my own. If I knew her name, I would be obligated to find her family.

As time went on and the woman's attempt to speak weakened, she fell into silence and all I could think about was her child. Her child could become my child. My own. I knew it was a selfish thought. What did I have to offer a child but a life of lies?

If she lived, I would take her and the baby in at the Door of Hope. I would help them find a new life. She would be my first real soul to save. One I could say was mine. Perhaps, then, God might forgive me.

I got down on my knees and prayed God would help bring her baby into this world safely and spare her life as well. I held her hand as I prayed. It was an unselfish prayer. One I believed could be answered. One I wanted her to hear. By praying, I had made a covenant with God that I would be there to guide this poor beaten woman and her child from the darkness of her past into the light of a new life.

When the doctor at last arrived, I could smell the liquor on his breath. The matron before me had warned me that when the doctor drank, and he drank often, he did not offer the women he treated at the Door of Hope any kindness. In fact, he became careless. Judgmental. Cruel.

I called out for Miss Rae, hoping that her presence would help turn the doctor's thoughts towards charity. How foolish of me. How naïve. Why would he ever care what a Negro cook saw him do or thought of him?

Miss Rae stepped into the room and took the woman's other hand.

You hold tight, misses, I won't leave you, and Mother won't either, she said.

Don't bother with her hands, the doctor shouted. Hold her legs. You better keep her still. You think you can do that? What'd she tell you about this baby?

I looked at Miss Rae, then at the doctor.

She hasn't spoken since she was brought here. She was unconscious when the police found her. They didn't know anything about her, or if they did, they didn't say.

The doctor slapped the woman's leg, as if by slapping her, he might dislodge her name and information about her pregnancy.

If you don't know and she's not saying then I need to find out for myself. Ain't that right? Right? Cut her clothes off!

Miss Rae ran to the kitchen and got her big scissors. Miss Rae took the scissors to the hem of the dress and began to cut, inching her way up to the woman's waist.

It's a pretty good bet that she ain't never going to wear these clothes again. Hand me those scissors, the doctor demanded.

Miss Rae handed the scissors to him and in one ugly move, he slit her dress open down her front like he was filleting a fish, exposing her naked breasts and stomach. He cut off her underwear and threw it onto the floor, and before I could scream for him to stop, he shoved his hand, hard, into her vagina. Blood and water streamed down her legs and onto the bed.

The girl's legs twitched and her head rocked from side to side. Her arms and legs began to shake. I could feel a fire of a fever rising in her body as if she were struggling to draw one last warm breath for her child.

You want this bastard baby? He asked.

I squeezed the girl's hand. I had no clear notion of what to do. I looked at Miss Rae. She nodded her head.

Yes, I said.

The doctor wiped his bloody hand on the front of the woman's dress.

This girl's half dead and no good to push this baby out on her own. There's chloroform in my bag, that brown bottle, he said to Miss Rae. I'm going to have to cut this baby out. You hold her legs, he said to me. And, you, he said to Miss Rae, grab one of those rags and douse it with a big splash of what's in that bottle and hold it over her face. Don't breathe while you're doing it or you'll pass out on me for sure. I need you upright to hold her shoulders.

When he made the first cut, the girl let out a muffled screamed like someone was holding a hand over her mouth. I could see the doctor's cut was too deep and something had gone wrong. Blood gushed from the sides of her open womb. Her arms and hands went limp. It was like her body fell through our hands. It softened then cooled.

She wasn't going to live anyway, he said.

Then the doctor reached into her body with a metal instrument to grab the baby as though he didn't want to get his hands dirty. The baby was limp. It was a tiny baby boy. Miss Rae let go of the girl's shoulders and grabbed the baby and wrapped it in the warmth of her big black arms.

You gonna breathe for me, baby, you hear? Miss Rae said. Ain't no baby going to die with Miss Rae holding it.

She began to hum an ancient kind of living song. The big body of Miss Rae rocked back and forth. Her humming filled the room.

The doctor pulled the ends of the girl's dress up over her body, as if the dress would close her wounds. Blood spread across the front of her white dress like a dirty rain soaked stain on wallpaper.

This here girl, the doctor said, wiping the blood from his instrument on the tail end of her dress, and shoving the bottle of chloroform into his bag. Ran away. Took one look at her bloody baby boy and ran. You never knew her name, never knew where she went, and she never came back for her baby. You hear?

What are you saying? I asked.

Miss Rae shot me a hard glance. She pressed her lips against the baby's lips and blew a deep breath into his lungs. The baby let out a jagged cry.

I said that this here girl got up from this table right after she gave birth to this bastard child and she abandoned him. Left in the middle of the night just like this here body is going to disappear and you ain't never going to say different. That is, if you want me to come running each time one of your girls stubs a toe or thinks she has a baby coming. You hear? You wrap her up in this blanket she's been bleeding on. Wrap her tight and wash the blood up off the floor. Then close the door. My man will come by later to get her. You don't know where she came from or who she was, and from now on, you don't know what happened to her. You understand?

He looked hard at Miss Rae.

Right, Miss Rae?

Miss Rae turned her head away from the doctor.

You like it here, don't you Miss Rae? Life in that kitchen of yours is pretty easy. You do what you want. No one bothers you. Pretty nice not to be picking cotton or working in the fields or doing whatever it is that you people do when you don't have an easy job cooking. From the size of you I know you like your cooking. You got a lot to thank me for, Miss Rae. You know I put in a word for you from time to time with the church. I say you're a good woman, a godly woman, someone who understands who these girls are and how to treat them. I expect you to explain a thing or two for the new Matron here when I leave. Got to get our stories straight if we want to work together. Let things run smooth and easy. Ain't that right?

Miss Rae picked up a rag that I had used to wash the woman's face, she dabbed the blood from around the baby's eyes, his silky brown hair, his long thin legs.

I was asking you something, Miss Rae. You hear me?

The doctor snapped his bag shut.

I hear you, she said.

Miss Rae dipped her rag in fresh water and wiped the baby's matted hair. He squirmed in her arms, nudging his face against her large breast, looking for something to drink.

I'm hoping, Miss Rae that we have established some kind of understanding. I came here, helped this woman deliver her baby then when I left, she ran. You didn't see where she was going and you didn't know who she was. Just left her baby and went on down the road and never looked back.

Mmmhmm," Miss Rae said, daring to look the doctor in the eye.

Gonna tell the Deacon when I see him on Sunday what a good job you're doing helping the new Matron settle into her missionary work with these girls. A really good job.

Then the doctor looked at me. I turned away from his gaze and pressed my fingers against the thin blue skin of the girl's eyelids, making sure she'd keep her eyes closed in death, and lifted her jaw so she had some dignity to her. She was so young. I had this urge to bend down and kiss her forehead, but instead, I walked over to Miss Rae and held out my arms for the baby.

He was a tiny little boy. Hard to know if it was his time to come or not, but he was here with us. I noticed that his left eye and socket looked bloodied and deep set almost hollow like maybe the doctor's surgical instrument had pushed it deep or tore something. I looked at Miss Rae. She tilted her chin as if there was nothing to say. Best to keep silent or we both might lose our jobs.

Let's take him into the kitchen and wash him good, Miss Rae said. And, I'll take care of the girl's body and clean up.

She took my arm and gently pushed me out of the room and out of the way of the doctor.

She was right, there was nothing to say and nothing to do about what had happened.

I had thought I had known cruelty when I woke every morning to an empty marriage bed. Had felt the sting of hatred when I understood what twisted bit of a husband I had was leaving me for someone else. Had tasted the salty shame of a lie when I said I was a widow so I could start a new life as the Matron, the Mother of the Door of Hope.

I was a woman who grabbed a second chance and now it was my turn to righteously dole out second chances to others who had even less than I had. I didn't know much, but one thing I knew for sure was that the chances they were going to get once they left the Door of Hope were as poor as a dinner of day-old biscuits.

That was the moment I decided to make good on my promise and raise the woman's baby as my own.

SEVENTEEN

Once the doctor had cut deep along the darkened ridge of my stomach, drew out my baby, and I knew he was safe and free, I let go.

Dying is not like what they say. It is not so much a reckoning as it is a strange moment of truth. It was all so clear. I understood everything that had happened before in my life and would happen in the future for my son. When the staff at Hull House told Mrs. Levy I had left and they didn't know where I was, she wrote to Georgette, hoping I had gone home. She did not tell her about my baby.

In that moment of dying, I knew that Georgette would come looking for me but she would never find me. She would, however, never give up trying. My brothers would work the land and have families and die on the land they worked all their lives. My father would never close his eyes at night without thinking of me, but he would never say anything of the kind to my mother. My mother would grow more silent, folding in on herself. She would dream about leaving my father and the farm but would never find the courage to walk to the train station alone. My brother's children would fill her final days. She would never quit wondering what happened to me and, like my father, would never talk about it to anyone.

As my spirit left my body, I saw my mother in her garden between two freshly planted rows of fall onions. Her pockets were full of onion sets, her knees were locked, her body bent at the waist, her hand on her worn trowel digging a hole, dropping one onion set after another along a row she had marked with a taut string. When my heart stopped, she dropped to the ground and began to sob.

I watched as she cried and dug the tip of her trowel into the earth. The hole she was digging grew larger and larger as she flipped bits of dirt from side to side until she had dug a hole nearly wide enough for a man's shoe or a small wooden box, and twice as deep as you'd ever dig to bury anything other than a cat. When she had cried as much as she was able to cry, without knowing why, she emptied her pockets of the last of the onions and covered them. She sat there next to that mound of earth and onions she had created until the sun went down and my father came looking for her.

You might say that my life had spun out in some divine plan and I had died when my time had come. But it had not. My time had been stolen from me.

I heard my baby cry, and his crying brought me back to the room, back to a life I had left too soon. But dying doesn't force you to leave if you don't want to, and I didn't want to. I chose in that instant to stay.

I hadn't done anything in my life of any significance but get pregnant. Hadn't seen anything but cornfields, church pews, the view of Michigan Avenue from the office I once worked in and, of course, the World's Columbian Exposition. The prettiest thing I had ever seen, except the Exposition, was Georgette's flower garden. A farmer had once wanted to marry me so I could raise his children. I had been raped and bore a child, but had never been loved by a man.

In truth, I had just begun to have a life with purpose that was mine.

Dying was like dreaming, but better than any dream I had ever conjured. There was light and music and colors and smells and the sound of the ocean rolling back and forth on a moonlit night. It was beautiful and I knew as I watched that it was everything I had kept hidden in my heart. It startled me. It was all I had ever wanted. It was like there had been a treasure chest inside of me that had been unlocked by death and these things were now given life.

I saw the pictures from the seed catalogues tacked to Georgette's walls and I had this gnawing feeling that I had always wanted to draw but had been too afraid of what might bleed out from my heart onto the blank page so I had never tried. I could feel the tug of a pencil in my hand, a wash of earthly golden brown brushed across a picture I was creating of my life.

There had been no space on our farm for foolishness like drawing or watercolors. I saw that sad grey suit I had made for my high school graduation unravel itself into a creamy yellow dress adorned with lace that was perfect for dancing. I felt the gentle rocking of the train and believed in my chilling bones that I had been meant to go to Florida. I saw the moon rise and knew I should have seen ten thousand more moons rise and just as many set. I tasted the salt from the ocean spray and felt the warmth of the sun on my cold flesh.

I saw books flying in the air: history books, art books, and a beautiful book about ancient kings and queens and all manner of treasures buried beneath my feet. The pages of a blank book tumbled by, and all the air I had once held in my body exploded like a fragile burst bubble. I ached. Some longing broke inside of me. What if I had owned that book, and filled it with drawings and my dreams? What would I have drawn? What would I have written? What things would I have done?

My spirit hovered over my child. His hair was dark chestnut brown. His head small and round. Perfect. He was still. Too still. I couldn't leave him. I waited in the room, unable to do anything but stay above him, watching. The woman they called Miss Rae blew a breath of life into his lungs and hugged him close to her warm black skin. When his cries broke free, they were frantic, as though he had been born with a broken heart.

Afterwards, Miss Rae swaddled my crying baby in a tea towel, tucking his flailing arms and legs into a tight bundle, wrapping him round and round as if he were a mummy. His small perfect face was the only thing left uncovered. The blanket I had knitted for him had been in my satchel, and like everything else I had owned, was stolen and thrown into the river by the man on the train, the one who beat me because I wouldn't give him what he wanted.

Georgette had been my one true friend but I had not trusted our friendship enough to tell her what had happened to me. Georgette would always wonder and grieve along with my mother that I was gone.

No one would ever know what happened or why.

Later, Miss Rae came into the room and crossed my arms over my chest and wrapped me with the blanket I had rested on, rolling me from side to side turning the blanket into a shroud. I looked ever so much like a moth spun into a cocoon.

Something about the way she wrapped me tickled my imagination. What if I might one day break free of that wrapping and become a butterfly! It was a lovely thought and one that would keep me going in the years while I waited for you, my granddaughter, to be born.

You are that butterfly that rested inside of me waiting to break free.

That evening, a man came to take my body away. He carried me in a cart through town and down into the cemetery to the edge of a big plot away from all the good churchwomen and businessmen buried higher up on the hill all around me. I could feel there were others in the plot near me. No graves were marked.

The man who dug the grave said the only prayer that was said for me. He took off his hat, leaned against his shovel and paused for a moment before he began filling my grave. He knew most of the Lord's Prayer, but not all of it, and said what few words he knew then stood with his eyes closed for a minute or two. I supposed it didn't feel like he'd said enough over someone who died with no one to claim her so he started singing. He didn't sing loud, just loud enough to be heard, but not so loud that anyone would notice what he was doing. His voice was sweet like a tenor, but dark from one too many hard days of working and drinking. He sang

Danny Boy. When he finished, he kept humming it over and over to himself as he dug his shovel into the earth then tossed each bit of dirt gently over what had been left of me.

There are choices in death, just as there are choices in life. I chose, in that moment when I heard my son's first cry that I wanted to stay. Heaven, or whatever was my due would just have to wait. That last breath I took anchored my soul to this world, not the other. It was the one choice I have never regretted.

Am I a ghost? A shade? I don't think of myself as something to be feared. I am, however, that which you, my beautiful granddaughter, can feel but can't explain.

You were the reason I had to stay. I had a favor to ask. A favor only you could grant. I could see it all spin out before me and knew that your father would falter a bit here and there, but would be fine. He had a sadness that came from growing up in that sad place I could not erase. But I was able to bring him comfort when he slept and give him the courage he needed to make a way free to find his own life.

There are many kinds of dreams. But, we only dare to share the little dreams, the dreams that won't expose us. That won't shame us because they are too bold. Always, there's that voice in our heads that shouts: Who are we to have big dreams?

Our lives have so many secrets. So many things locked in our hearts that we are afraid to free them. But death, sweet death, releases them in our last breaths.

I was so young. What did I know about the world other than what Georgette and I read about in books? What did I know about dreams?

Dreams take time. I didn't have time. But, you will.

I know you.

You are the best of me.

EIGHTEEN

GEORGETTE

I never quit missing her.

I had just put the spelling words for the week on the board. Jimmy Allen was having trouble settling down as usual, so I asked him to open the window. Things like opening a window or getting out the readers usually worked to get him focused. Getting Jimmy to concentrate and stay on task was a priority. Jimmy could sure get on your nerves.

It was an unusually warm day for late September, and, to tell the truth, I needed a breath of fresh air to keep me going.

When Jimmy lifted the sash, a gust of deathly cold air rushed into the room taking everyone by surprise. Red-haired Hilda Jenkins, who was sitting in the front row, let out a cry. My copy of *Huckleberry Finn* slid off my desk and drifted to the floor, pages fluttering on the way down as if someone were casually flipping through, trying to locate a favorite passage.

I told Jimmy to close the window, and when I did, that bit of cold air spun and swirled from side to side in the room as if it were looking for something.

Ain't gonna do it, Jimmy shouted. That thing's a banshee wind. We're all gonna die if it doesn't get out of here!

Mary Louise, who I was pretty sure didn't have the good sense not to play in the rain during a lightening storm, jumped onto her chair and gathered her skirts around her as though the classroom were flooding with water. Hilda began to cry. The two oldest boys in the class, Eugene and Otto, got out of their seats and stood back to back, feet spread apart and firmly on the ground, fists raised, ready to fight whatever ghost or strange wind that was coming at them.

I didn't know what else to do but to tell Jimmy to at least step away from the window, and when I did, that strange twisting thing gathered strength. *Huckleberry Finn*, that had fallen from my desk and was now lying on the floor, opened then shut with a snap. Hilda closed her eyes. The wind made one last swirl around my desk then roared through the open window.

Mary Louise straightened her skirts and stepped down from her chair. Eugene and Otto relaxed their hands and laughed as they took their seats. Jimmy closed the window and sat down.

Jimmy didn't move an inch the rest of the day.

No one talked about what happened.

I couldn't quit thinking about the afternoon. The wind had felt familiar. It had an urgency to it: a desire both to be there and to go somewhere else which made it twist and worry its way about the room.

A cock crowed in the middle of the night. Moonlight bathed my room. The curtains fluttered. When I sat up, I saw a shimmer of light in the slender form of a woman.

The room was still.

What do you want? I asked.

She turned. Her dress spun around her shimmering figure, wrapping her legs. I couldn't see her face.

He is safe.

Who? I asked.

A soft humming filled the room. It sounded like one of those songs you might sing to a restless child, or a song you'd carry under your breath at the end of a good day. I wondered if I should be afraid, but nothing about the light and the figure of the woman scared me. In fact, it felt like she had come to comfort me. I was grateful without knowing why.

When the humming stopped, the light began to dim. She, the light, the spirit or whatever it was, spoke again: *Human beings can be awful cruel to one another.*

Huckleberry Finn, I said.

He knew a lot about heaven, she said.

The light dimmed. The apparition disappeared and when she did, I experienced a dizzying rush of words, like a hurried confession, dancing through my head: a rape, a baby, and so, so sorry. The words came in a whoosh, like the wind that had cut through our classroom that morning. I got up, put on my robe and went to the kitchen. I lit the kerosene lamp and placed the Remington typewriter on the table and began to type a letter to my Aunt in Chicago:

I know about the baby, but I can't explain why. It's a boy. He is alive and well.

I fear she is dead. Please help me find them.

Your loving niece, Georgette

1967

NINETEEN

REGINA

My father is standing in my bedroom doorway. His feet are planted firmly on the ground, shoulder width apart, the palms of his hands pressed against the doorframe as though he is the door. I stop packing my clothes and turn to acknowledge him. I don't say anything. Don't want to hurt him.

"What are you doing, Regina? You had a full ride," he says, jamming his hands into his pockets.

"Where's a PhD in history going to take me?" I ask.

"How about to a job?"

"Teaching at a university. That's your job. Your dream. Not mine."

"I thought it was yours."

"Dreams change. I don't want to fight," I say, rolling a sweater and stuffing it into my backpack in case it's cold on the train.

"I don't understand why you are doing this. What did they say when you called them? Told them you weren't going to come, that you'd changed your mind and were going to go Chicago instead. To do what?"

I can't tell my father that I'm going to Chicago because I had a dream last night. That I have been hearing voices and that last night I heard her again in my sleep. Her voice, rising about them all, telling me to go. To look. To see. To find. That I was the only one who could fix something that had happened to her.

"Going to graduate school right now just doesn't seem, I don't know…"

"Seem right? Fun? Who said any of this was fun. It's just a way to get to someplace you want to be."

"I don't know if I want to be a history professor," I tell him, hoping that's enough of a reason to change my mind. To run away to Chicago.

"It's okay to be unsure about things. But to change your mind like this. At the last minute? Why? What happened?"

"I'm not saying I'll never go to graduate school."

"You can stay here while you decide what it is you want to do," he says.

"Going to Chicago is what I want to do right now," I say.

He pulls an envelop from his pocket.

"It's not much but it will help you get settled. Find a place to live. Tide you over until you get a job."

I wonder if my mother told him to give me the money. I know she worries. They both worry. They like things settled. Simple. No bumps in the road. Making a crazy last minute decision not to go to graduate school feels like a bump to them. I put the envelop into my purse and zip it shut. I want to show him that I'm responsible.

"Thank you," I say.

"You could probably get a job at the high school."

"I don't want to teach social studies to ninth graders."

"What kind of job are you going to get in Chicago with an undergraduate history degree?"

"I'll waitress," I say.

"At some bar?"

"How about a restaurant that serves drinks? There's nothing wrong with waiting tables. I hear the money is good in Chicago. Lots of business lunches. Tourists. I waited tables in college and you didn't seem to mind then."

"Waiting tables is fine if you're a student, not after you've graduated college."

"There are lots of restaurant jobs. It will give me time to think. Explore. Find out what I'm supposed to do."

"What are any of us supposed to do in this life? Was I supposed to have you?" he says, stepping forward, wrapping me in his arms.

"I sure hope so," I tell him. "In any case, I'm glad you did."

"You're the best thing that ever happened to me," he says, kissing my hair.

"And, Mom?"

"She's pretty good too. She puts up with me, feeds me, makes me laugh. Do I make you laugh?"

"You do."

"You'll call?"

"I'll call."

"I can't stop you?"

"Wouldn't be a good idea."

I want to, but don't tell my father about the dream I had last night about being on a train going to Chicago, watching long stretches of cornfields and tight little houses braced in a clutch of trees blur by. I don't know how to tell him about the room in my dream, the one with dark grey wallpaper studded with pink roses and a handmade quilt folded neatly at the foot of a single bed.

Last night, I felt myself unbuttoning a white blouse and slipping off a long black skirt then hanging it on the closet door on a hook in the room with the wallpaper. When I woke, the bottoms of my feet ached because the leather soles of the shoes in my dream were worn thin.

I don't know how to tell my father that when she, this dream, this ghost who haunts me, whispered to me last night, she said she is my grandmother. The mother my father never knew. The one I will never know unless I go where she wants me to go, do what she wants me to do.

I have to go to Chicago.

If I don't, I will never know what happened to her.

I will never be free of the past.

My parents drive me to the train station. We say our goodbyes. My mother hugs me tightly. Whispers in my ear that she thinks I'm brave, that she wished she had done something wild when she was younger. My father holds me for as long as he can as though he is afraid to let go.

"Be careful," he says. "It's a big city."

"Bigger than here," I say.

"Bigger than here," he responds, as though that's the reason for my going. It's a good enough reason for him to hold on to, so I leave it at that.

We say our goodbyes. I get on the train, press my hand to the window, and throw the two of them a kiss. When the train pulls out of the station, I settle into my seat, lean back and marvel at my audacity to pass up graduate school because of something I'm supposed to find or do to help a grandmother long dead whom I never knew.

I let the soft back and forth sway of the car and the click, shhh, click, shhh of the heavy metal wheels rubbing against the tracks become part of my heartbeat. No one else's heart. No one else's desires or dreams. Just my heart.

It's a curious thing.

The dreams I keep having don't feel at all like they are my dreams.

When I arrive in Chicago, the first thing I do is walk up and down Michigan Avenue dragging my two suitcases. It is late in the day and the sun glares off the dirt- streaked windows of the dozen or so tall buildings within easy sight of the Art Institute. I have seen some of these buildings in my dreams. I feel certain I've been here before and have looked out from one of their high up windows to the Chicago Art Institute below.

I look up and down Michigan Avenue at the various buildings trying to find something. Five stories up, I see a window in the Studebaker Building that feels familiar.

The window is dark. No one is there.

I pick up my suitcases and head North on Michigan Avenue to the YMCA. My parents made me call ahead before I left to book a room for a couple of weeks until I can find an apartment. They said I needed a place where I could rest for a moment. Figure things out.

They were right.

I take my time walking and looking. I buy a newspaper at a kiosk, roll it up and stick it into my backpack. I'll read the want ads later, once I get rid of my luggage at the Y and find a place to have dinner. Alone. I like the feeling of being alone in Chicago after living four years in a noisy crowded dorm at the university.

As I walk up Michigan Avenue on my way to the Y, Chicago begins to feel more and more like a home I have been missing all my life.

TWENTY

When I get to the corner of Michigan and Grand on my way to work, a gust of wind surprises me. I turn my back on it and just as I do, I think I see a bit of the gauzy hem of her white dress chasing around the corner and disappearing into a canyon of tall buildings.

I'm shaken. I want to run after her, ask her what she wants of me, but I can't afford to be late for work. My rent is due on Friday.

I push on the heavy front door to Guido's Pizzeria and jam my foot in the doorway to keep it from closing so I can let a little fresh air chase the dusky smell of booze and last night's stale cigarette smoke away before I have to start my lunchtime shift. I look down the street behind me. I worry the ghost, my grandmother, or whoever she is, might have followed me into the restaurant. Although she comes regularly into my room at night, invading the fine slender edges between sleeping and waking, I've never seen her in the daylight until this morning. She is getting closer, I think, to telling me what she wants from me.

"Hey, Regina, whaddaya want?" Clyde asks.

I watch as Clyde continues to top off opened bottles of Dewar's and Maker's Mark with water. The situation with the booze makes me nervous, but I'm happy to keep serving it. A watered down scotch can drive up a bill if someone is drinking to get a buzz. It's a win-win for the house and the waitresses.

"What do I want to drink? What do I want to do this afternoon? What do I want to do with my life? Which what are you asking about?"

"Pick one," Clyde says. "I've got all day."

I've been in Chicago almost a year now and still don't know what I want or what I'm doing here other than chasing a ghost I presume is my grandmother and having the same dreams I've had all my life: dreams about a woman standing by a window looking out on Michigan Avenue watching people rushing down the street. People dressed in long skirts and suits. Women carrying parasols. Men wearing hats. All going somewhere. Dreams of a struggle. A woman screaming. A baby crying. The sound of a train whistle.

Lately, when the woman in the dream looks out of the window she no longer sees people in long white dresses and men in suits. Instead, the people are in blue jeans and long flowered skirts. She sees them running and fighting. There are flashes of light. Broken glass. Screams. Anger.

"Okay, here's what I want. A tall glass of club soda." I say.

"Too easy, Regina, queen of my heart," he says, still waiting for me to tell him all my dark secrets. "You can have your club soda, extra ice, extra limes, two cherries, the whole deal, but I need to know once and for all why you came to Chicago."

"Inspiration," I say, looking over my shoulder to be sure the ghost of my grandmother hasn't snuck up behind me. I step into the cave-like darkness of the closed restaurant.

"Divine?" Clyde asks, handing me my drink.

"A sign from God might help." I pull my apron from my backpack and tie it around my waist.

"I think you're trying too hard," Clyde says. "You must have had some idea about what you wanted when you came to Chicago. I'm guessing it wasn't to sling pizzas, serve watered down whiskey and get hit on by drunken sales reps."

I laugh.

Clyde caps the bottles he was filling and puts them on the front row of the shelf behind him.

"I think you came to Chicago to meet me." Clyde smiles.

"That's a thought." I pick up the clipboard from the bar and check which station I'll be working.

"So, you'll go out with me?"

"How about I'll not hassle you when my customers complain that they're not getting buzzed by their expensive drinks?"

"How about dinner?"

"Sorry, busy slinging pizzas tonight. Looks like I'm booked for a double shift again. When are you going to fire Linda? I'm thinking this is the third time this month that she's called in sick or with some other excuse."

"Did you ever wonder why Chicago? Why this restaurant? There are lots of cities and lots of restaurants, and you chose the city I live in and the restaurant where I happen to work. I think we were meant to be."

"Maybe, but not tonight."

Clyde hands me a tall glass of club soda, extra ice, with three freshly cut limes and two cherries.

"For whatever twisted reason, I'm taking your response of not tonight to mean maybe another night. Maybe?"

I take a long sip of the cold drink.

"I came here because of this dream I keep having."

"Am I in the dream?" he teases.

"I'll let you know next time it comes around. If you'll excuse me, I need to get my station set up before the hungry hoards of drug reps break down the door and beg to be waited upon. Thanks for the drink."

I had the dream again last night. Clyde wasn't in it. He never is. This time the dream felt strangely real. Vibrant. It started with a woman standing by a window overlooking an earlier version of Michigan Avenue and the Art

Institute. I couldn't see who was standing, staring out the window, but could see through the window below to the crowds of people scurrying down the street: finely dressed women with their hair pinned up and tucked under their hats. Some were carrying parasols to shade their faces from the sun. The men were all in suits, some with spats and nearly all with hats. Everyone was walking in the same direction. I could see the Art Institute a couple blocks down, to the left of the crowds. Then the crowd changed. Everything changed. There was a flash of light and the people began running, and screaming.

As the dream spun out, the woman, ever vigilant, stood by the window, watching. I wondered if the woman in the window was my grandmother? I wondered what she was doing there. What she was looking for.

There was another flash of light and I saw a shadow coming from behind the woman. Tall. Dark. Foreboding. I woke with a start and tried to shake off what I saw or thought I saw. I felt uneasy.

I was alone in the room. The ghost of my grandmother was not there.

I wish she'd talk to me, tell me what she wants.

My lunch shift segues into the dinner crowd with barely enough time to refill the cheese shakers or Italian hot peppers on my tables. Fortunately, Clyde lets me stay on the same back station for dinner that I had for lunch so I don't have to reset another section.

The restaurant feels crazy. There is a big pharmacy convention in town. The place is jammed with salesmen intent on drinking and eating as much as possible on their expense accounts. By nine o'clock, I already have two offers of hotel keys accompanied by the slurred promise of a really good time, am stiffed by one man who didn't like the fact that I turned down his good time offer and got a twenty dollar tip on a ten dollar drink tab from another who said I was too pretty to be hassled. I give back the keys to the two jerks who thought I was easy-pickings, pocket the twenty and thank the generous man who wanted to make amends for my tough evening, and move on.

I am leaning on the bar, enjoying a couple of minutes standing still and not being hassled while Clyde fills my last call drink orders. When he finishes, I ask for another refill on my club soda. Clyde pulls a fresh glass from the rack and takes his time spearing a couple cherries and a lime on a toothpick before filling a Tom Collins glass with ice and club soda.

"Sure you don't want to live it up with some tonic instead? It's almost closing time. How about a splash of gin to celebrate living through another double shift of traveling drug salesmen hitting on you?" Clyde asks.

The phone rings. Clyde doesn't move. The kitchen is about to close and we quit accepting reservations or filling take out orders past ten so there's no reason to answer it.

"You should pick it up," I say. "It's my mother."

"How do you know?" Clyde asks.

"I just know things." I say, holding out my hand for the phone.

I do know things I can't explain. It has been that way my whole life. It is not always a good thing.

Clyde turns, picks up the receiver and hands it to me.

My mother is crying.

She tells me my father has died.

My body feels like it is heavy and sunk deep in water. I can barely move one foot in front of the other. I don't want to talk. I can't cry. Not here. Not now. I concentrate on breathing.

Clyde waves Marla over to deliver my last round of drinks. I have three more tables to close out. I hand her my checks and tell her to keep the tips. I go to the back and get my backpack. I tip my busboys; untie my apron, stuff it into my backpack and head towards the door.

"What happened?" Clyde asks as I pass through the restaurant.

"He ran off the road, hit a tree. They think he might have had a heart attack somewhere along the line, maybe before he lost control of his car, or afterwards when he hit the tree. The cremation is tomorrow. My mom wants me to meet her in Macon, Georgia. That's where he was born. He always said he wanted his ashes to be buried next to his mother, the woman who raised him."

"Your grandmother?" Clyde asks.

"I guess you could say she was my grandmother. I never knew her. She died when my father was in his early twenties. His biological mother died in childbirth. My father seemed to think there wasn't much in his childhood to talk about. He never mentioned anything about a father, biological or otherwise. He didn't have any brothers or sisters."

Clyde reaches into his pocket and hands me a hundred dollars. It's his tip money. I shake my head.

"Take it," he says. "You're going to need some traveling money."

"I'll pay you back," I offer.

"I won't let you. Someone did the same for me when my mother died. It's my way of squaring the deal. Take as much time as you need in Georgia. I'll get someone to cover for you. Would be great, however, if you can be back for the Democratic Convention in two weeks. I'll need someone I can depend on to keep this place from exploding. We'll be crushed for sure with delegates, candidates and protesters. Going to be a circus."

"Sure," I say. "I love a circus."

TWENTY-ONE

I leave without saying goodbye. I need to get away from everyone at work before I start grieving. I don't want anyone to comfort me. There is no comfort to be had. As soon as I step out into the night air, guilt washes over me. It was stupid that I left. That I passed up a chance to go to graduate school. That I came, instead, to Chicago in order to find the ghost of my grandmother and help her do, what?

I should have done what my father asked. I should have stayed home and taught history at the local high school. It doesn't matter that I didn't want to teach. What matters is that I have lost a chance this last year to be with my father.

My father and I always shared a warm silence whenever we were together. We didn't need to talk. We were always just happy to be together. I knew the minute the phone rang that I would miss him every day for the rest of my life.

I take my time walking down Michigan Avenue. The streets are crowded with tourists enjoying the cool of the evening. It is nearly midnight when I get to the last northbound bus stop on Michigan by The Drake Hotel.

The bus isn't crowded, so I take a seat to myself and press my face against the window. I watch the moonlight dance across the lazy waves of Lake Michigan. I hold what tears I need to shed for as long as I can.

When I get to my apartment, I drop my backpack in the kitchen and crawl into bed to cry. I am exhausted from the day. Exhausted from the knowledge that my father is gone.

I cry until I am empty from grief. When I at last fall asleep, the dream washes over me again.

The woman at the window. A whisper. A fluttering of white. Shadows crossing the room. Then something new happens.

The images come faster. A train. A shadow. A man. The smell of alcohol. Blood spreading down the front of a torn white linen dress. Dirty hands reaching into a womb. A heartbeat, like a drum, hard, strong, then stopping. Darkness. A baby's cry.

The dream plays over and over again in my head. I can't drag myself out of my exhausted sleep. I can't make the dream stop. It is like a film loop, the same scenes flashing forward and backward in rapid succession. I can't make it slow down. There are flashes of light. People fighting. More screaming. Broken glass. Sirens.

My mother meets me at the train station in Macon. She is wearing a pair of black slacks, a loose white blouse with her favorite yellow sweater tied around her shoulders. My father was sixteen years older than my mother. At 59, my mother is still tall and stately like a model. She is wearing a pair of drop pearl earrings my father gave her last Christmas. She looks contained and put together. Elegant. She normally wears what she calls pumps, but today she has on comfortable walking shoes. Shoes I've only seen her wear when she works in the garden. She is carrying a large Saks shopping bag. It looks bulky and a bit heavy. There's a box in it filled with my father's ashes.

I know from our last phone conversation that we are going to go directly from the train station to the cemetery. There's a taxi out front waiting for us. She has made arrangements to meet someone who can take us to my father's mother's gravesite.

"You okay with all of this?" she asks without waiting for me to respond. "Dad didn't like funerals. Made me promise that if he died before I did I would do this, bring his ashes to be buried next to his mother's. You know, I've never been here before. He never wanted to come back. I guess, except like this. Strange. How was the train?"

I know from a lifetime with my mother that the question about the train is not a question at all but rather a way to signal that she has come to the end of whatever she had to say. I give her a hug and say hello. She holds me a beat longer than usual. She starts to cry. Stops herself. Brushes a kiss across my cheek.

My father was the emotional one. My mother liked to knit: keep her hands busy and the conversation light and comfortable. She preferred to spend her evenings knitting and listening to show tunes on the living room stereo. My father needed a different way to unwind, so, while my mother knitted, we went downstairs together to watch television. We were rather indiscriminate about what we watched and would laugh at anything that was remotely funny and cry when necessary.

"Where's your suitcase?" she asks.

"Packed what I thought I needed in my backpack. Didn't think we'd be going out anywhere fancy. Didn't want to drag a suitcase all around town. Knew we were going straight from the train station to the cemetery."

"Good, good. I told the cab to wait for me while I came in to find you. He's going to take us to the cemetery. At first they had trouble finding Dad's mother. Seems like there's something funny about the way her grave is marked, but they found it. We can go now, take care of this. I didn't want to leave his ashes in the cab. Didn't want to put him in my suitcase, so I thought this was okay. Is it okay?"

"It's fine," I tell her.

Macon surprises me. There are stately houses everywhere. Tree-lined streets. Gentle rolling parks. It's clean. Bigger than I expected, and pretty.

Dad never said anything about it being pretty.

We ride along together in silence. The silence gnaws at my stomach. I think my mother is afraid to speak for fear of crying. She is not one for public displays of any kind. I am also afraid to speak because I don't want to cry. I had thought I had cried out my loss and grieved as much as humanly possible, but I know there's more to come. I will be blindsided by grief for the rest of my life.

The cab driver, for whatever reason, feels compelled to fill the silences between us and decides to provide a running commentary on the history of Macon and the cemetery.

"Rose Hill Cemetery is the oldest one in town. Early eighteen hundreds or so. Got some famous people buried there. Pillars of the society. People who made this town. Railroad people. Macon was a railroad town. Still is, but not so much anymore. Used to be a big hub. Fifteen different rail lines coming in day and night. Only a few trains travel this way anymore.

"I don't like driving in the old cemetery. Roads are narrow and the land slopes mighty steep down to the Ocmulgee River. Mighty steep. The Ocmulgee empties into the Atlantic Ocean. In the old days, the trains would come into Macon, and whatever was going out of the country was put on barges in the Ocmulgee, and whatever was going some place else in this country, would be put on other trains. It must have been something. All that coming and going.

"I don't like backing up. Prefer to go forward, but some of those narrow roads in the old part of the cemetery after you go down the only way out is to go backwards because there is no place to turn around. I'm going to take you into the gates and you can walk from there. It's a pretty day. I'll come back over and pick you up. How much time you gonna need? An hour? An hour and a half? You said there wasn't going to be any kind of ceremony or anything. Hour and a half should give you time to walk where you need to go, do what you got to do, then walk back again. I'll pick you up at the gates where I'm going to drop you off. Hour and a half. That seem right to you? If it's two, that's all right as well."

I look at my mother, hoping she knows how long all this is going to take.

"Hour and a half seems fine. If it's two, I hope you'll wait," she says.

"Sure," he says. "I'll wait. Not a whole lot of call for cabs on a day as pretty as this one. People around here like to walk unless it's raining, and it's not raining today. No call for rain. Hour and a half then. I'll wait. I've got my lunch with me so there's no hurry."

I'm grateful for his chatter. I strain to hear the cadence of my father's voice in his. My father always had a kind of sweet Georgia lilt to his words and laughter. He never lost it. Like it was a part of him that he couldn't shake.

The cab driver doesn't sound like my father except for the careful way he walks around an explanation. My father did that. Took his time making sure to paint a picture for you as to what was going to happen and when. He always spoke slowly as though the loss of the sight in his left eye had forced him to take his time to look at things and weigh what he needed to say.

There was no hurry in my father. I'm sure now that my father had a heart attack before he lost control of his car and hit a tree. He wouldn't have lost control for any other reason. Was probably dead long before he crashed. The tree just stopped him from going further.

The cab drives in through the arched stone gates of Rose Hill and stops. There's a small building on the right. A man is sitting on a stone bench under a tree by the building with a shovel in his hand. I suspect he's the man who dug the hole for my father and is now just waiting in the shade for us to show up with the ashes so he can finish his job and go home.

The cab pulls up next to the building. When we get out of the cab, the man with the shovel stands up to greet us. Says how sorry he is for our loss. My mother tells the cab driver that we'll be back in an hour and a half like she promised then we follow the man with the shovel down a narrow lane. My mother and I walk a few feet behind the man. It is a small funeral procession. Solemn. Silent. Respectful. Every few steps he lets the metal tip of his shovel hit against one of the cobblestones. It strikes like a bell. After a while, I hear him start to hum. He must feel that he owes this occasion some music. It's clear that he's walked down this lane a hundred times before to dig a hole and mark a soul's passing. I wonder if he expects us to say something when we bury my father's ashes.

"Do you think we should say anything?" I ask my mother.

"Dad didn't want a funeral. Didn't like that people felt like they had to say something nice when a person died whether they were telling the truth or not. He didn't want us to make up any lies or anything like that. He was a good man. That's what I want to say. He was a good man."

My heart catches in my throat. I ache with loss.

My mother continues. "He never talked about his childhood or his mother much except to say he lost the sight in his left eye when he was born. That his mother, the woman who raised him, used to snap her fingers when she came upon his blind side in order to get him to turn to look at her as though he had two eyes. She made him hold his head up straight on when he listened or spoke to her, and not to turn his head to the side. She didn't want him to be crippled by the loss of his eye. I don't know anything about her except that she took him in and raised him as her son. Don't know anything to say. I guess I should tell her thank you. Thanks for raising him to be a good man. Do you think that would be okay? Enough?"

"That's good," I say. "I think it's enough."

The man with the shovel stops near a grave marker and points to a narrow grassy path that cuts through a series of grave markers in various stages of tipped over decay.

"She's buried over there, down that hill," the gravedigger says. "It's a big plot. Biggest one in this part of the cemetery. Right on the edge of the cemetery overlooking the river. There's only one grave marker, hers. It's right in the middle of this big plot near an old tree. You'll see when we get there. I took a little time when I dug the hole for you to clear some branches that fell in the last storm and clean up the place a bit. Wanted it to be right for you. Only way to get there, however, is to wander through this here path around these old markers. It's kind of steep and there are a few loose stones and such along the way. Take your time and be careful. I'm used to making my way through all these souls. I'll go ahead and wait for you. Right before the land drops off you'll see a couple of steps that will take you down to where she is buried."

With that, he scampers down the grassy slope ahead of us using his shovel like a walking stick to steady his way.

We take our time zig-zagging through the grave markers, being careful not to step where we think there might be bodies below, which is hard because most of the engraving on the grave markers has been erased by years of rain and wind and an occasional winter freeze so it is difficult to know the head and foot of the burial plots. My mother's shoulders hunch up ever so slightly as if there's a cold breeze. She unties the sweater from her shoulders and slips her arms through the sleeves and buttons the top two buttons.

I reach the place where there are stairs and I am able to look down and see a small flat granite marker in the middle of a large plot. I guess it is for my grandmother, the woman who raised my father to be a good man. I look for the gravedigger. He is standing at the far edge on the other side of the tree from my grandmother. He is working his shovel idly in the hole he has created for my father.

"No!" My mother shouts.

Her voice is loud and irreverent in the hushed edge of this old cemetery. I have to stop myself from telling her not to be disrespectful.

Not to raise her voice.

"Ma'am?" The man stops what he is doing. He leans against the handle of his shovel and brushes his hands on his clothing.

"My husband wanted to be buried near his mother, not a half mile away. Next to her. That's what he wanted. That's what I told you on the phone. He wanted to be buried next to her."

"Can't," he says.

My mother comes down the stairs. I walk over to my father's mother's grave marker. There is no last name. No first name. Just the word "Mother" and two dates 1848-1928. My father was born in 1893. Mother was 45 when she adopted him. I was born in 1946 when my father was 53. Too old, some might say, to father a child. My mother was 37. They had tried, but failed so many times to have children they came to believe it would never happen and had given up hope. The story they always told me on each and every birthday was how surprised and full of joy they were the night I was born, as if my arrival was an unexpected gift of a new life together as a family.

I hear my mother arguing with the gravedigger. She wants my father's ashes, as per his wishes, to be buried next to his mother, the woman who raised him.

"I can't," the gravedigger insists.

"Of course you can," she says.

"I told you, I can't. They're everywhere," he says.

His arm makes a sweeping motion, and as I watch it swing from side to side over the expanse of this large plot I see fresh turned spades of dirt here and there where he must have tried to dig before he settled on a far place along the edge of the plot.

"Who is everywhere?" my mother asks.

Her hands are on her hips. She pulls the sleeves of her sweater up to her elbows as though she has a good notion to grab the shovel out of his hands and dig the grave herself.

"The others," he says. "The babies, the mothers, the girls who came to her for help. They're everywhere around her. He's not the first."

I step back afraid I'm standing on something or someone. I look all around. Babies. Mothers. Women in trouble. I know nothing about this woman who raised my father and feel as though I have fallen into a mystery. Have stumbled onto a lifetime of secrets.

"Who was she?" I ask.

"She was the matron of the Door of Hope. It was a home for wayward girls. Everyone called her Mother. Like on her tombstone. Mother. If she raised your father, then he knew some of these girls. Probably held some of these babies before they died.

"You ask me to dig a grave. I'll dig a grave, but I won't upset what's there already. Won't disturb the dead."

My mother and I hold the box with my father's ashes and together we lower them into my father's freshly dug grave. The gravedigger offers us his shovel.

"Where I come from," he says, "it's customary to help someone find eternal rest by covering the coffin or ashes with dirt. You should take a turn. Both of you. Say something truthful, something you won't regret. I'll finish up when you're done."

I take the shovel first. The handle is long, smooth and worn. I never worked in my mother's garden and find the long handle awkward. I choke up on the shovel the same way I used to choke up on the baseball bat when my father pitched to me in our backyard. The dirt is heavy. I tip in a small bit of earth I've managed to pick up, then another. I don't know what to say except to tell my father, thank you. I whisper it. The gravedigger nods his head. I say it again, louder. I start to cry.

My mother takes the shovel from me. She pushes the worn metal tip deeply into the pile of freshly dug soil. She turns the shovel, dumping the dirt she has scooped up into the grave. Over and over again, she digs then tips the shovel so the dirt slides like water back into the ground from where it came. Tears are streaking down her face.

"He was a good man," she says with each turn of the shovel. "A good man."

When my mother stops, the gravedigger takes the shovel from her and pushes the rest of the dirt into the hole he has dug. He tamps down the soil with the toe of his boot.

"If you don't mind," he says. "I'd like to sing. I always sing a little something to the ones that come to me for burying."

My mother takes my hand and nods her head. We stand, hand and hand, close. She leans her head onto my shoulder. I feel the warmth of her along the side of my body. The gravedigger starts to sing. It is his version of *Amazing Grace*. The melody wanders a bit and he hums some of the words as though he has sung them so many times before they no longer need to be said. When he finishes, he brushes the few bits of remaining soil over the spot he has dug and tamps it down again with the toe of his boot. Then he reaches into his pocket and sprinkles grass seed onto the bare earth.

"Going to rain tonight," he says. "Life starts fresh. These seeds will grow. I'll come by next week to check on it. You gonna put up a marker?"

My mother shakes her head no.

"He just wanted to be near her," she says. "I guess, just like all the others."

After dinner, we go to the hotel. I can't sleep. I tell my mother I'm going to go out for a walk. I grab a cab. I go to the cemetery. I find Mother's grave again. I sit with my back against the big tree in the middle of the plot. It starts to rain. Soft at first. Silent. It feels comfortable, familiar, like the many hours my father and I sat next to each other not talking, but just being.

The moon rides in and out of the clouds and rain. My eyes feel tricked by a flicker of white that could be moonlight or the hem of a white dress. It's her. She's here. I'm beginning to feel that it wasn't a coincidence that I saw her for the first time in daylight, when I was walking down Michigan Avenue the day my father died.

I let the moment wash over me. I am trying to think my way through the notion that my father grew up in a home for wayward girls. That he knew these girls. That he held their babies. That life died in his arms.

His mother is near and wants something from me.

Coming to Macon to bury my father's ashes has challenged whatever notion I once had about my father, his life, my life, and where we came from together. I try to imagine how he must have felt to at last have his own daughter, and the fear he must have wrestled with every day of my life to keep me safe from death.

I do not speak. I wait for his mother to talk to me.

Her white dress drifts off to the side as if the wind has blown her away.

Another form takes shape. One I have never seen before. Tall. Elegant in the way some elderly women walk straight-backed and reassured they have done right in their time on earth. Her dress is brown. Her hair grey and pulled back in a kind of no nonsense bird nest affair at the nape of her neck.

It is the first time Mother comes to me. The whistle of a cool breeze through the tree branches above me takes on the shape of music first, then words.

I raised him to be a good man. He was born with a strong will to live. A strong will to be someone despite his rough start and blind eye. I took him from his mother's cold womb. Gave him my name. Called him mine.

The wind blows harder. There is a shrill whistling sound. The swirl of white reappears. A slim figure takes shape.

I am your grandmother. It is time for you to know what happened to me and how I died when your father was born. And, what you must do now to make it right so your father, as well as all the others who came to the Door of Hope, can at last rest easy.

TWENTY-TWO

Around ten o'clock, two young priests, black shirts, turned white collars, and cheap dark sports jackets, get seated in my section near my workstation. They order two drafts and a medium supreme pizza with extra sauce.

I take their order and deliver their beers. I am standing by my station, cleaning up condiment containers and filling cheese shakers when I overhear their conversation. They are talking about ghosts.

I walk over to their table.

"Anything else I can get for you? Salad?"

"Do you believe in ghosts?" They ask in unison.

"I'm assuming you mean, as in Holy," I reply.

My mind flashes on the bit of white dress I saw disappearing down Grand Avenue on the afternoon my father died. I see the stern figure of Mother at the gravesite, feel a chill as I recall, once again, the young slight figure of my paternal grandmother floating above the freshly turned earth of my father's grave.

It's been a long day and it's late. I'm still struggling to get my feet on the ground after my father's death. I've only been back from Georgia for two days and I'm wiped out. I have been unable to sleep. Ever since I came back to Chicago, the dreams have become more vivid, more detailed. My mind and heart ache with loss.

I want to hear what these two priests know about ghosts. Want to ask them if my father's ghost is close at hand and will come to me as well. I want badly to talk with my father again, to know what he knows, to understand what his two mothers want from me.

"I'm Father Tim, and this is Father Paul. But, we prefer Tim and Paul and apologize about the turned collars.

"Holy is a whole different ballgame. What we're talking about right now are ghosts of the white sheet variety. Ghost stories. Visitations from the beyond. Those kinds of ghosts."

"I'm not Catholic," I reply.

I look around at my tables making sure no one is waving an empty beer mug at me to ask for another. I still have a couple tables to close out but don't want to rush anyone. I'm too tired and in no mood to turn another table and take yet another customer. I'm focused now on ghost hunting.

"Not being Catholic doesn't count for an answer. Besides, it doesn't matter. We're Jesuits, which means we look like we're Catholic but we ask too many questions about everything. Most Catholics wish we'd just get over the whole Rome thing and announce that we're really Episcopalians. However, to be or not to be Catholic is not what we're talking about right now."

"How do you feel about ghosts? Have you ever seen any? Felt any?" Paul asks.

I hear the kitchen bell ring.

"Your pizza is ready," I say.

I serve them their pizza. While they linger over their last call drinks, we chat about religion and the possible reality of ghosts. I don't tell them about my father's two mothers in the graveyard.

They are the last customers in my section to pay their bill and leave.

"What if," I say to Clyde, "life and death aren't opposites? That it's more complicated than turning a light on and off?"

Clyde is closing out the register. I'm standing at the bar, drinking a gin and tonic. I can't decide what I want or should tell him, but I need to talk. The priests have stirred a restlessness in me. Everyone else has gone home. The place is empty.

"I'm not sure I understand," he says.

"If being alive is defined by breathing and dead is defined by not breathing, what is breath? Is it soul?"

I'm feeling a little edgy talking to Clyde about the idea of breath and soul. I know what I saw in the cemetery was real. Since my time in Macon, I can feel my grandmothers' dreams and whispers creep into my consciousness and deep into my bones. Being in the ghostly presence of these two women felt like breath. My two grandmothers are very much alive within my life. Are we dreaming for each other? Breathing for each other? Are we one soul stitched together through circumstance and fate?

"I don't know," he says. "I guess if the conscious, engaged person is alive and the breathing one is alive, maybe one is more alive than the other."

"I think I agree. And, if so, then perhaps there is a state of being dead, really dead, and something less dead, like, maybe just not being fully alive. Does that make sense?"

Clyde pours himself a healthy shot of bourbon from a bottle in the back of the shelf: one he hasn't watered down.

"Like a coma?"

"I was thinking more about ghosts," I reply.

"Ghosts?"

"Is a ghost alive? Half dead? Can someone be almost dead, but not dead enough to go to Heaven or Hell? Some people see ghosts."

Clyde looks at me a little sideways.

"When did you see a ghost?" he asks.

I hold up my empty glass indicating I want another drink and start telling him about what I happened in the cemetery.

Clyde takes the money from the cash register and zips it into the bag for the bank. He opens the safe under the bar, throws in the bag, closes the door and secures the lock. He takes a fresh glass from the rack and pours me another drink.

"Did you see your father's ghost?" he asks.

"No," I tell him. "Only the ghost of his mother and the woman who raised him. I also saw his mother's ghost the day my father died. I saw the hem of her dress as she fluttered down a side street. I wanted to follow her, but couldn't. I would have been late. She's in my room sometime, at night. There's a soft rustling noise and the air around me feels like a whisper."

"What about your other grandmother, the woman who raised your father?"

"I haven't seen her since I've been back."

TWENTY-THREE

Whispers. A fluttering of white. Lights flashing. Images rushing through my mind. Sleep last night was more like a restless trance than rest. There is a now a new half consciousness to the dreams. I see as well as sense a train, a shadow, a man, and the smell of alcohol. I both feel and see warm blood spreading across the front of a white dress, see blood on my hands. Not my blood, but someone else's blood.

Right before I wake up, I hear a baby's cry. My father?

The phone rings.

I roll to the edge of my bed and lift the hem of the window curtain. I put my hand on the windowpane to judge how far the August heat has already risen from the pavement. I'm anxious for September and the return of cooler nights, tourists leaving town and children going back to school. The street below is bathed in sunlight. A woman is calling to her dog. Two kids ride by on bicycles teasing the dog as they pass the woman. There is much barking and a bit of swearing on the part of both the children and the woman with her dog. I hear a garbage truck rumble by. I pick up the phone.

It's Clyde.

"Hope you don't have plans for the next few days."

"You going on vacation?"

"It's Friday and the city is already mobbed. The Democratic

Convention doesn't start until Sunday and it looks like there's a hundred cops on every block from Grant Park across from the Conrad Hilton where the delegates are going to stay up to Lincoln Park, where the hippies, yippies and protesters say they're going to camp out. Daley is threatening to bring in the National Guard tomorrow morning because the protesters are making noise, dancing, singing, doing all nature of drugs and getting high and having sex on good clean Chicago soil. The Mayor is not having any of it. Oh, yeah, I'd appreciate it if you could get here without getting on television. Just talked to the owners. They'd like us to do everything possible to stay out of the fray of all this. Stay out of the news. There are reporters and camera crews everywhere just waiting for the first push to come to a shove so they can have something to broadcast. They're pretty aggressive about getting their news. One of them stopped me on my way in and wanted to know if I was a hippie or whatever and what type of protest had I planned to do during the convention. I didn't think it was wise for me to say I planned to serve some beer.

"It is, as predicted, a circus complete with freaks. To top it off, I had to walk through a mob of cymbal clanging, drum beating Hari Krishna, in order to get here. What do they want? Money? My soul? I can't figure them out. The delegates are rumored to start arriving tonight with most of them coming on Sunday morning. The circus is in full swing and we are going to get slammed. It's ten o'clock and we already have people lined up on the sidewalk for lunch. I'm calling Jess, Marla, Mindy and Lucy asking them to pull a week of double shifts. Cindy is out of town, so is Jen, so we're going into this ordeal short handed. I need you near the door to keep things calm, handle the seating, as well as the tables in the front of the house. I want customers to think this is a safe place, a friendly place, and you're the only one I can count on to manage all this."

"Cops don't tip," I say, letting go of the curtain. "And, I'm willing to bet the hippies don't either, which only leaves the delegates, the gawkers and the tourists who don't have the good sense to leave town when Mayor Daley decides he's going to call in the National Guard to pick a fight."

"Honest to God, if you take the front of the house and help me control the situation, I'll split my tips with you."

"Fifty-fifty?"

"Plus dinner at some place with white linen when it's all over."

"What if the hippies and the cops decide to bring the fight indoors?"

"Already thought of that. The owners agreed to hire a couple of bouncers."

"Big ones?"

"One is called Moose, the other Truck. I offered them cash and all the pizza they could eat. They asked me to define ALL, as in all the pizza they could eat. They didn't seem too interested in the money. Seems like they do some kind of body slamming work for the Italian guys in town and don't really need the cash."

"When do these double shifts start?"

"As soon as you can get here."

When I round the corner from Michigan Avenue I see a crowd of folks lined up on the sidewalk waiting for Guido's to open. Some are standing, leaning against the building, others are sitting with their backs against the wall: legs crossed or stuck out across the sidewalk like broomsticks. The ones in comfortable shoes and fanny packs are tourists. The longhaired unshaven men and the women in bright colored cheap Indian skirts for sure are hippies.

Cops are everywhere. Some are walking up and down the sidewalk letting their nightsticks tap against curbs and lampposts as they pass by. The tourists seem alarmed, the hippies unimpressed. The press is everywhere, soaking it all in, waiting for the fight to begin.

The air is thick with humidity. Ten-thirty in the morning and it has already hit a muggy eighty-six degrees. Noon will be ninety for sure. Not a cloud in sight. The National Guardsmen, as well as the cops, are dressed out in riot gear. They look hot and unhappy.

There's a colorful crowd of hippies standing along the side of the building waiting for the restaurant to open. They look shockingly tired for so early in the day. I'm getting the impression not many of the out of town protesters have slept since they arrived in Chicago.

I push my way through the crowd. I knock hard on the door, hoping Clyde hears me. The hippies cheer when the door opens and a blast of refrigerated air conditioning spills out into the street. They stop cheering when I squeeze through the crack in the door and lock it behind me.

"Where are Truck and Moose?" I ask.

"Called right after I hung up with you. Said they might be a half hour or so late. This political show has turned the whole city into some kind of congested nightmare. That was forty-five minutes ago. I hadn't planned on opening until they arrived, but I'm thinking folks baking on the sidewalk out there might not remain civil if I keep them waiting any longer."

I pull a clean apron from my backpack and toss my bag behind the bar.

"Anyone else get here?"

"Mindy is here. She's working the back room. Jess and Marla said they wanted to work the big section together, rather than split it up. They're getting changed. Lucy had planned to take this time off, said she can't make it today, could be here tomorrow if we really need her. So, that's it. Think you can handle the door and seating parties as well as your section? I'm hoping if you seat them, you can kind of slow things down a little so the place runs smoothly. I gave your three back four tops to Jess and Marla, which leaves you with six four tops and a deuce. Let's keep the hippies together. Seat them near the kitchen. That should make them a little less visible and vocal. Put the cops and National Guard up front in your section and spread the tourists in between the cops and the hippies. Rumor has it that the National Guard and Mayor Daly's crew of goons, have orders to make the protesters feel as unwelcome and as uncomfortable as possible. Not sure how they're going to do that without freaking out everyone else, including the natives. But, I'm hoping the tourists can act as a buffer between the two aggrieved parties and all remains calm. "

"Give me a couple minutes to check the stations. Make sure everyone is ready for the rush. When I come back, you can open the doors."

By the time I get the initial lineup from outside seated, the place is nearly full and feels oddly charged and ready for a fight. The tourists are nervous and not sure what to order. The hippies want the music turned up and won't quit yelling about it until I go back there and tell them I'll see what I can do. I walk up front to the bar, pretending to muscle Clyde a little. Clyde takes my cue and messes with the sound system for a few moments before he yells at me and says it's as loud as he can make it. I go back and complain to the hippies that the bartender, who is also the manager, is a real jerk and refuses to change either the volume or his choice of music.

I can see that Mindy is less than happy that I've given her the hippies. She's overwhelmed with the noise and the odd threat hanging in the air that anything could and might happen with them. The last thing I need is for her to quit, so I stick around asking our special guests where they're staying, how things are going, and what they want to do in Chicago.

"Stop the war!" One of the hippies shouts and the others start in chanting: "No more war, no more war."

I don't know what I think about the war, but hearing them chanting raises the hair on my arms. I look over and see Mindy turning her back like she might be thinking of taking off her apron and calling it a day. At the moment, it doesn't seem like there is much that we can do to stop the chanting or the growing edge of chaos they're creating. The one who started the chanting has jumped onto his chair and is pumping his fist in the air, leading the chanting.

"There's no war in here," I say. "Let's make a little peace."

I go over to the station and fill half a dozen pitchers with coke and iced tea, tell Mindy and the busboy to fill glasses with ice and we start giving out cold drinks on the house. I promise everyone that if the chanting stops and things stay civil, the free tea and soft drinks will keep flowing. The cheerleader one sits back down in his chair and downs his coke and holds up his glass for a refill.

When Mindy gives me the nod that she's okay and can handle the orders, I go back to my station.

Two cops come in, I offer them seating in my section and comp them a couple of beers to keep them from exploring the back room where the hippies are drinking free cokes. I don't want a scene.

"Nice work," Clyde says, filling the two beer mugs for the cops.

"You do what you have to," I say, picking up the mugs with one hand and two menus with the other. "A dozen pitchers of coke and iced tea along with a few beers is a cheap price for the house to pay for keeping the peace. You are definitely going to owe me big time."

Clyde laughs, tips his head in the direction of the door. Two men the size of refrigerators muscle their way through the line, come into the restaurant and immediately lean on the bar.

"Which one is Moose?" I ask.

"The one who's not called Truck," says Clyde.

"Where should we put them?"

"I'm thinking I'll keep them with me at the bar. Let everyone who comes in get a good look at them."

"They are big," I say.

"How much pizza do you think the two of them can eat?"

"I'm guessing we'll find out."

The lunch shift runs surprisingly smoothly. It's crowded. The National Guard has gotten word of the free beer the cops have been drinking and are hoping to get the same treatment. They're hot and hungry like the cops. I put all the uniforms in my section and keep the hippies and tourists tucked safely in the back. I don't want trouble.

I step up to the bar to talk with Clyde about what to do about closing the place between lunch and dinner. It's almost three. The lunch shift should have been over and our doors locked by now so we can run the vacuum cleaner, refill the condiments and get ready for dinner, but the day has a kind of slow motion action flick feeling to it and I'm thinking we should take things easy and just stay open and segue into dinner around five. Half the tables in both the front and back are still filled with people nursing cold drinks and picking at pizza crusts. The wait staff is puttering, wiping tables, filling shakers with cheese and Italian pepper flakes, while not trying any too hard to push folks to leave. They're all pulling a double shift so closing or staying open doesn't really matter all that much. No one is planning on going home.

The two bouncers are working their way through their third large double sausage double cheese pizza at the bar.

"How about we work out a plan to give everyone a half hour break before the five o'clock rush and just keep the place open and quiet. I don't see any reason to kick out anyone right now. Neither the hippies nor the tourists seemed to want to leave because it's not just hot outside. It's damn hot."

"What about the cops and the National Guard?" Clyde asks.

"As long as the hippies are here, the boys in uniform are happy to be sipping on their free beers and sitting in air conditioning. Probably already called in a report to Mayor Daley that they have captured a group of protesters and have them cornered, disarmed and under house arrest in a pizza joint."

"What's going on with the hippies?" Clyde asks.

"They seem to be having a good time making plans. I caught a few bits of conversation on the back and forth. Sounds like there may be some bonfires, dancing, and general protesting in Lincoln Park tonight. They're hoping to catch the attention of the news media. Also heard a few things about a march from Grant Park down to the Chicago Amphitheatre where the convention is taking place. Seems like Daley has blocked their attempts to get a parade permit and they're trying to figure out what to do and how to do it without getting arrested.

"You know anyone in Vietnam?" I ask.

"My cousin, Lenny. He writes me letters when he can. Asks me not to tell either my parents or his where he is or what he's doing. He says it's pretty awful. The fighting doesn't ever seem to stop and he says you never know sometimes who the enemy is and who might be friend. He said they've got kids over there carrying explosives and women too. He says it's like you can't talk to anyone. Can't trust anyone. The only way he and his friends can remain sane is to stay high. He says it's pretty messed up."

"Why didn't you go?" I ask.

"Don't like the idea of getting killed. I ran straight to this bar after college. Figure I'll keep my head down and my fingers crossed that the war ends before they decide to draft middle class folks like me. Truth be told, I rather like hanging out here and staying alive."

Clyde delivers all the food orders for the customers sitting at the bar along with my tables up front so I can give the rest of the staff enough of a break to keep them from going crazy before we lock the doors around midnight. When breaks are over, I'm nice, but firm, and ask all the left over customers from lunch to cash out and make room for our dinner crowd. There's some push back from the folks in the back, but eventually the busboys are able to get the tables cleared, the floors swept and the place ready for dinner.

Dinner is a blur. We're serving so much beer and pizza and flipping so many tables in order to accommodate all the folks lined up at the door wanting to eat, I wind up asking Truck to man the door and Moose to hand out menus and seat folks as soon as I can get tables cleaned and set up.

We are flipping tables like we're staffing a high school cafeteria with a hundred chairs and two thousand hungry students pushing at the doors to sit down and eat before the bell rings. I overhear the dishwashers complaining loud enough that I know they're just a dishpan away from threatening to call it a night and walk out the backdoor. I go to the front of the house and look outside. There's a line all the way down the block. We've got a long way to go before we can lock the doors.

I don't feel like washing dishes and I'm not so sure either Truck or Moose have ever washed a dish in their lives, so I dig into my tips and give each of the dishwashers twenty bucks and beg them to stay.

"Ten more if we stay around to clean up when we close?" one of the dishwashers asks.

"Ten more if you stay," I promise.

Around nine o'clock, I hear the big Hobart mixer in the kitchen crank up and I realize we're running low on pizza dough. I'm praying we've got enough sausage, cheese and sauce to keep the food coming. I have no desire to start turning away customers and locking the doors. I'm not looking for a scene and don't want a fight. The tips are flowing and I know it's going to be a good night for the wait staff and a just reward for working a double shift. Running out of pizzas is not an option. Nobody wants this to stop.

I go to the bar to talk with Clyde.

"I need five twenties," I tell him. "From the cash drawer, not your pocket. The kitchen staff has been pushing hard all day to keep up.

They're mixing more dough right now. I'm thinking we don't want to tell folks we're out of pizza. An extra twenty all the way around for the five cooks in the kitchen might be the best way to keep pizzas coming."

"Good call," Clyde says, opening the cash register. "I knew you could deal with this."

"You are going to be my slave," I tell him. "You are so in debt…"

It's one o'clock in the morning before Clyde flips off the lights and locks the front door.

"See you at ten tomorrow morning?" he asks.

As promised, he splits his tips with me which more than makes up for the money I gave the busboys and dishwashers.

"Ten o'clock," I say.

I start walking down the street. Clyde catches up and walks with me, as though we are together going somewhere. He's mumbling something about how much he likes me and appreciates how I handle the house. I smile and tell him thanks. He tries to reach for my hand, but I turn away, saying I need to get home, that I'm tired. I leave Clyde standing by himself on the sidewalk as I hurry down Michigan Avenue alone.

That's when I see it again: the flip of the hem of my grandmother's white dress.

I start to follow her. She's moving fast, like a wispy cloud on a windy day. I walk as fast as I can, but I can't catch up. I don't see her anywhere when I come to the corner. I flag down a bus. Take my seat. Press my face against the window all the way home, thinking about the hippies chanting "No More War" and wondering what my grandmother wants me to see, as well as what I'm supposed to be looking for.

TWENTY-FOUR

Before I can tie on my apron to work, Clyde starts rambling.

"Saturday night was the biggest we've had in a long while. Big enough that I don't think we need to try to top it tonight, but I'm thinking we might. The rest of the delegates are checking in tonight and tomorrow morning. Convention starts tomorrow afternoon. National Guard is out on the streets and in the parks again in riot gear. So are the cops. It's like some goddamn birthday party where they all get to dress up in their hard hats and shields and push people around. Rumor has it that they plan to teargas the crowds. Mayor Daley seems to be enjoying the muscle show and is doing his best to declare his toughness to any news source he can step in front of. Hippies are threatening to have some kind of love-in or dance-in or something or other this afternoon when the convention convenes. We've got press crawling all up and down Michigan Avenue looking for a fight to photograph. There are hippies, cops, delegates, candidates, and tourists who don't know what bus to take to get to the aquarium. It feels like a madhouse. Like some kind of weird sideways history is being made. We already have half dozen reservations for big parties of six or more for the various delegate groups at both lunch and dinner. Not taking any more reservations. Thinking we can set up a couple long tables in the back and leave them in place all day. I tried to stagger the reservations to make it more manageable. Tell everyone to add on a 15% tip to anything bigger than a party of four for the rest of the week. Some of these big shots with votes to buy and sell might think they're too big to tip. It's worse than a drug convention."

Clyde is talking a mile a minute, not looking up from his work watering down the scotch while he prattles on and on. He hasn't bothered with hello or turning on the house lights. He looks like he spent the night sleeping behind the bar and didn't bother to go home to shave and change his clothes.

I can hear the kitchen staff cutting dough, pounding it out in the deep -dish pans and stacking the pans on the shelf to grab and finish off when the orders start pouring in. The dough mixer is grinding away. Cheese is being grated. They're getting ready.

"I slept well, last night," I say. "How about you?"

Clyde stops. Laughs. Caps a now watered down full fifth of Jack Daniels and looks up.

"You want a club soda?" he asks.

"I had the strangest dream last night," I start to tell him.

"Was I in it?" he asks.

"No, but my grandmother was."

I need to tell Clyde about my dream. I want him to stop what he is doing and listen, nod, and reassure me that I haven't lost my mind. That I'm just tired from working two double shifts in a row with at least three if not four to go, which makes me even more tired just thinking about it.

The door opens and Mindy comes in.

"I'm okay with the hippies again today," she says. "They're growing on me. They told me they're coming back today and bringing friends. They pooled their money last night and left a decent tip after stiffing me the first night. You know, they honestly think they can do this. Stop the war."

I look at Clyde. Last night, my grandmother told me to listen. That's what she said: *listen*. Dreams talk. When I woke I heard her whisper: *There are many kinds of war.*

"Keep giving them free iced tea and cokes. Doesn't cost us much, and worth the good will it buys," Clyde says.

"Thanks." Mindy replies.

"Let me know if you need help," I add.

"Will do," she says.

Marla and Jess come in.

"They're already lining up for lunch," Marla says.

"Cops are everywhere," Jess adds.

"You okay sharing the big middle room again?" I ask.

"Okay by me," Marla says.

"Can you give us a break again if we don't shut down before dinner?"

"If it slows down, we'll close between lunch and dinner. If not, I'll make sure everyone gets a break. I'll start the breaks around 2:30 and plan to give everyone a half hour. You all should go outside this time, get some fresh air. We have days to go before we get to normal again."

"Don't know how we could have made it through to midnight the last couple nights if you hadn't given us a break. Thanks."

"We got set up for today before we left last night," Marla added. "Open the doors whenever you want. Might as well get this double shift started!"

The cops and the National Guard don't start showing up until late afternoon. They're hungry, tired of walking and are barely able to squeeze into the booths with all their riot gear.

There are many kinds of wars.

I seat them in my section. Offer beers. Take my time getting their orders and serving them because I'm listening.

I want to hear about the war they're fighting.

Listen.

I don't know what I'm supposed to be listening for.

I go to the back and help Mindy serve iced tea and cokes to the hippies who have pulled up spare chairs and are crowded around a couple of tables talking, planning, looking over their shoulders to see if people are watching them. I hear them talk about last night, in Lincoln Park, how the cops sent up flares lighting the park, ordering them around shouting through bullhorns, eventually pushing them back and out of Lincoln Park by shooting tear gas at them. They talk about throwing rocks. Running away from the tear gas. Sleeping on church steps and on park benches. Coming back in the morning to reclaim Lincoln Park.

I overhear talk about Allen Ginsberg planning a love-in or dance-in or another OM meditation. The media seem to love Ginsberg. Everyone agrees they need to go along with whatever he wants to do. People shuffle in and out of the hippie cluster throughout the day. The tables they have claimed have become a de facto resistance headquarters. Mindy keeps the various pitchers of cold drinks filled while the busboys do a decent job of clearing dirty glassware and bringing fresh. Everyone is working overtime to keep tempers down and things running smoothly.

The tables we pushed together for the large party reservations, mostly for various groups of convention delegates, are crowded from lunch through dinner all the way to closing. They talk about strategies. Who they will support, how they plan to cast their ballots, and if there's a chance they can persuade others to back McCarthy since the dream of ending the war is a lost cause now that Bobby Kennedy is gone.

Listen.

There are many kinds of struggles, many kinds of wars.

TWENTY-FIVE

Wednesday. The hippies aren't in the restaurant today. They're in Grant Park listening to the convention on transistor radios. The cops are down there too trying to keep things contained. Clyde has his radio on low at the bar. While ordering drinks, I overhear a commentator say the demonstrators still don't have a permit to organize a march down to the convention. The police and National Guard have instructions from Mayor Daley to use muscle. I notice everyone, including Truck and Moose, are moving more slowly, talking more softly, as though they have the power to keep everything in the city contained as long as they don't rush or raise their voices.

Even without the protestors and the cops, we stay busy. It's mostly tourists and locals. The tables turn fairly quickly and the shift feels busy. The tips are good. We are able to fall back into our old routine of closing between lunch and dinner. By ten o'clock in the evening, the place is empty, the stations cleaned, refilled and ready for tomorrow. The kitchen staff does a quick inventory before clocking out. We're running low on just about everything. Clyde puts in a rush order for supplies to be delivered in the morning.

I have this funny sense of digging trenches, battening down hatches, checking supplies, gathering the troops, getting ready to fight.

There are many kinds of wars.

Clyde and I are the last to leave.

It's only 10:45. The earliest either one of us has left the restaurant in days. I half expect to see the sun shining when we open the door to go outside. The moon doesn't disappoint. It's full and bright and so low in the sky I feel like I could touch it if I were just a little taller.

The night air is fresh and cool. It feels good on my face.

"You want me to call you a cab?" Clyde asks.

"The night is young," I say.

"Can I walk with you?"

"Sure."

"Really?"

"As long as you understand it's not a date."

"I heard talk at the bar today that there are hundreds of people, local and otherwise, organizing to demonstrate tonight in front of the Conrad Hilton where the delegates are staying. Stir things up a little. We could walk down there. There's a nice bar in the hotel that stays open until 2."

"We're not on a date. Just taking a walk."

"And, if we get thirsty, we can get a drink?"

"If we get thirsty."

"Let's walk."

Clyde is a good four inches taller than I am. I have to walk fast in order to keep up with him. I can feel the muscles along the backs of my legs stretch and let go of the tension of the day.

"Do you ever get tired of smiling? Of listening to people talk?" I ask.

"I don't mind listening," Clyde says. "Makes the time go faster. Plus, listening is easy. Truth is, I like everything about the rhythm of the restaurant, the people coming and going, the smell of food, all the chatter. I'm thinking of going to law school."

"Law school?"

We have been walking fast for fifteen minutes or so, as if we can't slow down from the last couple of days in the restaurant. We are passing the Prudential Building when a gust of wind from Lake Michigan catches us at the corner and pushes me off balance. Before I can regain my footing, my body brushes against Clyde's arm.

I don't know what I want.

The streets are full of people.

"You might find this surprising," he says, not bothering to step away from me. "But while I have been masquerading as a bartender, I have been developing some fine lawyer skills."

"Like?"

"Listening and being able to recognize BS from the truth. Plus, when things were slow or when we actually did close between lunch and dinner, I studied for the LSATs. Looks like I have my choice between Northwestern and Loyola. I'm thinking Loyola because they offer a night school option. I can keep my job working the lunch shift, have a hot meal before going off to school, and cover my tuition with my tips. What do you think?"

I am about to congratulate Clyde. Tell him I think he'd make a good lawyer, but I can't get the words out because there's shouting and chaos all around us. He grabs my hand and starts running. I run along with him into the crowds. We are being pushed from side to side. I hold tightly to his hand and fall into step with his steps. My lungs are beginning to burn. I can see the Art Institute in the distance being lit by flares. We hear sirens and police shouting through bullhorns to get back, go home. People are pushing forward and getting pushed back. I get my first choking whiff of tear gas.

I see a flash of my grandmother's white dress again. A wedding dress? Why is she wearing a white dress? Who is she? Why is my grandmother here? Where is she going? Why did she want me to come to Chicago?

I break loose from Clyde and start running after my grandmother, going deeper into the crowd. I look down the block and see the building I have seen so many times in my dreams. There's a light on in a window five stories up. Another flare lights the sky. Someone is standing by the window. I look where they are looking.

A hand grabs my arm. It's Clyde.

"Where are you going?" he shouts above the chaos.

"Over there," I say.

I can see her dress flashing through the crowd.

"Okay," Clyde says, grabbing my hand. "I'm going with you."

We run. The air is thick with shouting and body heat. A canister of tear gas rolls by our feet. My lungs burn. I start to choke. Clyde kicks the canister away, but it's too late. The air is fouled. My hands and face are burning.

He pulls at my backpack.

"Your apron," he yells. "Did you put your apron in your backpack?"

I hear an explosion of broken glass. Screaming. I look over and see the window of the bar at the Conrad Hilton has been broken, maybe been pushed in. Bodies are tumbling through the broken glass. Nightsticks catch heads, shoulders, and knees. People stumble. Some fall.

Clyde unzips my backpack, pulls out my apron and forces it into my hands.

"Cover your face," he commands.

He pulls off his shirt and covers his mouth.

"Over there!" I yell.

There's a woman crouching on the sidewalk. Her arms are wrapped around her knees. There's blood in her hair. Her face is hidden in her skirt.

My grandmother's dress surrounds the woman in a swirl of white and light. The wind whips through my hair. My grandmother whispers to me: *This one. There were so many like this one. Like me. Help her!*

"She's hurt," I call to Clyde. "We have to get her out of here!"

TWENTY-SIX

Her name is Cassie. She doesn't give us a last name. She's tired, needs to sleep, and probably is not sure yet if she can or should trust us. She thanks us for helping her. She says she hitchhiked from Urbana where she goes to school. Her parents don't know she's in Chicago.

It is two o'clock in the morning. I manage to get the blood washed out of her hair. She tells us a blow from a policeman's nightstick caused the gash in her head. It is nearly two inches long. It looks like it needs stitches. She doesn't want to go to an emergency room. She says they were told that if they went to a hospital they would be arrested for disorderly conduct, for inciting a riot, for trespassing, for harassing police.

She showers and gives me her soiled clothes to wash. We are about the same size, so I give her an old sweatshirt and some fresh underwear. I don't own pajamas. I did my best to clean and close the wound on her head using all the band-aids I had. Clyde brews a pot of tea and scrambles an egg. Cassie eats it all in a matter of minutes and asks for more. Clyde scrambles another egg. I put fresh sheets on my bed and tell her to get some sleep. I put her clothes in the washing machine along with the bloody towels and start the machine.

"Shouldn't she call someone?" Clyde asks when Cassie is at last asleep on my bed.

"In the morning," I say, knowing how my own mother would freak if she got a call in the middle of the night informing her that I had been hurt in a riot.

"You saw something," Clyde says. "What was it?"

The quiet of two o'clock in the morning hugs me like a worn quilt. Clyde is sitting on my one and only kitchen stool. I'm curled up in an old upholstered rocking chair I dragged out of the alleyway when I first found this apartment. It's my one and only piece of comfortable furniture. I don't have a table. I eat my meals sitting on the stool pulled up to my kitchen counter. My place is small: a bedroom, bathroom, and a tiny living area with kitchen and one window. Not much, but it also has a small washer and dryer stacked in the corner of the kitchen, which means I don't have to suffer Laundromats. The apartment is cozy in a post-college, no ambition-no money kind of way. My mother would want me to paint the walls white. Buy a nice rug. Hang some art.

"Cup of tea?"

"I'll get it," Clyde says, jumping up from the stool. "Do you have honey?"

Without waiting for my answer, he starts rummaging through my cupboard.

"In the fridge," I say.

"Why?"

"That's where my mother always kept it. She says it keeps the ants out."

The kettle whistles. It was a graduation present from my father. It has two tones. Like a train whistle. It's probably the most expensive thing I own.

Clyde fixes me a cup of tea. He's found a box of vanilla wafers in the back of the cabinet. He puts three cookies and the teacup on plate and hands it to me.

"Why three?" I ask.

"It's late. Two didn't seem like enough. What were you chasing?"

I hear Cassie stir. I get up and check on her. She's rolled to her side, pulled the sheet up over her face. Her legs are tucked up under her in a protective fetal kind of way. She looks small and frightened. The blanket has fallen off the bed to the floor. I pick it up, cover her, and back out of the room, closing the door as softly as I can. I want her to sleep. She told us she's been sleeping outside wherever she could find a place: on a park bench, a church step, or curled up under a tree. Her clothes were filthy.

"You were just about to tell me what you were chasing," Clyde says. "And, why you wanted to help Cassie. Do you know her?"

"My grandmother was there, all around Cassie, she was trying to tell me something I need to know or maybe asking me to help. I'm not sure which," I say. I let the words sink in. Take a sip of my tea. Pop one of the vanilla wafers in my mouth, whole.

Once I start talking, I can't stop. I tell him about my dreams. I tell him about seeing a woman in a white dress standing by a window watching people in Grant Park.

I tell him about seeing the same white dress on the day my father died. That I have also seen it the same bit of dress floating down the street and when I've tried to follow it, it disappears before I can catch it.

I start talking about the cemetery in Macon. About Mother's tombstone being the only marker. I tell him what the gravedigger said about the babies and the women buried all around her. About how quietly the rain fell that night while I was sitting under that tree waiting for something to happen.

I tell him I didn't go to graduate school, but instead came to Chicago because this ghost, my grandmother, told me I had to come to help her do, I don't know what yet. That asking me to help Cassie is the closest she has come to telling me anything about what I need to do. I tell him that sometimes I don't know whose life I'm living, mine or hers, and that I don't know who I am anymore. I tell him that I miss my father more than I thought it was possible to miss anyone.

Clyde listens. He doesn't judge. He doesn't ask any questions. He doesn't say anything. He just listens.

"I saw her again tonight," I say. "Her white dress. It flew into the crowds. I ran after her. I thought I had lost her and then another flare went up. The canister of tear gas rolled by our feet. When I looked up, my grandmother's ghost was swirling around Cassie. I don't know why, but I could hear her talking to me. Like she was standing beside me, whispering in my ear, but I knew she wasn't, that she was in my head. Like she was part of me, like how when my father and I would sit together watching movies or having dinner, that we didn't need to talk because we understood that somehow we were part of each other, that it was just enough to be close to one another. That's what it felt like. I could feel her asking me to do something."

Clyde leans forward.

"What did she say?" he asks.

"This one," I say. "She said, 'This one. There were so many like this one.' I don't know what that means, just that I need to help Cassie. I think it's a piece of the puzzle of why I came to Chicago."

TWENTY-SEVEN

The sound of helicopters crisscrossing the lakeshore wakes me, tying and twisting one knot after another in my stomach. They are riding low and slow, stirring up dust and menacing the morning. It's exactly what Mayor Daley ordered: tension, chaos, and a hint of impending danger.

I wrestle myself out of sleep and try to stretch my cramped legs. What little sleep I got last night was grabbed uncomfortably in the chair. I do not know what time it is, what time we quit talking, when I fell asleep, or when Clyde covered me with the beach towel he found in the bathroom closet, and left. I only have one blanket and I gave that to Cassie. She needed it more than I did.

I get up. Pull the cord on the venetian blinds and watch a disturbance of dust drift through the morning sun firefly-like in my living room. I look at my clock radio. It's 11am. I should be serving pizzas.

I hear the Howard L rumble by. I go into the kitchen to get a glass of water and find a note from Clyde: *Got you covered for lunch. Let me know if you can make it for dinner.*

I hear the toilet flush. Cassie opens the bathroom door. She has showered and her hair is wrapped in a towel.

"The shower last night felt divine and I just had to have another. Haven't had a good wash since I got here. Hope you don't mind. The bandage you put on my head came off when I washed my hair. Can you take a look?"

She leans forward. I untangle her long wet hair away from the wound on the back of her head. The area around the gash is swollen, dark purple and raw looking. I'm not a doctor, but I'm pretty sure it hurts like hell. I'm afraid to touch it.

"You sure you don't want to go to the emergency room? See a doctor? It's deeper than I thought. I'm worried it might get infected. I think you need some stitches. Does your head still hurt?"

"My mother always said you should keep a wound clean and moist. I never knew what moist meant or what it was supposed to do but she had this way of saying things with a lot of authority so I believed her."

"I might have something that will work."

I go into the bathroom and find a tube of Neosporin, some cotton balls, and the bottle of hydrogen peroxide I used last night to clean the wound.

When I come out, Cassie has combed through her wet hair with her fingers and has carefully parted what she could of her hair away from the wound.

"What does it look like this morning?" she asks.

"It's bruised pretty badly. The cut seems to be closing up some, but not completely. I'm going to dab it with some hydrogen peroxide like I did last night. Clean it out some more."

I work slowly, trying my best not to push too hard against the damaged flesh. I don't want to reopen the wound.

"Feels funny," she says. "Cold, wet, and a little numb. Numb is good, yes?"

"It's probably numb because it's swollen a little and the peroxide always feels cold. The bleeding has pretty much stopped. Are you sure you don't want to see a doctor?"

"I can't go to the hospital. They'll arrest me for rioting, or worse, call my parents."

I squeeze a line of Neosporin along the jagged two-inch open cut on her scalp.

"There's going to be a scar," I say.

"A souvenir," Cassie says. "Proof that I've been here. Done battle with the pigs. Do you have my clothes?"

"Washed and dried," I said. "One of the only perks of this tiny abode is a small washing machine and an equally small dryer. They're not the best machines, but they get stuff clean enough."

I gather up the various medicines and bandages I've been using to fix the wound then pull her clothes out of the dryer.

"I don't have an iron, but I do have a toaster. Want some peanut butter toast and tea? It's about all I've got in the place. I usually eat at the restaurant."

"You're a waitress?" she asks.

"At Guido's in the Loop. Pizza, beer, and salads. It's decent enough food and we get mostly businessmen and convention people on expense accounts. The tips are good. Pays the rent and gives me something to do while I'm trying to figure out what I want to be when I grow up."

"The guy who helped me last night, he works there too?"

"Clyde? Yeah, he's the bartender and manager."

She drops the towel she wrapped up in after her shower and takes the clothes I've pulled from the dryer. She is naked. I turn my head.

She fumbles with her underwear. Laughs.

"Sorry. I have two sisters. The three of us have shared a room since we were born. We've been borrowing each other's clothes and changing in front of each other for as long as I can remember. I guess you could say I have no shame."

"I'm an only child. My college roommate had a boyfriend she lived with, and it was my job to lie to her parents about where she was every time they called looking for her. I don't think she spent more than ten nights in the dorm with me in the whole four years of school we lived together. I guess you could say I'm used to being alone."

"I'm sorry," Cassie says.

"For getting dressed?"

"For sleeping in your bed. For crashing the party last night."

"What party?"

"Your boyfriend, Clyde," she says.

"He's not my boyfriend. We work together. That's all."

I shower, dress, then make some toast and tea for Cassie and myself and apologize that I don't have more to offer. She inhales the toast and asks if she can have more. I make more and have another slice myself.

"Where are you going to go?" I ask her.

"Back to Grant Park. Wait for the voting to take place. The SDS guys are planning some kind of demonstration, one way or the other. Win or lose. Except I'm not sure anymore what winning would be given that the war will probably go on no matter who is in charge in Washington. War is a funny business," Cassie says, nibbling on a dark half moon of crust from her third piece of toast. "You can usually figure out when a war starts, but it's another to know when it has stopped. Doesn't seem clear to me that anyone knows for sure why we are fighting a war in Vietnam. I mean, had you ever even heard of Vietnam before this war?"

There are many kinds of wars.

"Do you know anyone in Vietnam?" I ask.

Cassie licks toast crumbs from her fingers and takes a sip of her tea, blowing across the top as though she is stalling for time trying to figure out what she thinks is safe to tell me. I told her last night I was not sure I could travel somewhere without telling my parents where I was going or what I was going to be doing.

"I kind of know this one guy. We dated a little in high school. I ran into his sister when I was home last Christmas. She told me told me that he volunteered. Can you imagine?"

I shake my head. "Maybe he figured it was better to volunteer than get drafted."

"Whatever. She said he couldn't tell them where he is or what he's doing. Just that he's somewhere. Fighting. Or, I guess, waiting to fight. Do you think they're fighting everyday? All the time? I mean, everybody, even the bad guys, have got to sleep and eat, right? So, this guy I know is someplace he has never even heard about and can't tell his sister what he's doing. It's really messed up. He wrote her once that it's hard to tell sometimes who is fighting whom and why. Even some of the women are carrying guns and fighting. He says he really doesn't know anything and mostly just does what people tell him to do. I guess that means someone knows what the enemy looks like. Someone in the park the other night said that sometimes the Americans are the only ones wearing military uniforms, so they're the only ones that the other side knows for sure are the enemy. The uniforms make it easier to shoot at them. I don't know if that's true, but it sounded right when he said it.

"From what I've seen in the movies about World War II, after Pearl Harbor, we were in the war fighting against the Japanese. And, of course, we were also fighting the Nazis. It seemed simple enough. But I don't know. Who are we angry at in Vietnam? What have they done to us? Why are we there? What do we want? What kind of war is this?"

"There are many kinds of wars, I guess, and this one seems complicated."

When Cassie leaves for Grant Park, I make another cup of tea and sit in my one chair in the living room watching the cars and people go down the street. It feels like an ordinary day.

I call Clyde and tell him thanks for the pass on lunch and that I'll be there an hour before the dinner shift to help clean up and get ready. He asks about Cassie. I tell him she left for Grant Park and that I told her that she could come back to my place again in the evening, after my shift, or come by the restaurant around closing time.

He asks if I want to go to Grant Park again after work. That if I did, he'd come with me. I ask him what he thinks about the war in Vietnam. He gets quiet. He says he thinks it's bad. That it has no good ending to it. If he had to, he'd go to Canada rather than fight in Vietnam.

Clyde tells me his father was a pilot in WWII, and his mother told him that his father was never the same when he came home. That he couldn't sleep.

That's all Clyde said he remembers about his father: that he couldn't sleep. He paced the house. He couldn't sit still long enough to eat. He sometimes hid in the garage. Under the bed. Behind the curtains in the living room. He was afraid to leave the house and afraid that the planes that flew over their house were going to drop bombs on them. He couldn't hold a job.

Clyde's mother worked every shift she could as a nurse's aide in order to pay the bills. Day or night, it didn't matter. She once told Clyde that working for her was more than just the money: she had to get out of the house because she couldn't help his father.

Their home was strangely silent and uncomfortable. All those fun father memories that most people talk about, Clyde says, are just blank film to him.

That he has no memories of ever tossing ball in the backyard with his father, watching television with him, talking or reading books together. He doesn't even know who taught him to ride a bike, just that someone did and he knows how.

The one memory Clyde has of his father is when he walked home from school by himself on the first day of fourth grade and found his father, dead, sitting in his car in the garage, the motor running, and the doors closed.

TWENTY-EIGHT

"I've been here before," I say, grabbing Clyde's arm in order not to fall.

There is no flicker of my grandmother's white dress this time. No whoshing of wind. No whisper. Just a strong feeling that I had been down this street before, not last week, but in another life. I'm dizzy from the feeling. Need to hold on. Keep grounded, as though not holding on to something or someone might send me flying through time and space.

I could lose myself.

It's midnight and Clyde and I are walking down Michigan Avenue towards Grant Park again. The Art Institute is on our left. The broad stone staircase entrance is littered with protestors and police. Clyde heard on the radio this afternoon that there were 10,000 protestors and possibly as many as 23,000 police and National Guard. There is not room for everyone. There's a faint whiff of tear gas in the air. There doesn't seem to be enough oxygen to go around. I'm afraid to take a deep breath.

"We walked down this street last night," Clyde says.

"No, before," I say, glancing up the brick front of the Studebaker Building to a window five stories up. I half expect to see a woman in a white dress, the back of her head pressed against the window. A sharp pain shoots down from the crown of my head to my toes. There's a strange sensation of warmth spreading across the back of my head. Someone's hand? My blood? I struggle to breathe. My throat is choked with fear. It's impossible for me to scream or call out for help. The smell of fetid breath laced with sweat, garlic, sausages and stale beer makes my stomach lurch. I cannot stop myself. I vomit. I empty my stomach while Clyde holds my shoulders. My head starts to hurt as if someone big and half drunk is pushing against my body, breathing in my face, tearing at my clothes and slamming my head against a wall. I double over again even though my stomach is empty. A searing pain shoots up from my pelvis tearing me in half. My heart skips a beat, it lodges in my throat. The air is too warm. Swirling. I kick out, trying to free myself. I'm wrestling with a ghost.

Clyde grabs my shoulders and eases me down to the safety of the sidewalk. He surrounds my body with his then spreads his arms wide, creating a barrier between my crumpled body and the people rushing by.

I hear screams. Breaking glass.

Clyde starts yelling.

"Help, medic, anyone!"

I feel the crowd pushing forward. Clyde's body can't stop them. A tear gas canister rattles along the edge of the sidewalk.

Clyde picks me up, and starts running.

"What happened?" Clyde asks.

I am on my rumpled bed, in my apartment. Clyde has unlaced my shoes, taken them off and is rubbing my feet. My left hand is throbbing. A deep purple bloom of bruise is spreading from the tips of my little and ring fingers to my wrist. The same two fingers that have always been a little twisted ever since I was born. My fingers feel stiff and painfully broken. I rest my elbow on a pillow, elevating my hand in order to keep it from swelling. I vaguely remember my mother telling me to do the same when I fell once and sprained my wrist.

"I must have hurt my hand when I fell," I say.

"You didn't fall. I put my arms around you trying to calm you and carried you to the ground. You were fighting something, someone. You pushed me away, but I held on. You were crying and seemed to be in pain. I didn't know what to do. I tried to be gentle. Be careful not to hurt you. I didn't know what was happening. I'm sorry if I bruised your hand. Let me get some ice."

I grab his arm with my good right hand. I don't want him to leave me, even for a minute.

"You didn't do it," I say.

My mind is racing. I close my eyes. See that fifth story window again. Feel myself being pinned to the wall. Smell the struggle, sweat, sour breath, and blood.

"He raped me," I say.

Clyde pulls away for a moment then crumples to the floor.

"Who?" he asks, his voice a softened whisper.

"I don't know. It was me, but wasn't me. I think he broke my fingers. I can't move them. God, they hurt."

"When?" he asks.

"A long time ago. My father's mother, my grandmother, me. She's part of me. I can't explain it. It's the reason I came to Chicago."

Cassie is ringing the buzzer. Clyde gets up to answer it. He lets her in. Makes a pallet on the floor in the living room with the blanket from my bed. He finds a clean pillowcase in the closet, stuffs a towel into it to make a pillow and gives her the beach towel to use as a blanket. He tells her there's bread and peanut butter in the fridge. Says he'll get some bagels and cream cheese in the morning. He comes back into my room and closes the bedroom door.

I've already told him most of what I know to be true. The dreams that brought me to Chicago. The questions I never asked my father. My father's death. The unmarked graves. My father wanting to be buried near the woman he called Mother. Wanting to rest next to all the others.

When I hear the slow even breathing of Cassie sleeping, I roll to my side and tell Clyde about that night, when I sat with my back against the one tree in the middle of those silent graves waiting for something to happen. How Mother, the woman who raised my father appeared first, then afterwards when I saw the swirling specter of my father's birth mother. Heard their voices twine together. Felt them drawing me into some kind of circle.

"Ghosts," Clyde says, nodding his head.

"Have you seen a ghost?" I ask.

"I felt my father move across my room the night I found him. Thought I saw him once a couple of years later when I was walking down the street. Just a shadow across my vision, a cool breeze on a still hot August day. It was nothing I could tell anyone or explain."

"Sometimes I see the white hem of my grandmother's dress. She's here in Chicago. She wants me to know…"

"About her rape?" he asks.

We talk until we can't talk anymore. Clyde falls asleep on the floor. I pull the blanket off my bed and cover him. The sheet is enough for me. I open my bedroom window. The air is soft, warm and still. I think about what Clyde said to me the day my father died: that I came to Chicago to work at Guido's in order to meet him.

Maybe.

I hear Cassie and Clyde talking in the living room. I drift back to sleep and am awakened when I hear the front door open then close.

"Hello," I call out.

"Fresh bagels," Clyde says. "Want tea?"

I pull my left hand out from under the sheet. My fingers feel stiff, but nothing hurts. Was I dreaming?

"My twisted fingers. The bruise. It's all gone."

Clyde is standing in the doorway of my bedroom. "Let me see," he says.

I hold up both of my hands. Press my palms together. Move them apart. Wiggle my fingers.

He doesn't seem surprised.

"You saw the bruises. Didn't you? Saw that I couldn't bend my fingers last night. That they were bruised and twisted."

"Do you feel like working?"

"Is that what you were worried about last night when you carried me home? That I wasn't going to be able to work if my fingers were broken? Really?"

"How about you get off your angry high horse for just one minute. If you didn't feel like going to work today, I was calling in sick as well. After what we talked about last night, I'm worried. Really worried. Not about you. There's nothing wrong with you. But, there are some pretty scary things happening to you. That white dress you talked about. It came into the room last night after you had fallen asleep. It woke me. It swirled around the bed. Hovered over you, your broken fingers. The room got warm. Still. Intense. It doesn't surprise me one bit that your fingers are healed this morning. Powerful is how I would describe it. I've got a feeling that whatever that white dress thing is, has been a part of your life for a long time and it's not going away anytime soon.

"I think the broken fingers, the rape, everything about last night happened just to get your attention."

I don't tell Clyde that I also felt her in the room last night. Or, about her whispering in my ear:

Your father, your father, your father…was born from this.

TWENTY-NINE

"She was raped here, I mean, there."

We are sitting on the top step of the Chicago Art Institute. I am shouting. Pointing down the block to the fifth floor window of the Studebaker Building. Clyde has his arm around my shoulders, making sure I won't get pushed off of the stairs.

It is nearly midnight. Traffic is blocked on Michigan Avenue. There are still thousands of people in the streets. Shouting. Pushing. The air is thick with the smell of crowded anxious bodies, mace and tear gas. Homemade signs calling for PEACE, NO MORE WAR, and McCARTHY FOR PRESIDENT wave like begging, praying hands, casting a benediction over the restless crowd. The police are pushing against the crowd trying to get people to go home, to get out of their way.

The police and National Guard are tired of the singing, the dancing, and the constant, irritating demonstrations. The crowd is angry. No one looks like they've slept or showered since the convention began. Periodically, someone somewhere throws something: a bottle, a rock, or an empty teargas canister. The raspy blare of a bullhorn cuts a jagged rift through the crowd. Police take one more step forward. Protestors push and then rock one step back. It's a dangerous dance.

I'm exhausted and am pretty sure Clyde is as well. Both lunch and dinner at the restaurant were rushed and hushed, as though no one felt comfortable sitting still in one place any too long. Antsy. I could barely get the food on the table before people were waving me down demanding the check. Drinks flowed. Fast. The front door opening and closing so often, the room was thick and muggy with August heat. The kitchen was a furnace. Tempers were short. One cook walked out in the middle of the lunch shift, throwing his apron across the room. Knives chattered on cutting boards. The backroom ice machine sputtered and spewed then quit working. I filled plastic pitchers with ice from the bar and gave them out to the staff in the hopes of cooling things down. We couldn't afford to have any more walkouts. We were already short staffed and slammed.

The muffled drone of Clyde's radio under the counter near the cash register was a constant reminder of the world outside. Things were changing. Uncomfortable. Out of control. The Kennedy brothers both dead. Martin Luther King, dead. Hope dead. The war in Vietnam grinding on indefinitely.

Whenever there was a drink order, the waitress who brought it stood for as long as she could leaning against the bar, listening to Clyde's radio, bringing back news of the convention to the rest of us as she passed through to her station.

The vote came. Clyde adjusted the volume. Turned the radio up just loud enough to be heard over the din of dishes scraping on trays and thudding as they hit wooden tabletops. There was a sudden swish of the kitchen doors swinging open, cooks standing in the doorway anxiously waiting to hear what was happening. People holding their breath. Not eating and drinking. Silverware resting uncomfortably in closed hands.

Humphrey. Hubert Humphrey. Johnson's VP. It was going to be Humphrey battling Nixon. Hardly a fair fight for the soul of the country.

"Je-sus," someone hissed: steam escaping.

"Hey, can I get a beer?"

A stack of dirty dishes clattered to the floor. The front door opened wide. A half dozen people paid their bills and rushed out. In response, a blast of summer air and sunburned customers rushed in, demanding tables and something cold to drink to chase the news of the day. I grabbed a menu to fan myself. I could barely breathe. Clyde flipped off the radio and started pouring beers.

"There," I say, again. "In that office, that room."

"You okay?" Clyde asks.

"She was raped there. Maybe she worked there. The man was probably her boss. It was late. He smelled of stale beer, sausages, and garlic. He was big. She was frightened by the assault. Terrified she was going to lose her job. He tore her clothes. Hurt her. She tried to fight him. He broke her fingers. No one witnessed what happened.

"She wanted me to know. For someone to know. To bear witness, I guess. But, it feels like there's more."

"What about your father?"

"She died giving birth. That's all he knew about her. Never knew her name. Where she came from. Or who his father was. I don't think she came to him, made herself visible or whispered to him when he dreamed. It would have been too much of a burden for a little boy."

"What about for you?"

"That night in the cemetery, she told me she had waited for me. She said that we are connected by our dreams. I don't understand it. She's a grandmother I never knew, a mother my father never knew. I don't know what she has to do with our lives. I don't know where she came from, or if she had a family or not. I only know she was raped here, in that building over there and that my father was born of that rape.

"But it feels like there is something else. Here. On this side of the street, in this building. She wants me to know something that happened here as well. It's not the same feeling I get when I look at the Studebaker Building. I feel different here. At peace, yet full of life in a way I've never been full of life before."

"My mother used to bring me to the Art Institute on Sunday afternoons," Clyde says. "We'd ride the bus, spend the day. I still love the Impressionists. All those beautiful colors and soft lines where the world doesn't look as much as it feels."

"I walk the galleries with my eyes closed," I say. "Listening. Feeling. I couldn't tell you anything about the artwork. It's as though there's nothing on the walls. Just rooms. People. I feel people. Lots of people. There's an amazing energy. I love it here."

"The white dress?" he asks.

"I felt, then saw a shimmer of light once, in a corner. It was still. Not moving. I walked towards the light, reaching out my hand to touch whatever might be there. Then a school group came into the gallery and the shimmer vanished."

"When was your father born?"

"He was older than my mother. Older than almost all of my friends' fathers. He was born in 1894, in Georgia. Macon. Why?"

"The World's Columbian Exhibition happened in 1893. The Art Institute was brand new then but there was no art in it. It was used as a meeting place for the International Congress. My grandmother was a Suffragette. She was really proud of that. Whenever I went to visit her at her apartment, we'd sit on the couch together and she'd get out this album she had filled with clippings, pictures, and programs. She was one of the leaders of the Chicago Suffragettes. She had these ribbons, sashes she wore. Even had a small twisted gold ring with purple and green stones and tiny pearls. She wore it all the time. She called it her Suffragette ring. The colors of the Suffragettes were purple, pale green and white. She was very proud that she marched for women's right to vote.

"She had this one program tucked into the pages of her scrapbook. It was stained and tattered as though she had taken it out and touched it a thousand times, remembering what happened that day. The program was for the World's Congress of Representative Women. Susan B. Anthony was there. Here. In this building, before it became a museum. My grandmother met Susan Anthony that day. Talked to her. It was like one of those moments that defined who she was and how she lived the rest of her life."

"Our grandmothers could have met, could have been together in the room that day." The possibility stuns me, makes my grandmother come alive for a moment.

"My grandmother also had a white dress," Clyde says.

"A wedding dress?" I ask, closing my eyes while trying to piece together the bits of the many images in my mind of my grandmother's dress. "I don't think my grandmother's dress was a wedding dress, but a simple soft white long-sleeved linen dress tied in back with a broad sash. A summer sort of dress made with the kind of material you'd find in a man's handkerchief."

"That's what my grandmother's white dress looked like," Clyde says, his voice soft with memory. "She called it her Suffragette dress. Said she wore it that day she met Miss Anthony. Said she wanted to be buried in it."

Around midnight, the protestors form a snaking chain dance that twists itself together and wiggles out of the crowd of cops in a kind of joyful protest. They haven't won anything, but they haven't lost everything. The television cameras are rolling the whole time, showing the world what is happening.

We wait for the protest procession to pass and the camera crews to pack up before we leave the steps. As the park and the street clear, the police spread out, filling the space as though they half expect the protestors to come back and storm the place.

"Someone needs to tell the cops to go home," Clyde says.

THIRTY

I dream about Clyde's grandmother's white dress, her wedding white Suffragette dress that she was buried in. In the restless early morning of my sleeping and waking, the torn hem of my grandmother's white dress fills the space between night and day. I see her. Feel her. I am swimming in a dream-memory of a grandmother I have never met. She is part of me. I am part of her. The other grandmother, the woman called Mother who raised my father, the only mother he ever knew, floats above it all, like a warning.

Find her, find her, find her, she sings.

I feel the warm exhaustion of restless sleep begging me to wake. The sun begins to sift through the slates of my window blinds, I hear someone knocking at my door. I stagger across the bare floor of my bedroom and pull on the dirty clothes I wore to work last night. They smell of pizza, spilled beer, sweat and tear gas.

"Did I wake you?" Cassie asks.

"It was time for me to get up," I say. "Come on in."

"I was wondering if I could get a shower. Have a cup of tea. I was up all night. There were bonfires in Lincoln Park. Drinking, and well, you know. I smell like wood smoke and sex. I need to wash. Get clean. Move on with my life. I should never have come. They're all misogynist assholes. All they cared about was being able to say they'd been here and made history. That's what one of them told me. That they had made history. They, the men. Not the women. They didn't care about the women. We had things we wanted too. Equal rights, equal pay, equal chances. But they used us. Stepped in front of us. Pushed us aside unless they wanted us for sex. Free love, they called it, as if love is ever free. It isn't, you know. It's never free. Someone always pays.

"The bonfires, the demonstrations, the shouting, the pushing, the cops, the tear gas, the news cameras. The news cameras! Like it was some holier than thou news conference about a stupid war that none of them will ever fight in because they've got money and have a way to get out of going. It's like a game to them: some big horrible war game. They're all playing it: the cops, the politicians, and the hippies. It's all about power, not about peace."

"You okay?" I ask, putting my arms around her shoulders, drawing her into my apartment.

Cassie lets her head sink into my shoulder, her arms circle my back. I smell the campfire in her hair. She starts to cry.

"Did someone hurt you?" I ask.

"Stupid. How could I be so stupid?"

"Did he rape you?"

"What's rape? I was drunk, high, whatever. Like everyone else, we were dancing around the campfire like we had won some great victory. There were helicopters flying above. Circling like great hungry birds of prey. It was like the more outrageous we could be, the louder we could sing, the harder we could dance, that we were putting it to the man. Stupid. Just stupid.

"It was kind of like some big orgy. The helicopters flying above us: shining their searchlights on us. People took their clothes off. It felt kind of crazy wild. Mooning the cops. Then this guy, he'd been looking at me and I had been looking at him. He offered me a joint. Said he liked my hair. Liked the way I danced.

"So many people were smoking dope you could get high from just breathing. He kissed me. I guess I kissed him back and then it just happened. When I woke up, he was gone."

I make tea while Cassie takes a shower. I throw her clothes into the washing machine. I find a bra and a pair of clean underwear to give her. Hers are ripped. Mud stained and bloody. I throw them out.

The fingers, the ones on my left hand that I thought had been broken then mysteriously healed, begin to ache again.

"New day," Clyde says, taking his time to pull a beer. "Any wild dreams last night?"

"You once said that you thought I must have come to Chicago to meet you."

He laughs, puts the beer onto my drink tray and pulls back a step.

"So, did you?" he asks.

"That thing about your grandmother meeting Susan B. Anthony and wanting to be buried in her white dress. Was that for real?"

"Yes," he says, picking up a rag and polishing the bar as though we're not talking. Another waitress comes up behind me and gives a gentle nudge with her hip, pushing me out of the way.

"Two Budweisers," she says, giving me a wink. "Clyde, if you've got time, that is, once you're finished flirting with Miss Regina here."

I pick up my drink tray and walk away.

I finish my lunch shift and leave.

I start to walk my usual route down Michigan Avenue to the last bus stop before Lake Shore Drive by The Drake Hotel. It's the first day in almost a week when I've been outside in full daylight. The sun feels good on my face, my shoulders. I try to relax, to let go of the ache in my hand. I reach the corner of Michigan and Oak and a gust of wind from Lake Michigan swirls around my legs. I stop walking, as though the wind is a rope and I am caught.

I look up and see a bit of white, a flash of hem, hear a buzzing sound in my head, a whisper.

There are so many like me, like her. So many. So very many.

I cross the street. Take the next bus going south instead of North to my apartment. I sit by myself, my face pressed against the window watching as we near the Art Institute then the Studebaker Building. The street cleaners are busy sweeping. There's a rattle of empty tear gas canisters, trash, beer bottles, an occasional item of clothing. I'm looking for a white dress.

Someone pulls the cord to signal they want the next stop. The bus pulls to the curb, opens the door. Several people get off, tourists mainly, clutching maps, trying to decide where to cross Michigan Avenue in order to get to the Art Institute. Or, where they should stop for a drink, a sandwich, a bit of shade. When the bus pulls back into the traffic, I close my eyes and hear the faint dreamy clang of a bell and the high squeal of metal against metal as though I've been thrown back in time and the bus has become a long forgotten trolley. When I open my eyes, I half expect to see men in hats and spats and women wearing white summer dresses and carrying parasols.

I stay on the bus when it turns west. When it nears Halsted, I get off and start walking. All up and down Halsted, houses are being torn down, while at the same time, huge buildings are going up. I see a sign about a new university. I wonder what was here before, and why I am drawn to this place.

I reach a corner and the wind whips by creating a small swirling of white dust. I stop walking and watch, wondering if I will see a hem of a white skirt beckoning me on. I continue walking.

Nestled in the midst of fresh grey cement buildings, tall birdlike cranes and hunch-shouldered bulldozers, I discover a building with an elegant red façade, clearly from another time. The brass sign outside announces it is Hull House, founded in 1889. The time is right. I push open the front door and walk in.

It's a museum of sorts. I ask the woman at the desk what happened here before it was a museum, and she tells me it was a settlement house for recently arrived European immigrants.

"Did they live here?"

"Mostly they took classes. English classes. Sewing. Cooking. Childcare. Things young women would need to know. And, sometimes women who had no one or no place else to go lived here, upstairs," she says, pointing to the wide stairs and polished banister going upstairs.

"What kind of women lived here?" I ask.

"Mostly single women who worked here," she said. "Some women who were in trouble, you know, and their families didn't want them."

"Can I walk around? I'd like to go upstairs to see some of the rooms. I think I might know someone who lived here a long time ago and I'd just like to look around."

She glances at her watch.

"We close in an hour. I guess it's okay for you to go upstairs. We usually only allow visitors upstairs when there's a tour. We ask you not to touch anything. Oh, and if you see the ghost, please let us know. She comes and goes but lately she's been around more than not."

"A ghost?"

"Legend has it she was one of the residents. Lived here for a bit, then disappeared without a word or a notion as to where she was going. She rattles around in the kitchen sometime. She is said to have been the best pie maker in Chicago. There used to be a kind of café in the building. A place where women could bring their children and have some apple pie and a cup of tea, and men could visit after work for a slice of meat pie. Lots of people came for her pies. Even Jane Addams, our founder, loved her pies."

"When did she disappear?"

"I don't know the exact date. We think it was sometime in the 1890s, or at least that's what we tell visitors. We know she was a Suffragette. Jane Addams was also a Suffragette. Susan B. Anthony was her friend. You know, she came here to speak once."

"For the World's Congress at the Art Institute," I say.

"That's right. Most people don't know that bit about the Chicago World's Fair, that there were these intellectual congresses taking place among all the hoopla at the Fair."

"Did all the Suffragettes wear white dresses?"

"Most but not all. Miss Anthony wore black. All black. We've got a picture of her with Miss Addams. It's down the hallway, there, right before you go up the stairs. You should have a look. The two of them together must have been a force of nature."

"Did the ghost have a name?"

"I'm sure she did, but we don't know it. Just know that she lived here, became a Suffragette along with Miss Addams, and made wonderful pies, or at least that's the story we tell."

"Any chance she could have been pregnant when she was here?"

"She could have been. Quite a few women who lived here had no place else to go because they were unmarried and pregnant. Or, they had run away from a drunken or abusive husband and needed a safe place to start a new life. There weren't many places or choices for women back then."

I take my time and wander through the big sitting rooms downstairs, then walk through the dining hall and the kitchen. I am tempted to run my hand along the smooth worn surface of the large butcher block island and pick up one of the heavy rolling pins, just to feel what she must have felt, but I step back and look instead. There's a stack of tin pie plates on a high shelf. If I could reach one of them, hold one in my hand, I wonder if she would appear.

I walk up the stairs. The banister is silken to the touch. Polished by hundreds of human hands sliding along up and down the stairs. The house, with its outsized parlors and polished wood, feels more like a cathedral than a home for desperate women. It feels like a place of care and rest. I hope it was so.

There are small bedrooms on either side of the hallway. Some doors are open. Others are closed. The ones that are open are cordoned off, so you can't enter but can only lean in the doorway to see a narrow single bed pushed against a wall along with a small desk and chair, a washstand and a mirror. Several hooks hang on either side of the mirror for clothes and/or towels. It has the feeling of a dormitory, or perhaps a convent. It is scrubbed smooth and plain. Spare. Austere. A place to hide. Not the kind of place where people might shout or sing or even talk to one another.

I walk down the hall, stopping at each door. I close my eyes. I wait. I listen. I keep walking. I go to the end, turn, and start to walk back down the hallway to the staircase.

She walks with me. I hear her whisper.

Here. Here. Here. I made pies. I waited for you. To see. To understand. I couldn't. I couldn't. The midwife told me they were going to take my baby away. Away. Away. Away. Give him to someone with a husband and the means to take care of my child. I want you to understand. I had to run away.

I walk back down Halsted and take the bus downtown to the Art Institute. I sit on the steps. Watch the sun go down against the glass and steel edges of the skyscraper giants. The Studebaker, one of the first of the tall ones, now dwarfed and easily missed in the shadows.

Streetlights go on. The evening air begins to cool. People slow down. Stroll. The city breathes in the night air. I decide to walk home. I take my time, stopping at each corner. Looking both ways to see if my grandmother might be there. Might reappear.

The pieces of my grandmother's life are coming together. Her boss raped her. Broke her fingers. Later, she discovered she was pregnant. Then she went to Hull House to hide, bake pies, be part of the Suffragette movement, meet Jane Addams, Susan B. Anthony. Then she disappeared. Ran away. Where did she come from? Who was her family? Did anyone know where she went? Why did she go to Macon? What happened to her there? Why does she want me to know?

Questions tumble through my mind. When I press my key into the lock to open my apartment, the evening light slants through the venetian blinds and dances on the wooden floor. The place is empty. Cassie is gone. I say a prayer that she might be okay. The air is still. I wash my face. Even though it is too early to go to sleep, I take off my clothes and crawl into bed.

I toss and turn. My legs twitch tired from walking. I fall fitfully into a dream of the room at the end of the hallway in Hull House. I see the single bed. It feels like a safe haven. I go downstairs, my hand skimming along the smooth banister. I step back into the kitchen and am left alone to bake pies. I can taste them in my sleep: plump apple pies, tart lemon meringue, cherry pies sweet with ripened sunshine, bubbling chicken pot pies, shepherd's pie stuffed with beef and gravy all dressed up with golden mounds of yesterday's mashed potatoes.

I pull myself up from sleep. My door is rattling. I hear a knocking.

"Regina," Clyde calls out. "Open up. Please, open up."

I remember I was supposed to work the night shift.

"I lied," he says. "Told everyone you called in at the last minute. Said you were sick."

"I found the place where she lived. Baked pies. Was safe, probably after she was raped. You should see this place. It's called Hull House. The woman at the desk told me about a ghost. A woman who once lived there, who baked pies, disappeared. The white dress. She was a Suffragette with Jane Addams. I took the bus back to the Art Institute and walked home. There were so many things. So many questions. I'm sorry. I didn't even think about work."

"Are you okay?"

"When I walked back down the staircase to leave, it was as if she was leaving too. I've never felt so lonely in my life. Do you think she'll come back?"

"I don't know."

THIRTY-ONE

Clyde makes tea for the two of us. He sits on the edge of my bed. He talks about his father, about how sometimes he would feel him standing near, putting a hand on his shoulder, never talking, but just standing there, his head cocked to one side as though he wanted to listen.

"Then one night I had this dream. It was very real. Something I felt as much as imagined. My father and I were standing on either side of a narrow river, fishing. My father would cast his line. I would wait until his hook was in the water, his line pulled taut by the current, then I would cast mine. My father would then pull his line back, I would pull mine, and he would cast again, then it would be my turn. It was like a conversation, him saying something, me replying, always careful not to interrupt each other or get our lines tangled.

"There was just the slightest breeze. The sun was shining, but my hands and face felt cool. I could hear the soft whistle of my line as my rod whipped through the air. At first, I also heard my father's line singing out. I strained to hear what he was trying to say. With each cast, the sound of my line grew stronger and his weaker until I didn't hear his anymore. I pulled my line from the water, waiting for my father to throw his so it would be my turn again."

"What happened then?"

"I looked across and he was gone."

"What did you do?"

"I cast my line one more time and let the water carry my hook down the river, through the rocks, into a patch of sun. I'd like to say I caught something, but I didn't. I just stood there waiting, knowing he was gone. Gone forever, and I was left alone fishing."

"Did you tell your mother?"

"No."

"Did the ghost of your father ever come back?"

Clyde shakes his head and takes the empty cup from my hands. He leaves my bedroom and walks to the kitchen. I can hear him washing the dishes, drying them and putting them away in the same methodical way he washes glasses and dries them at the bar in the restaurant. Never rushed, always careful, putting things in order.

When he finishes straightening the kitchen, he turns off the light and stands in the doorway to my room. He doesn't come in.

"How long has your grandmother been in your dreams?" he asks.

"For as long as I can remember."

After Clyde leaves, I fall into a long dark sleep. It is the first time in months that my sleep has not been interrupted by dreams of my grandmother or by the sense that someone is with me, watching over me.

When I wake up, I realize I've overslept from sheer exhaustion. I call Clyde at the restaurant.

"You're not coming in," he says, before I have a chance to say anything.

"Not today and maybe not for a while," I answer.

"I can hold your job for as long as it takes," he replies. "I'd like it if you came back."

"I need to go home," I say. I hadn't really thought about where I was going or what I was going to do until I told him. But, when I say it, it feels right.

"That's good," he says.

"I'm keeping my apartment," I offer.

"Need me to look after anything?"

"No plants, no pets. I travel light," I say.

"Plants are good, makes things feel like home. When you get back, I'll buy you a philodendron. It's good to start off easy with plants. Philodendron plants are not very demanding. It's good if you water them from time to time, but I've known them to go without water for weeks."

"You don't need to worry about me."

"Is it okay if I do?"

"It's okay."

"Okay," he says. "Thanks."

I pack a suitcase. Summer clothes only. I stop by the landlord's apartment and give her a check for two month's rent. Tell her I'm going to be gone for a couple of weeks. Remind her that I don't have any pets or plants, so no one needs to get in to do anything. She tells me she's sorry about my father and knows how hard it can be when a parent dies.

I nod my head and tell her I'm going to spend some time with my mother. I give her my mother's phone number in case she needs to reach me. She gives me a hug. It feels awkward. I have failed to mention I'm going looking for a grandmother I never knew and I don't know what happened to her.

I take the bus to the train station and buy my ticket. When I board the train, I realize I have forgotten to tell my mother I'm coming home.

When I approach my parent's home, my mother is outside trimming the rose bushes. My father used to always trim the roses. They were his roses: a long bed of them running red, yellow, white, lavender and pale pink down the full length of our backyard fence and along the side of our driveway. They are a flowering history of my parents' love. Each bush rooted from one stem of whatever color of roses he gave my mother for each birthday, anniversary, and Mother's Day. The pale pink rose bushes have grown from the flowers he sent me for all my birthdays.

The roses always came in beautiful long white boxes that were tied with red satin ribbons hiding a card tucked underneath the bow. Before my mother began working on making an arrangement with the roses in her big crystal vase, my father choose one rose from the box, trimmed it, dipped it in a secret rooting solution he had created then planted the stem in the ground, watered it and covered the rose and stem with a Mason jar, carefully nestling the glass jar into the ground so it made a tiny sealed greenhouse. Once the stem had born a new shoot and my father had determined the weather would be kind to the small sapling, the glass jar would be removed and a new rosebush would begin to grow.

Long stemmed, red, yellow, pink, white…a parade of color, pride and love. As I approach, my mother is working her way down the line of roses, deadheading the ones that have bloomed and gone, snipping the withered branches and the ones that have grown unruly.

I stand at the edge of the driveway watching her work. She is wearing my father's long leather gloves, using his favorite pruning sheers. She is working slowly, moving from one bush to the next taking her time to examine each flower. Snipping one perfect bloom from each bush and plunging the stem into a pail of warm water as she moves down the side of the yard.

"Hello," I call out.

"Oh! Oh!" she cries before she drops the sheers and runs to greet me. "You've come to see me!"

"I should have called. I meant to. Made the decision this morning to come. I was all the way to the station before I remembered I hadn't called. Just wanted to see you, be here for a while. Hope it's okay."

"More than okay," she says. "Fine. Wonderful. I'm delighted! I was just thinking about stopping. Tea?"

"I'd love a cup."

"I haven't been able to sort through your father's things. Kind of silly, I guess, but I can't seem to get it started. Like, if I do, that's the end somehow."

"I can help," I say.

She has her back to me. She's making grilled cheese sandwiches for the two of us. Cheese and mustard with thin slices of tomato tucked into the sandwiches.

"Thanks," she says. "Thanks for coming. I didn't think I'd be lonely. You know, before he retired he worked so much and was gone much of the time I thought I knew what it was like to be alone. But, I guess you are never prepared for what might happen, what really being alone feels like, are you?"

"No," I say. I put two placemats on the table. Get glasses for water and plates for our sandwiches. I look in the cupboard for chips. My father loved potato chips. So do I.

"Top shelf," she says, over her shoulder. "In the back. I moved them so I wouldn't eat them. You shouldn't eat chips alone, like drinking alone, because you can't stop, or at least I can't stop. I don't want to become one of those women who eats to feel less lonely."

I get a chair.

"Right hand side," she says.

"Found them," I say.

It's a fresh bag. Unopened.

"I bought them yesterday. I wanted to be sure to have some here just in case you came to visit."

"Did you know I was coming?" I ask, surprised.

"Hoping, I guess."

"Work has been crazy," I say. "The Democratic Convention really hit town hard. We were slammed. Couldn't even close to reset for dinner."

"You like waitressing?"

Her question doesn't surprise me. I half expected it. I know she's really asking in the easiest way she can if I know what I'm going to do when I grow up. I don't.

"I've been trying to figure out what I want to do," I say. "Part of the reason I came home, I guess."

"Is there something you want to keep?" she asks. We are sorting through the odds and ends from my father's office. My mother is handing me things and I am putting them in piles: things to take to the Goodwill, some things to keep, and others to throw away.

"Maybe a book or some photos," I say. "Did he have a picture of the woman he called Mother?"

She shakes her head.

"Not that I ever saw. He didn't talk too much about her except to say that she was strict."

"Did he ever talk about where he lived, about the Door of Hope, the girls who came there? What happened to them and their babies?"

"He kept all that tucked away. Secret. I can only imagine it must have been a hard, strange kind of growing up with all those women who needed so much help coming and going in all hours of the day and night. I suspect it was more sadness than he was able to talk about. So he didn't. Sometimes it's best to just let go of things."

I open the top drawer of his desk. It's stuffed with envelopes, typing paper, a dozen pens and pencils, and a box of paperclips.

"Do you want any of these?" I ask.

"I've got a place in the kitchen where I keep supplies. Give them to me and I'll put them away. Then let's load the car, and make a little order from all this mess."

The room is quiet with her leaving. I start to close up the desk but something tugs at my hands and I pull the top drawer out as far as I can. Fast. A small notebook slides out from the back. It's one of those hard cover black speckled notebooks we used to write our spelling words in at school. I open it. I see my father's handwriting. Tight, perfectly formed upright loops. Punctuation marks firm and precise. It feels secret.

I take the book to my room, tuck it into my backpack and close the door.

I don't tell my mother what I've found.

I take out the garbage. Fill my mother's car with clothes and books to take to the Goodwill. My mother asks me if it's okay that I go to the Goodwill by myself. She doesn't think she can be the one to give his things away. It would feel too final. She can't quite face it yet.

I drive around town. I need some time to think about what I've found. I brought my backpack with me. The book is tucked inside along with my wallet. I could go somewhere. Park the car and read. I could.

Instead, I take his clothes and books to the Goodwill. I unload the car. The woman at the backdoor asks me if I want a receipt for tax purposes. I don't know the answer, but decide that if my mother wants it I should take the receipt and if she doesn't want it, then I will throw the receipt away. Nothing is lost.

When I get home, my mother is in the kitchen getting dinner ready.

I can smell the meatloaf cooking when I step into the kitchen. Hear the potatoes bumping against each other as she drops them into the boiling pot. She salts the water.

"Smells good," I say.

"Mashed potatoes and meatloaf," she says.

"His favorite," I say. I put out placemats, get silverware and water glasses, plates and napkins. "Do you want me to make the salad?"

Mom is peeling carrots. She stops, pushes the carrot peels into the compost bucket in the sink and wipes her hands on her apron.

"I heard him," she says, turning to face me. I can feel her words dangling in the air between us. "I was here, peeling carrots. The meatloaf was in the oven, the potatoes boiling in the pot just like they are now. His footsteps. He was walking down the stairs, stopped on the landing for a minute like he was thinking maybe he forgot something upstairs and he was trying to decide if he needed to go back to get whatever it was he thought he forgot. I wanted to, but was afraid to walk into the dining room to see him. I didn't know what he would look like, what I might find. My heart was pounding so fast, it was hard to breathe. I didn't call out. Didn't try to say his name or ask him if he wanted a beer with dinner. I just stood here, a carrot in my hand, waiting."

"What happened?"

"He always used to say that he loved coming into the house and smelling meatloaf cooking. Loved the warmth from the oven, the earthy steam from the boiling potatoes. He didn't like being cold. I don't think he ever went barefoot except at the beach.

"I don't know how long the two of us waited for the other to say something. It was like everything in my life had been standing still for as long as I could remember. But at the same time, I felt like I was in the middle of a tornado, like Dorothy in the Wizard of Oz. Warm air swirled around the room. Made me dizzy a bit. I tried, but couldn't move my feet. Opened my mouth but couldn't speak.

"The backdoor opened a crack and closed like the wind was pushing it. He didn't say anything like he was going to the store and would be right back and we'd talk then. I was here, washing carrots just like I am now and looked out the window into the garden hoping to see him pass by. The leaves on the trees rustled as though a sharp quick wind had just blown across the yard or someone had reached up and shook the limbs as they passed by. Then there was quiet.

"Quiet like a storm was coming or something was about to happen. They say that before an earthquake the birds quit singing and dogs quit barking and the earth is still. That's what it felt like, like the earth was still."

"Have you seen him since?" I ask.

My mother shakes her head and begins slicing carrots for the salad.

"When he left the house that afternoon, he was gone. Gone forever and I knew I would never feel him near me again."

I mash the potatoes, adding cream and butter and more salt and pepper than most people would use, but that was the way my father liked them, the way I had grown up eating them: salty with a strong bite of pepper. I put them in the mashed potato bowl, the funny oval one with the turned rim decorated with tiny painted flowers. I think my mother found the bowl at a yard sale and long ago declared it perfect for mashed potatoes.

We eat, talking about finishing emptying the closets tomorrow, the garage maybe Saturday. Neither of us seems to have the energy to go up into the attic to see what might be there. My mother wonders if we should have a yard sale with his tools and the odds and ends we have yet to uncover. We both decide it would be too sad of an affair and that it would be better to just take things to the Goodwill and be done with it.

We each have this need to let go. There is no sadness in it, just a feeling that we have to move forward. He would have wanted it that way.

"How long are you going to stay?" my mother asks.

I don't know how to answer the question.

"Are you going to keep the house?" I ask.

"I don't have anywhere else to go for now," she says.

"I need some time," I say. "At least a week. Maybe more."

"Good. That's good. Shall we clean up? I don't use the dishwasher since he died. Hope you don't mind. It's usually just my one dish. A coffee cup or two. A pot and a pan. It doesn't take long to do the dishes. Besides, I like to stand by the window. Look out. See the garden."

"I don't mind. I don't have a dishwasher in my place in Chicago. Washing the dishes always gives me time to think."

"Do you think I'm crazy? That I heard him? That he let me know he can't come back. That's what it feels like, like he had come to a place in life where he wanted to move on. Not to leave me, but to leave something."

"I don't think you're crazy."

"He was here. He really was, I heard him."

I carry our dishes to the sink. I turn on the water, add the dish soap, and take a moment to gather my thoughts before I speak.

"What if, when your heart stops and you are no longer alive, a moment comes when you can choose to leave or stay around to walk down the stairs, and go on with your life as usual. Say goodbye to someone you love without speaking," I say.

"He did that, didn't he," she says.

"Yes," I say. "I think he did."

I open my father's book. The house is quiet. My mother has gone to bed. The streetlight shines against the window shade. I turn on the lamp at my desk and start reading.

MOTHER

She snaps her fingers. I try not to flinch, but turn instead, to meet her snap with a smile, a gaze that lies and says I can see with both eyes. No one is to know I am half blind. Half an orphan. Half here for however long she lets me stay.

No one, not even the cook, Miss Rae, speaks about my blind eye. How it was blinded. How I got here. Or what happened to the woman who really was my mother. No one speaks about any of it. So much is unspoken. Silent.

Mother named me John and gave me her last name. Like everyone who comes to the Door of Hope, I call her Mother.

She calls me Sonny.

I do not know from love. Just from a bed to sleep on. A roof over my head. Wonderful afternoons in the kitchen with Miss Rae peeling potatoes and carrots, cutting biscuits from the fat dough she rolls out onto her big wooden pastry board.

Some days I think that I could stay in Miss Rae's kitchen forever. It is my safe place in this house. It feels like home, or at least what I think home must feel like. I often wonder what this house feels like to the women who come here because they have nowhere else to feel safe. Safe. I'm safe here in the kitchen with Miss Rae.

I run here from school each afternoon anxious to open the kitchen door and put my books down. Breathe. I can breathe in Miss Rae's kitchen. The air is warm in winter. It's cool in summer. I can dream here. When the bad things of night hound me, I come to Miss Rae's kitchen and crawl under her big worktable to sleep. She keeps a blanket there for me just in case I need it.

She understands how hard it is to hear the women screaming through the night as they struggle to bring their babies into this world, and the fearful crying of all the hungry babies in this harsh place. Miss Rae also knows how dark and desperate the nights can be when the whole house is hushed into silence because something terrible has gone wrong. She knows, because she is always there holding a hand, rocking a baby, saying a prayer. I don't think she ever sleeps.

I never go in or out of the front door. Never sit on the front porch in one of the wooden rocking chairs. Never take my meals at the big table in the dining room with the women who come here. They come. They go. There is never time enough in their being here to know them. To care.

The sorrow they carry through our front door, and leave behind when they go, seeps into every cracked board of this big house. The bitter salted tears of their regrets dampen the air even on the most glorious of mornings. Life here always feels like a thunderstorm breaking free of the heat of August. Whenever I have to go somewhere else in the house to deliver fresh linens, fetch Mother, sweep, clear the dining room table of dishes, I always walk as quickly as I can back to Miss Rae's kitchen.

I take my meals with Miss Rae. She helps me with my schoolwork. I help her wash the dishes and feed the chickens out back. She says we have a good life.

There is a blank page, then another entry.

Before I left the Door of Hope for the last time, Miss Rae came out back while I was feeding the chickens and told me how my mother died when I was born. That she was half dead when the police brought her to them. How the doctor pulled me from her cold body, gripping a little too tightly with his instrument in his hurried effort to save me before I too could have died, damaging my eye, the one that's blind.

When I asked Miss Rae about my father, she said nobody at the Door of Hope ever knows anything about the fathers.

Sometimes when the girls at the Door of Hope worried her too much, she'd tell me things. We'd be side-by-side chopping vegetables, stirring a pot, or peeling apples for a pie, and I'd get quiet when she talked and just listen as though I was grown and Miss Rae's confessor. I knew better than to interrupt her. Better than to tell her what I thought about what I heard in the house. I'd just listen and eventually she'd pull out whatever meat from the cooler there was to serve that night and start pounding it into something tender and edible all the time saying: No good has ever come from the fathers of the babies of the Door of Hope and no good is expected to arrive any time soon.

Then, as if to make a point, she'd start waving her big wooden meat mallet my way adding: If there's any hope to be had in this life for these babies brought to the world here by their poor mothers, it is that the fathers will stay gone forever.

With Miss Rae's help, I have completely forgotten my father. I never knew him, or knew of him. I do not dream of him. Never have, as though I lost any memory of a father when I was born as well as the sight in my left eye.

My real mother, the one who died carrying me into this world, is with me at all times. She is like a second shadow. She never speaks to me. I wish she would. I wonder if she will follow me when I leave the Door of Hope.

I think Miss Rae can see my mother hovering around sometimes and that's why she told me what happened.

When I close my father's book, I feel Miss Rae's presence in the room. Mother is there as well. The room hums with their energy. The torn white hem of my grandmother's dress stirs the air around me.

THIRTY-TWO

Clyde leans over the bar and hands me a tall club soda, two limes, one cherry and lots of ice.

"Nice to have you back," he says.

I've come back to Chicago. Come back to work.

"I got back a week ago. I wasn't ready. The apron, the sensible black shoes, the white blouse and black skirt…the whole thing, didn't fit anymore."

"Looks good to me."

"Nothing fits. When we finished cleaning out my father's closet, his study and all, I tried on all the clothing I'd left behind in my room. Picked up all the books I once read. The silly things I kept from high school and college. Nothing felt right. I took most of it to the Goodwill or threw it away. Like it wasn't me anymore. Maybe never had been."

"And?"

"You always used to say that this is where I'm supposed to be. Is it?"

"I'd like to think we were supposed to meet."

"You've been…"

"Wonderful? Helpful? Please don't say I've been a good friend."

"I need something to hold onto."

"Then hold onto me."

I finish the club soda and leave the empty glass on the bar. The other waitresses are starting to close out their checks, fill ketchup bottles, salt and pepper shakers, wipe tables and flip chairs.

"I need to close out," I say.

"Can I walk you home?" Clyde asks.

I hesitate. Worried I don't have the right words anymore.

"Sure."

When the rest of the staff leaves, I take off my apron. Instead of shoving it into my backpack, I fold it neatly and set it on the bar.

"It's okay," he says.

"If I could, I'd give you two weeks notice," I say.

"Not necessary," he says.

"The ghost thing…"

"Did you see your father when you went home?" Clyde asks.

Clyde turns off the lights, we step outside and he locks the door.

"My mother did. Once. He came down the stairs while she was cooking dinner. His favorite. Meatloaf, mashed potatoes and salad. Came down and stood for a minute before going out the backdoor."

"Did he say anything?"

"No, he just left. She's okay about it. It was like he forgot something. Like he wanted to come back and say goodbye. Let her know he was fine. There was nothing sad about it. Getting rid of the clothes was hard. That and the books. Like they were a part of him and that part was gone forever. She kept all the pictures. I kept one of his books."

"Which one?"

"A notebook he'd written in. Stories about the woman who raised him. The woman he called Mother. There was a hardness in what he wrote. Like it was something he wanted, no, needed to leave behind when he left home. I found it shoved in the back of his desk drawer. Hidden. He was blind in one eye."

"What happened?"

"His real mother died when she was giving birth. The doctor did an emergency C-section. Used forceps, damaged his eye and the eye socket. He had a lot of surgeries to fix it. Make it look normal. He wore a glass eye. He never talked about it. It looked natural. If you met him you wouldn't have noticed anything unusual."

"And the ghosts are…"

"Still around."

"How do you feel about them now that you're back?"

I stop walking. We are standing at a corner. I turn to let the coolness of the evening air blowing from Lake Michigan flutter across my face. I close my eyes. Try to imagine the ghosts of the women who have become part of my waking and my sleeping. They are the ones who have made me feel uncomfortable in my clothes that once fit. Who have stirred a desire within me for something I need to do. Make something right. Put other things to rest. I don't yet have the words to explain it to Clyde.

I hear footsteps. A snapping of fingers. I turn my head. Keep walking. Take Clyde's hand. The wind teases me. Makes me dizzy.

"My father's birth mother was lost to this world too soon. The other, the mother who raised my father, has begun to demand my attention as well. I feel the urgency, the energy of her sometimes. She's pushing me to do something, but I don't know what. She inhabits my dreams. I'm not sleeping much these days.

"The one who bore my father, his birth mother, wants, I don't know what. It's like she wants me to be her and do the things she didn't have time or couldn't do in her life. I can't be a waitress anymore. When I'm in the restaurant I can hear both of the mothers talking to me while I'm trying to take orders, serve pizzas, move through the evening carrying pitchers of beer, making small talk. And, now, there's a third. The cook. Miss Rae. A woman I believe my father loved because she made him feel loved. She pushes me in the same way she must have pushed my father to leave, to find his own life."

"It's okay," Clyde says.

"No. It's not, because I need a friend. I need for you to be a friend. And I know that's not what you want, but I'm afraid to let you go. I don't have many friends. Don't know what to do exactly with friends. But, I need someone I can talk to. I miss my father. My mother is hurting. I can't burden her with the things I hear, the things I see. When I try to talk with her about it, about how I don't know what it is I'm supposed to do, all she says is that she wants me to be happy. What's happy?"

"You're not crazy." Clyde starts to reach out to touch my shoulder, but pulls back. "This going to law school thing has been going on for a long time. I first took the LSATs right after college and passed them. I could have gone anywhere. My grandfather was a lawyer. So was my father, but he wasn't happy being a lawyer. I think that's why he killed himself. I was worried I wouldn't be happy either, so I didn't go because I was afraid to be a lawyer. To be unhappy like my father. Instead, I started tending bar."

"And now?"

"I'm not doing it for my grandfather or my father. I'm doing it for me. Sounds easy, but it hasn't been. Every night for the last five years, standing behind the bar, pouring whisky, pulling beers, I thought about what of them is part of me and what part is just me. I don't know anymore. It's been a strange wrestling and reckoning. The ghosts you see, the things you feel. They're real. I know."

"It's a pretty night," I say, taking his hand. "Would you walk me home?"

"And be your friend?"

"If you're okay with that."

"What's next?"

"Lately I've been dreaming about making pies."

Fruit pies, lemon custard, chicken pot pies, shepherd's pie piped with crusty golden mounds of mashed potatoes. Pies. I smell them cooking in my dreams.

I've never baked a pie in my life.

When I got back to Chicago, I didn't call Clyde. Didn't go into work. Instead, I walked down alleyways hoping to be able to follow the flicker of my grandmother's white skirt again. I stood in front of the Studebaker building, sun in my eyes, scanning the windows on the fifth floor trying to catch a glimpse of her.

Eventually, I went back to Hull House. I told myself I went because I wanted to, but the truth is, my grandmother wanted me to. I could feel her tugging at me. Pulling me back to discover something new. When I got off the bus and walked down South Halsted I stood in front of the hulking red brick building of Hull House for a long time before going in, hoping my grandmother would appear so I would know why I had come.

There was a different receptionist at the desk. I told her I was interested in taking a self-guided tour. She asked if I could go upstairs. As I walked down the long empty hallway, looking at each convent-like room, I was once again drawn to the last room on the right at the end of the hallway.

I stepped inside. Touched the edge of the narrow bed. Brushed my hand along the tiny stitches of the faded quilt. Looked into the mirror hanging over the washbasin sitting on the top of the dresser. Touched the yellowed towel hanging from one of the two hooks on the wall. Let my hand rest on the thin fabric of the white cotton dress hanging from the other hook.

I slipped off my shoes and let my feet brush against the thick braids of the wool rug at the foot of the bed.

I closed my eyes. Tried to summon my grandmother. This, I asked. Is this where you slept? Is this what you ran away from? Did someone hurt you? Were you scared? What happened here?

Nothing happened, so I put my shoes back on and walked over to the window. I tried to open it. It wouldn't budge. It was painted or nailed shut. I don't know what I thought opening the window would do. Provide a cool breeze or perhaps give my grandmother a way to come in?

I sat down on the wooden chair by the window and stayed in the room for as long as I dared. I didn't want some other tourist or the receptionist to come upstairs and find me, waiting for my grandmother to appear.

When my grandmother didn't come, I got up, went down the hallway and descended the long polished staircase to the reception area. As I went down the stairs, a perfume of cinnamon and sugar filled my head.

As I walked down the hallway toward the kitchen at the back of the building, the smell grew stronger. It was intoxicating. When I found the kitchen door open I looked in and saw the thick wooden rolling pin on the counter where it had been the last time I had been there.

"Can I help you?" the receptionist came up behind me.

"Pie," was all I could say.

"Did you smell apple pie?" she asked.

"When I walked down the stairs."

"It happens sometimes. There's a ghost in the house. She wears a white dress. We never see her face, just a flicker of a hem of her dress as she scurries up the stairs. Sometimes we hear a bedroom door open or close. We think it's the room at the end of the hall, the one on the right. She must have lived here, in that room. The story is that when the residents started saying that room was haunted, Jane Addams had the window nailed shut. She thought it might keep out the ghost. It worked for a while, but then she came back. When I unlocked the doors this morning. I thought I saw her, or at least a bit of her white dress, going up the stairs. Lately, she's been more active. Often when we see her, there's this apple pie smell. It fills the house. Cinnamon and…"

"Sugar, butter and tart apples."

"Always apple. I don't know what it means."

"Neither do I," I say.

THIRTY-TWO

I hear a thud, then a flutter of pages. My father's journal has tumbled off my bed and onto the floor. I wake up. There is a loud sharp sound. Like fingers snapping. Snap. Snap. Snap. I can hear the sound moving from corner to corner in my room. I turn my head to follow it as it flies around circling the room. Four snaps then silence. The room stills. I take a breath. Then it comes again. One loud snap. Just one this time. Signaling something is about to happen. I pull back the covers and sit up.

Mother is in the room. More than a shimmer of light this time. Her long brown dress has a kind of fullness to it, a sense of being in the room in an altered state. But, being. Real. Her hair is drawn up in a lose bun at the nape of her neck. Her eyes are blue. So blue. She is straight backed and commanding.

I listen.

I only wanted the best for him. His eye, the one that was lost. Damaged in his birth. Not his fault. How do you tell a child that the world won't understand? Won't see him as whole, as having value unless he looks like them. That's it, you see, we want people to look like us. To be like us. To be normal. I wanted him to be normal. I didn't want him to have to carry the scars of his uncertain birth. Didn't want people to stare or turn away.

I didn't want for him to have to explain.

That's why I did what I did. I gave him a name. My name. He called me

Mother. And, I was his mother, although I do not fool myself to think that I was more of a mother than the woman who carried and gave birth to him. Or, for that matter, that I was a better mother than Miss Rae was to him. She was the one who nurtured him. I knew it. I let it happen. He needed her. She needed him. I kept out of the way of the two of them and their private little world in the back of the house.

I would like it to be known that I was the one who gave Miss Rae the blanket and told her to keep it under her worktable for those nights when he was afraid and needed the comfort and privacy of the kitchen to help him sleep.

It was Miss Rae's job to nurture him, and it was my job to teach him to live in this world. I couldn't be soft with him. I had to make him stand up straight when he walked. To look at people when they spoke to him and he spoke to them. To be fully sighted. Not half blind.

Yes, I snapped my fingers. Tapped the soft underside of his chin in order to force him to lift his head when he walked or talked. Taught him to turn his head in order to see when someone or something approached him from his blindside.

It wasn't what you think. Or what he wrote about in that notebook you found in the back of his desk drawer. The one you keep reading, hoping to find…what?

That his life was horrible? That he wanted nothing more of it and so therefore ran away?

Yes, he ran away. But, he didn't tell you that. Didn't tell you anything. Kept it all to himself. I tried to make him talk about it. I knew it wasn't good that all that sadness stayed locked inside. The dead babies. The mothers…so young…so very young…who came expectant to our front door and left alone out the back. The bruises he witnessed on their bodies and their faces. The terrible life screams he heard night after night as the women pushed and fought to bring their babies safely into the world. The hard tears they cried when they gave their babies away.

I was there, just as your grandmother was, when you were born. She stood on your mother's right side. I stood on her left. We were there to witness.

Your father was out in the hallway, waiting. Miss Rae sat beside him the whole time. We were all fearful of what might happen if something went wrong. We both knew what he had witnessed, had carried with him in his heart and dreams all his life. We were there for him as well as for you. You must know that.

It was not the best life. But, it was the only life we had to give him. I knew there would be no one who came to the Door of Hope who wanted him. No family desperate enough to take a child so marked by tragedy.

When you took you first breath and cried, a damn broke in your father's heart. His tears came in a rush. A flood of forgotten tears: hot and bitter, and mixed with salty new ones celebrating your birth.

Miss Rae cried, too. But he couldn't see her. Could only feel her warmth beside him. He buried his face in his hands and shook with years of anger, of loss, of so much sadness. He cried until there were no more tears. No more nightmares.

You carried him that night. Carried him from the past to the future. You tore open his heart and made him forget what he had once known. Your cries were like an incantation that closed the terrible ache inside of him.

Our hands, the hands of your two grandmothers, reached out across the bed and our palms touched, forming an arch above your mother. She was holding you. You were wet and slippery and so raw and new to this world. We held like that, eyes closed, for as long as it took for you to make your decision to breathe, to stay in this world and grow.

There is this moment in the coming and going of life where you can decide what you want to do.

It is time for you to choose.

"To stay?" I ask.

There is an icy silence.

"To stay?" I ask again. I twist and turn from side to side in my bed, trying to find her, bring her back. In my search, I have wound my nightgown around me like a second skin, a shroud.

I get out of bed and unwind the fabric that has temporarily bound me. I pick up my father's book and put it on my bedside table.

I snap my fingers. Nothing happens.

I am alone.

"How did you decide? I mean, was it really your decision? Are you sure?" I ask.

It is seven o'clock in the morning. Clyde is sitting at the counter in my apartment kitchen. He is drinking coffee and eating apple pie. It is the apple pie I baked in the middle of the night after Mother left. I couldn't sleep.

"Great apple pie," he says, as though it is his habit to drop by my place at seven o'clock in the morning when I call him to come over to eat a slice of pie. "You might want to add a pinch of salt to the filling, next time. Brings out the tart flavor of the apples."

"I'll make a note of that," I say.

"I don't think I ever got over finding my father dead in the garage. I still have nightmares that I did something wrong. Something that made him not want to stick around to find out who I was going to be, like he already knew and was disappointed.

"My mother often worked double shifts. They'd call her to come in early sometimes and I'd eat dinner alone. Or, she'd phone me when it was time for me to wake up and tell me someone just called in sick and she'd be working another shift so I'd have to make breakfast for myself and pack a lunch to take to school. One time when she called, I started to cry. There had been a bad storm that night. The wind was wild and I had this crazy feeling that my father was in my room. I didn't know what to do, so I hid in my closet. I was afraid of him, of what he did, how maybe he was in me and I was like him. I didn't want to be alone. I didn't want to eat by myself. I cried and told her I didn't want her to work another shift. I wanted her to come home. She started yelling at me. She called me ungrateful. Said she worked all the extra shifts so I could have what I needed. What I needed. I think about that a lot, like there's some kind of magical quantity of stuff that you need in order to survive.

"I didn't need stuff. I needed to have breakfast with her. I needed to come home from school and be able to say hello to her, eat dinner with her, and listen to what happened in her day and tell her about mine. I needed to be able to say goodnight to her before I fell asleep.

"I hate eating alone. When I know it's going to be rough, like near the anniversary of my father's death, or just any day when my brain is traveling a million miles an hour carrying carload after carload of guilt and confusion I ask the kitchen to fix a small mushroom and cheese pizza and box it up before they shut off the ovens and close the kitchen. I don't take it home. Instead, I put it in the cooler at the bar and eat it the next morning when the delivery guys arrive. Anything not to have to eat breakfast alone in my apartment."

"You like cold pizza?" I say.

"I've come to like it. It's not bacon and eggs, but it's better than grabbing a donut and chugging a black coffee. Couple slices of cold pizza can keep me going until after the lunch rush."

"Why guilt?"

"Why not? I mean, why did he do it? Was it my fault? Could I have stopped him? Should I have?"

"Did you know he was unhappy?" I ask.

"I was ten. What does anyone know about happy or unhappy when they're ten? I play that day over and over again in my dreams, when I'm wiping down the bar, when I'm trying to decide if I should order a mushroom pizza or a pepperoni one for a change. Everything about the memory of that day takes hold of my life and I can't think of anything else. So I order the mushroom pizza because I don't know what else to do. What else I want to do."

"It wasn't your fault."

"It doesn't matter. He haunts me."

THIRTY-FOUR

"Come to Macon with me," I say.

It's midnight. Clyde is sitting at my kitchen counter eating his second piece of chicken pot pie. I pour us each another glass of wine.

"You have a recipe for this?" he asks.

"Not really. I don't have recipes for any of them."

"This one is a really good idea."

"When was the last time you took a vacation?" I ask.

"Going to Macon, Georgia, to chase ghosts doesn't sound like a vacation."

"We can take the train."

"Because?"

"She probably took the train. I mean, that's where they found her, on the train station platform."

"Is she coming along?"

I pick at a mushroom that has fallen away from the filling onto the pie plate. Lick my fingers. Pull a potato chunk out from underneath the top crust. Then another mushroom.

"Why don't you cut yourself a slice? I'm more than happy to share," he says.

"We could take a week, or if you think that's too much, maybe just a long weekend. Is there someone else who can manage the bar?"

"You didn't answer my question. Is your grandmother coming along?"

"Which one?"

"Both?"

"Maybe. I mean I don't expect them to ride along with us on the train. But I suspect they will be there."

"They know we're coming?"

"I don't know. I guess."

"You guess because?"

"I can't just keep making pies day and night."

"Why not?"

"Is there someone else who can manage the bar? Can you get away for a couple of days?"

"When?"

"I was thinking maybe we could leave Sunday morning. Probably wouldn't be good to try to push this thing out any longer than I have to."

"Because?"

"Aren't you starting law school in two weeks?"

"What's the rush? Is something going to happen? Some reason you need to be there ASAP? I'm going to have to find someone to fill in for me. Jess has done it a couple of time in the past."

"So you'll go?"

"Tell me what we're going to do there."

"It has something to do with the cemetery. I need to go there. Talk to them. Find out what I'm supposed to do to help them."

"Have they told you?"

"Last night, in my dream, I was there, both of us were there, sitting in the moonlight, waiting. Then they came, all three of them. My grandmother, the woman who raised my father, and Miss Rae stood before us. My grandmother's dress was torn and bloodied, her face tired. It was like she was working as hard as she could to be present with us, to be more than a tattered hem of a dress. Mother, the woman who raised my father was the first to speak."

"What did she say?"

"She was whispering this one phrase over and over again but each time she said it the leaves on the big tree began to rattle as though the leaves were speaking, joining her. Dozens of voices. Maybe even hundreds of voices. All speaking together as one."

"Could you understand what they were saying?"

"Not at first, and even now, I'm not sure I understand, except that I have to go there. Sit in the moonlight under the big tree and listen again.

"The dream was so real. I keep hearing them calling to me, the rhythm of their voices in unison like a heartbeat. Rest easy. Rest easy...Only you can help us rest easy..."

"I'm going with you."

"It's strange, but I can feel them. All around me."

Clyde is walking around the large bare plot. He has a stick in his hand, tapping the ground as though he is divining for water.

"I know," I say.

"Your father?" he asks, standing at the edge of the plot by a patch of new grass.

"His ashes," I say, because I no longer understand anymore where life ends and death begins.

"There's someone next to him on either side. Crowded together. So many. When you talked about what happened when you buried your father I never imagined so many other graves."

"How many?" I ask, letting my eyes sweep across the flat grassy surface before me. I squint, looking for signs: a small bulge, a shallow place, or even a handful of stones left by someone in remembrance.

Clyde slows his walking and tapping. He paces off the perimeter surrounding the only marker: my other grandmother's tombstone with the word Mother chiseled into it.

"Could be fifty," he says. "Or, a hundred, depending on how many babies, how many women."

Mother's grave and small flat marker sits in the middle under the shade of the tree. The plot is the largest and the last one at the very edge of the cemetery. Far away from the politicians, the preachers, businessmen and church ladies marked by impressive monuments, and separated by a swell of land, a short brick wall. Below, there's the Ocmulgee River with railroad tracks running parallel along the upper part of the bank. A train passes. Its whistle blows a soft greeting out of respect for the dead. The leaves on the tree flutter.

The moon pushes through a billow of clouds. The night is still again. Clyde walks the perimeter of the plot, tapping his stick as he goes. The wind picks up.

I hear it first as a whisper, a warm wind whistling through the branches of the great tree.

Rest easy, rest easy, rest easy.

Clyde sits down beside me. He bounces the point of the stick against the grass. I feel the heat from his body. The silence between us like held breath.

"Do you hear it?" I whisper.

He nods his head.

I was raped, a voice calls out.

Beaten, shamed, forgotten…

Raped, raped, raped…

The individual voices, now a chorus.

No one believed me. No one, no one, no one. They couldn't listen. Could only see. But not believe. No one believed me when I told what happened. What I didn't want. What I couldn't fight. What I couldn't stop.

My baby, my baby, my baby, the chorus cries.

My father tried to beat the Devil out of me.

Harlot. Slut. Whore.

When I knocked on the Door of Hope I came with no other name. Only shame.

Shame, shame, shame…

No one knows, no one knows, no one knows.

A swirl of wind. The long brown skirt of Mother takes form from the dust.

I did my best. I held the babies when they died. Wrapped them in torn sheets, old petticoats, whatever we had to cover their bodies for burial. Rocked and sang to them. Listened when their mothers cried.

What else could I do but listen? I let them sleep. That was the only comfort I had to give. A bed. A meal. A place to hide.

The tree branches rattle.

Other voices cry out:

I was fifteen.

I was twenty.

I was twelve.

When I found out I was pregnant, my family abandoned me.

No one believed me.

No one.

No one knows I am here.

My uncle did this to me.

My brother.

The man I worked for held his hand over my mouth, tore my clothes away.

The voices howl and cry. The air is electrified. The moon makes its lazy way across the sky. My skin feels tight and worn thin. Clyde is beside me. He brushes his hand against mine. I reach out. Clutching. I need something to hold on to. I dare not close my eyes.

Their words are like stones thrown into the bucket of my soul. I feel so very heavy. I think about Cassie. Wonder where she is, who is holding her. Who will believe that she couldn't stop what was happening to her? Who will know where she has gone when she runs away?

Clyde squeezes my hand. I turn and see what he sees. My grandmother. She is standing at the edge in the moonlight in her blood stained white dress. Strands of her hair fall free from the tight bun at the nape of her neck. Her arms are bruised. I can see the fingers of her left hand are twisted and broken.

Her face is my face. It shocks me. Her blue eyes are my blue eyes: her fair skin, my fair skin. We are the same.

The midwife told me they would take my baby away. That's why I ran. Ran as far and as fast as I could. But I didn't get far enough. Couldn't escape what was going to happen. And then there was the man on the train. Even crueler than the first. I fought back. He beat me. I held on. Held tight to this world as long as I could. As long as I had to in order to keep my baby safe. In that moment from here to there I saw you. Saw my face in your face. My fate in your hands.

She spread her arms out wide, stretched her fingers out like stars welcoming the coming of morning. I ached to touch her. To be held by her.

And, so I stayed, to bring you here so you would know my story, all our stories, so many stories no one wants to hear, no one wants to know.

Your father is here now. Lying next to me as he has always wanted to be. He was so very tired of carrying all these babies, all these sad stories in his heart. It was time for him to rest.

Rest easy.

That's what he wanted. What we all want.

To rest easy. To be marked in this world as having been here. Of having knocked on the Door of Hope because we had nowhere else to go. No one to run to. No place to call home. Our names were lost. Forgotten.

You will know what to do.

The woman my father called Mother walks to the center of the circle. She sits down and stretches her tall legs out in front of her on the ground. Rests her head on the grave marker. She begins to hum, and as she does, she slowly disappears.

My grandmother lies down on the ground near the freshly turned earth where my father is buried. She rolls to her side as though she is holding his soul in her arms. I see her shoulders relax. Her head rest on the ground. Her torn white dress swirl and tangle around her thin legs.

She is gone.

The wind is still. The voices quieted.

There's a rustle in the grass.

Miss Rae approaches.

I loved him. Rocked him to sleep. Made apple pies for every one of his birthdays. Lord, he loved apple pie. I watched him grow. Cried when he ran away. He did, you know. It was too hard. I knew it was. Too hard for any soul to hold. He wanted to know about his mother, the one who birthed him, so I told him. I had no choice. He was nearly six feet tall. He was a man by then because of circumstance. He was only fifteen. He had lived a lifetime in that sad house of desperate women and hard born babies who wouldn't have a chance to know their true mothers. It was funny, but he never walked through that front door. Always came around the back to the kitchen. Was afraid to I suspect. That coming through that door marked him as one of them, as having come from something terrible.

We had finished with supper that evening when he left. When the last dish was dried and put on the shelf he turned to me and demanded to know where she was. I had no choice but to tell.

I knew where she was buried.

And, he knew where the babies were buried because he had helped me. It was my job to bury the babies. The doctor, in his shame, had the women who died under his cruel knife, taken away by his man and brought here. Buried in the middle of the night so no one would know where the girls had gone. If we wanted to keep our jobs, to do what little we could to comfort and care for these poor souls, we had to say they had run away. Had birthed their babies and run. The lie was bitter in my mouth.

Mother always washed the babies who died then wrapped them in whatever clean linen we had. When the others had gone to sleep and the house was quiet, she would bring the infant to the kitchen. I'd be waiting.

That first time your father helped me had been a night of much screaming and carrying on. The poor girl was just a child. Almost too young to understand what had happened to her when her brother raped her. She was maybe thirteen, too young to be believed or to do anything about it. She didn't even know there was something wrong with any of it. When her baby couldn't draw breath, wasn't strong enough to make it to this world, she started screaming. She wanted to hold it. Keep it with her like it was a doll that she could play with. She didn't understand that even if her baby had lived it would have been taken from her arms and given away.

Her carrying on woke everyone in the house.

Your father couldn't sleep and had come into the kitchen and crawled under the worktable as he had done so many times before trying to find a quiet place to rest. He was eleven years old. His birthday just passed.

When Mother came into the kitchen to give me the baby, he stayed quiet like until she left. Then he came out from where he'd been hiding and asked me about the small white bundle I was cradling.

I held those small angels for as long as I could. Hummed to them, rocked them in my arms, trying to make sure they were going to find eternal rest. A life so short should have some comfort.

I told him the baby had died and I was going to go out into the night to bury it. I remember it all like it was yesterday. The baby was a girl. I named her

Tabitha. I named them all in secret. You shouldn't pass through this world without a name.

He asked if he could hold the baby. I gave her to him. He held that small bundle so close to his chest it was as if he were trying to give that poor child one last chance to steal the beats from his own heart.

I asked if he wanted to carry her to the cemetery, help me bury her. He nodded his head. The two of us left. Me with a garden shovel I kept by the backdoor and him with the baby in his arms. The moon was full, a harvest moon, so bright we didn't need candlelight.

It was the first time he came with me to the cemetery. Like you, he walked the whole of this big plot until he came to that spot over there. I didn't need to tell him. He could feel her.

I sat where you are sitting and watched him. He sat down on the ground with the baby still in his arms. He didn't cry. Didn't say anything. I guess he didn't need to. He'd found his mother.

After a while, he got up and came over to me. Said it was time to dig the grave. He put the baby in my arms and went to a place near this big tree and started digging.

It was like he knew that was where the other babies were buried. I always put them there so they could feel the change of the seasons and hear the rustling of the leaves when the wind blew.

From then on he helped me each time a baby died. Then one day he said he couldn't stay any longer. Couldn't live in that house full of sorrow. Couldn't bury any more babies.

Each baby we buried silenced him a little more than the last until he hardly spoke. We'd work, cracking eggs for breakfast, peeling potatoes, rolling biscuits, plucking chickens like two old people who had done the work so long standing side by side that there was nothing to say anymore. I guess his silence was his way of trying to make his own space in the world.

When there were women crying and babies anxious and angry, wanting to be fed and he couldn't sleep, he'd pace the house or leave out the kitchen door and walk the streets.

You see, when things weren't right in the house, he didn't have any place to go. He was too tall by then to hide under my big worktable waiting for a new day to come. Sometimes I'd find him the next morning asleep on the kitchen stoop as though he were on guard and it was his job to keep the house safe from intruders.

The air in the house grew heavy with his stillness, like a storm was coming. Everyone could feel it and did the best they could to stay out of the way of whatever it was that was going to happen. I ached for him.

One evening, after we finished with supper and everything was washed and put away, he asked if I'd walk with him to the cemetery and tell him all what I knew about his mother.

It was early spring and still cool in the evenings. I went to my room to get a shawl. While I was there, I took the money I kept hidden in an old shoe under my bed and put it in my pocket. It was money I had from selling eggs and making pies and sweet cream cakes for the churchwomen.

While we walked I told him everything I had remembered. I told him the police had found her at the train station. That she had been badly beaten. Unconscious. No one knew who she was, where she came from or where she was going. That the doctor thought she was going to die but he could save the baby. I told him that she was gone before he arrived. Her face smooth with death when I blew that first breath into him and he cried.

I didn't tell him about the doctor's cruelty or that he had been drinking. I didn't tell him how the doctor tore his mother's flesh and had blinded his eye with his carelessness. These were things he didn't need to carry.

He asked me what she looked like. I told him that she was beautiful. That he had her fair skin and her blue eyes. That I thought he favored her. He seemed happy with what I knew, what I could tell him.

When we got to the cemetery he walked the whole of the plot, just like he had done when we buried that first baby together, but this time, he paused at each small grave he'd dug and any of the others where he felt some soul lay. When he came to that edge, over there, where his own mother was buried, he sat for a long time whispering like he might be praying.

When he was done talking with her, he came to me and put his arms around me. I kissed him on the cheek and put the money in his hands. It was all I had to give him. He thanked me for the money. For everything. He said he'd hid his satchel underneath the porch and would walk me back to the home to get it.

That was the loneliest walk I ever took 'cause I knew that, come the next morning, the kitchen and my life wouldn't ever be the same again. With him gone, there would be this unbearable quiet in the house. I knew Mother would feel it too.

We didn't say much to each other. The silence between us was enough.

I didn't ask him where he was going because I understood he didn't know. That he had to find some way to make a life away from what he'd been born to and he had no idea where that life was going to take him.

He never came back. Not even for Mother's funeral.

Sadness can bury your heart.

That night when you were born and I came to sit beside him, he leaned into me like he knew I was there. When his mother, the one who birthed him, had breathed her dreams into your tiny life she came and sat by his other side. When she did, his shoulders slumped as though the weight of all the babies he had once buried had been draped like a mantel on his shoulders. His head was bent in prayer, or maybe exhaustion. When Mother, the one who raised him, saw him like that, she ticked him on the chin, making him look up, like she had done a hundred times before when he was little and she wanted with all the love that she had for him to make him normal, to make him believe he wasn't half a person, half blind.

His head jerked hard to the left and right. Looking for her, or some memory of her. I put my hand on his arm to steady him.

The three of us have been here all along, waiting. And, now it's time. Time for us to rest easy and time for you to put down the burden we've asked you to carry and be free.

You are everything he dreamed for you. Everything we knew you would be.

I felt a cool breeze kiss my cheek. Watched as Miss Rae walked to her place on the other side of my father, lay down and was gone.

THIRTY-FIVE

We are sitting in the H&H Soul Food Restaurant on Forsyth Street in Macon. It's not quite 7 am. The place is filling up with people stopping for a biscuit and a black coffee on their way to work, and others who can take their time to read the morning paper and linger over the H&H regular: scrambled eggs, sausage, bacon, grits, two biscuits and coffee.

I butter a biscuit and stuff it with a firm round patty of sausage. I am cold, hungry, and shaken. Clyde is methodically stirring bits of his scrambled eggs into his grits. He picks up a piece of bacon and starts to crumble it onto his plate.

"Thank you," I say.

He moves the broken bits of bacon into his carefully assembled mess of eggs and grits. He takes a bite of a biscuit. Holds his coffee cup up motioning to the waitress that he wants another one. A fresh one, not the cold one he's been staring at.

"You're welcome," he says.

"I couldn't do it alone," I say.

The waitress comes, takes our cold coffee away and brings back two clean cups. She puts them on our table and pours hot coffee into them from a fresh carafe.

"Cream?" she asks.

"More sugar would be nice," I answer.

"Cream," says Clyde.

The waitress leaves, comes back with the sugar and cream. Clyde thanks her.

"You needed a witness," he says. "If you're going to tell someone. I'll back you. Tell them what I saw. What we saw."

"You okay?" I ask.

"How long have you been dreaming these three women?"

"Do you think they are dreams?"

"Visions, ghosts, dreams, demands: I'm not sure which, but they were as real as this biscuit." He takes a bite out of his biscuit. Puts it down. Leans forward and waits for me to speak.

"For as long as I can remember, someone was there. One of them. Maybe all three. They always seemed to be there, like Miss Rae said, from the moment I was born. Probably before. At first I didn't realize there was more than one. Mostly, they came in dreams, until the last couple of years. That's when she started speaking to me, telling me I had to go to Chicago."

"Which one told you?"

"My grandmother. She was the first to speak to me. You know how dreams are usually just pictures. Silent movies where the words you hear are the words in your head. Your words, usually. Or, at least, that's how my dreams worked. Then one night, there was another sound. Someone else was speaking. The voice was different. It wasn't mine. Later I realized it was hers."

I pinch off a bit of my biscuit. I'm trying to quiet my heart by taking things slowly. Being deliberate. Not rushing. I need some time to think.

"The time I dreamed about fishing with my father, I was standing on one side of the bank calling out to him. He'd answer by throwing his line into the water," Clyde says. I notice that he is looking over my shoulder when he says this as though he is worried someone else might hear.

"I remember when you told me," I said.

"But it felt bigger than just a dream."

"I know."

"Did they, the ghosts, the dreams scare you?"

"Never. And, I don't know why. I guess I should have been afraid, but I wasn't. Maybe I should have been, but I wasn't. Over time, the dreams, the voices, I guess, the apparitions, just became part of me. Of the things I thought about. The things I saw when I walked down the street. The dreams I had at night."

"Are you going to tell your mother what happened last night?" Clyde asks. "Would she want to know that you saw your father's birth mother? That she came to you and you witnessed her lying down beside him at the edge of the plot. That your father is where he has always wanted to be."

"That's the word, isn't it?"

"What?"

"That we witnessed. That's what they wanted. They wanted someone to witness what was there. To know that there were unmarked graves all around. The Door of Hope was a last hope, but a harsh one, because no one either cared or believed that they might be innocent, that there were circumstances. That some of them tried to fight and were hurt. I guess, by not being believed, the women became nameless. Nobody. Forgotten. Buried in unmarked graves."

I hear myself rambling. Talking a zig-zag of a blue streak, trying to make sense of what I witnessed, and what my two grandmothers want me to do.

I take my time. I want the words I'm going to say to come out right. I want Clyde to understand. I want him to agree with what I think I should do. I want him to help me.

"They won't be able to rest easy until someone else knows where they are and what happened to them. They want someone to believe. They don't want to be forgotten."

Clyde stirs cream into his coffee. He nods his head.

"Cassie was part of it, wasn't she?" Clyde says. "They wanted you to help her because the man who used her would never know, would never care about what he did to her. But you know what happened to Cassie and how it is going to change her life. And, now you know about the babies and all the young girls buried in unmarked graves, and about what happened to your grandmother."

"I need to call my mother."

"Where are you?"

I can hear an edge of fear in my mother's voice. I'm not quite sure what or how much to tell her about last night: the cemetery, the ghosts, and the voices of the women telling their stories asking for help.

"I'm in Macon."

"Is anyone with you?"

"Clyde, from the restaurant. I think I told you about him. He's the manager, the bartender. He's going to law school in the fall. We're friends. He came with me. We took the train. We're staying at a youth hostel. In different rooms."

I'm in a phone booth at the train station. It's probably the very same station where my father's mother was found so many years ago. Clyde is standing outside the phone booth. He has a handful of dimes and quarters that he's giving me when the time runs out on my call.

"Are you okay?"

I look at Clyde, he hands me some coins, nods his head. I am so grateful he is here. I tell my mother I just had this feeling I needed to go back to Macon because I wanted to show Clyde the cemetery and show him where we buried Dad. I don't tell her about the dreams. The voices I hear sometimes.

"When I was home you told me about hearing Dad, maybe his ghost, walking down the stairs, going out the backdoor."

"I was cooking meatloaf, his favorite."

"The night after we buried Dad's ashes, I went back to the cemetery. I didn't tell you where I went or what I saw because I wasn't sure how to explain everything then. I saw something that night. Not Dad, but his mother. His birthmother. Her spirit, I guess, a ghost, she appeared."

"Mother, and the one he called Miss Rae, who he said raised him," my mother says.

"How did you know?"

"When you didn't come back right away. I guessed that you went back to the cemetery. I followed you. As I was coming down the lane to the plot, I saw the ghost of the woman they called Mother. She was tall, thin. She had on a plain brown dress. I kept my distance. I was afraid if I came close, she would disappear. Miss Rae was standing out in the woods, waiting."

"You didn't say anything."

"There were so many things I wanted to ask about what was happening, why you weren't afraid. Your face was turned away from me, but I could see by the way you sat, how you listened, that you had seen all of them before. They seemed to be part of you and you of them."

"The three of them have been in my dreams, in my life, for as long as I can remember."

"They were why you went to Chicago, aren't they?" she asks.

"Mostly Dad's birth mother, my grandmother. She was the one who spoke to me the most. Came into my dreams. When I came to Chicago, I started seeing her, not just in my dreams but also in the daylight. Sometimes when I was walking down Michigan Avenue, I'd see a quick flash of the hem of her dress and I'd try to follow. She wanted me to see where she had been hurt, the home where she lived and learned to bake pie. She wanted me to know what happened."

"And then Dad died. The two of you were so close. Sometimes I was jealous that the two of you could laugh so easily. Could sit for hours without talking. Could be so much a part of each other's lives. When he died, I felt angry that he was gone and angry that I hadn't been a better mother."

"You are a wonderful mother. I loved him and I love you."

"Did you tell your father about the ghosts? About your dreams?"

"I didn't know what to tell either you or him," I said. "I wasn't always sure until just the last few months of what I was supposed to do or why they were in my life. I guess I didn't understand it enough to try to explain it. Sometimes I worried if I told anyone they might think I was crazy."

"Maybe I would have thought you were crazy if you had told me you saw ghosts before Dad died, but not now."

"Remember what the grave digger told us, that there were other people buried all around Mother?"

"I was so angry with him that he didn't bury Dad where I thought he wanted to be. Your father didn't talk about growing up in Macon that often, but when he did, he always said he wanted to be buried near his mother and I guess I thought that meant that he wanted to be buried next to the woman who raised him. I had no idea there would be others buried there."

"Some of the women buried there wanted to be there," I say. "And others are there because they had no place else to go. No one wanted them. Their families disowned them because had gotten pregnant, as if it was their fault. No one believed these women when they tried to tell what happened to them. The violence. The shame. Like the grave digger said, there are many babies buried there as well as the women."

The operator breaks into our call. Clyde hands me more coins. I drop them in, one at a time in order to reconnect.

"How many? Do you know their names?" she asks.

"Miss Rae told us about one of the babies she named Tabitha. She named them all, you know, before she buried them. She thought it was the least she could do for them. That, and she held them and sang to them."

"Did she tell you the names of the others?"

"No, she only told us about Tabitha. Miss Rae talked the most of the three of them. It was like it was her job to reveal all the missing pieces, the things I needed to know in order to understand what it was they wanted me to do. Miss Rae said that Dad helped her bury the babies. That he was the one who buried Tabitha.

"He had just turned eleven. I can't imagine growing up in that house full of women whose families had thrown them out. Forgotten their names. Didn't want anything to do with them. Women who had nowhere else to go, but the Door of Hope, to bear their babies, their shame."

"That must have been what happened to his mother," my mother says.

"She was running away when she came to Macon. She had a job in Chicago as a typist. She worked in the Studebaker building. Her boss raped her. When she fought him, he broke her fingers so she wouldn't be able to be a typist ever again. Her family didn't know about any of it. She wound up at Hull House, a resettlement house west of downtown Chicago for women who needed help. While his mother was there, right before she was ready to give birth, the midwife told her she that once she had the baby, the people at Hull

House would take it from her and put her baby up for adoption. That's why she ran. After that, no one knew where she went or what happened to her."

"Who beat her up?"

"Another man, from the train. Beat her and left her to die. The police took her to the Door of Hope."

"What about the others?"

"Some of the mothers died in childbirth. Others, like Dad, left the Door of Hope then came back to be buried with Mother when they died. Many of the girls were beaten, raped and disowned by their families. Some of the women were young. Very young and didn't know how to stop an uncle or a brother from repeatedly abusing them. No one believed them. No one knows what happened to them, who they were, how they died, why they died or even where they are buried. All the graves are unmarked. Dad's mother is there and Miss Rae, the cook, the woman who cared so much for him. They're buried on either side of where we buried dad. He's where he wanted to be. He didn't want to be buried next to Mother, but next to his birth mother. I wanted you to know. He's resting easy."

My mother is quiet. She never talks on the phone without a scrap of paper in front of her, a pencil in her hand. I hear the scrape of a pencil move across the paper. I can guess that she is nervously doodling, and has possibly written down Tabitha's name.

"Clyde stayed with you through all of this? He saw what you saw? Heard what you heard? He believes you?"

"Yes. He saw the three women. When he walked around Mother's tombstone, he could feel the others as he passed over their graves."

"How many?" my mother asks.

"I think there are quite a few. Clyde thought maybe as many as 50 or even more. The babies are buried under the tree. That's what Miss

Rae told us. The mothers are buried all around the edges. Like sentries guarding their children."

I pause for a moment to give my mother a chance to take it all in. I hear the point of her pencil making small scratches and dots on the paper like she's trying to think of the next word, the next question to ask.

"Your dad and I didn't have a big wedding. I wore a rose colored suit rather than a white dress. He bought me a beautiful red rose corsage. We got married at the courthouse then had a dinner with friends and my family afterwards at a restaurant. We drank some champagne and had a small wedding cake. I asked if he wanted to invite his family and he said he had no family, that the woman who raised him had died and he had no father or brothers and sisters."

The operator interrupts the call again. Clyde hands me more money. I push two dimes and a quarter into the slot.

"Did you ever ask Dad about his childhood?"

"He didn't want to talk about it, so I didn't ask. I think that's how marriages work sometimes. Things go unsaid. After you were born he changed. It's like having you caused what had been hurtful before to become easier to remember. One night after he'd sat in your room for a long time rocking you to sleep, he came into our bedroom and told me about running away from his home and never going back. I think he might have been afraid that you would grow up and run away like he did and that's why he told me.

"He never talked about the Door of Hope, never told me about the babies, about having to help bury them. I wish he had. I wish he were here, just for a moment more, so I could hold him."

"He loved you," I say.

"Is there anything we can do?"

"For Dad?" I ask.

"For all of them."

Clyde and I are sitting on the grass in Washington Park across from the Washington Library in Macon. We are taking a break from doing research in the Genealogical Archives of the library, looking at microfiche birth and death records, census records for the Door of Hope, anything we could find.

Clyde is idly picking blades of grass and arranging them like cords of wood stacked this way and that.

"There's no record of Tabitha," I say.

"There's no record of anyone," Clyde replies.

"There's not even a record of my father's birth."

Clyde stops what he is doing.

"There are no records because they were nobody. Nobody wanted them. Nobody cared. Nobody came looking for them. Their babies were born in shame and they died and were buried in unmarked graves. They didn't matter. There's nothing to find."

"We found them," I say.

"We don't know what we found."

"Do you believe we saw the three of them? Mother, his mother, Miss Rae?"

Clyde uses his fingers like a rake and stacks up the bits and pieces of torn grass in a pile as though he is building a small campfire.

"Yes," he says, softly, looking away from me. "Where's Cassie in all of this?'"

"I believe my grandmother wanted me to come to Chicago so I would know what happened to her. So I would come to understand that what happened to her was no so different than what happened to any of the women who found their way to the Door of Hope, or to Cassie.

"You once said that I brought you along because I needed a witness. I did. And, maybe they do too. I think they deserve at least that."

THIRTY-SIX

The man who dug the grave for my father is pulling a small flatbed wagon carrying his shovel and the marker. Clyde is walking behind the wagon, helping to guide it down the steep path. My mother is holding my hand.

"Where shall we have him put the marker?" my mother asks.

"Clyde and I came last night again. Sat on the edge near the path. I had this idea that maybe if I spoke to them, they'd help me, help us know where to put it."

"Was Mother there?"

I leaned into my mother. Pulled her close. Felt her warmth along the length of my body.

"No," I whispered.

"Going to have to find kind of a level place if you don't want it to crack," the gravedigger calls back to us. "Earth is always shifting here, so close to the river. Plus, the train going by on the tracks down there is always rattles things lose. I'm forever having to right some of the old tombstones that have been rocked lose. Flat is good. Easier too to dig it into the earth, make it look good."

He picks up a big rock off the wagon and kicks it under one of the back tires so the wagon won't roll while he looks for a place to put the marker. Clyde grabs the shovel and follows him down to the gravesite.

The two of them slowly begin to circle around Mother's headstone like tightrope walkers searching for their footing.

"You feel them too, don't you?" the man asks, turning to Clyde.

"I think I do," Clyde says.

"Kind of a whisper or a bit of a twitch rising through the soles of my feet. I saw a dowser once. He was carrying a forked stick in his hands. I watched how he walked. It was a lot like I've learned to walk over this cemetery. You know, there are lots of unmarked graves all around here. People didn't always have the money to do right by those that died, especially if it was a little one. They usually just gave me money to dig close to someone in their family and put the baby there.

"Anyway, this dowser was walking, not talking, back and forth with that stick then all of a sudden he stopped and his stick started twitching and he said, dig here. And sure enough, there was water. You've got to be quiet to feel it. Got to quit talking, quit thinking and let yourself get connected to the earth."

"So many," Clyde says.

"Hmmm," the gravedigger replies.

They keep walking, circling, not talking. My mother puts her arm around my shoulders. I let myself be pulled close. It's a hot day, but the shadow of the big tree cools the air. Leaves rustle.

"Here?" Clyde calls out. He is standing at the edge of the shadow of the tree near the path where there are three stairs going down to the gravesite.

The gravedigger turns and moves deliberately to where Clyde is standing. Careful, it seems, to not miss anything. I hear him counting under his breath.

"I've counted thirty-seven graves, including the one I dug the other week. And, of course, Mother's. Did you count the babies?"

Clyde nods his head.

"I found thirty. Maybe thirty-five. Some are so small."

"My God," my mother whispers.

The gravedigger stands shoulder to shoulder with Clyde. The two of them fan their feet out on either side, brushing the grass with their shoes.

"Is it big enough?" Clyde asks.

The gravedigger takes his shovel and marks the area.

"It's a good spot. People will see it if they pass down this way."

"How deep should I dig?" Clyde asks.

"Clear the grass. Dig another three or four inches. You want the stone to sit comfortably. You'll need to pick out the pebbles and roots. Has to be a smooth bed so the marker won't rock, won't get broken if someone happens to step on it by accident."

While Clyde clears the area of grass and dirt, the gravedigger walks the plot again, stopping from time to time to stoop down, touch a spot here or there. My mother and I walk to the furthest edge where we buried Dad's ashes.

"This is where his mother is buried," I say, pointing to the spot where we saw her disappear. My mother puts her hand on my grandmother's grave.

"Do we know her name?"

"No."

My mother and I sit together by my father's site and watch as they carry the marker and set it into the ground.

"It's good," the gravedigger says. "A righteous thing to mark these poor soul's passing."

He puts the shovel back on his cart. He brushes the dirt from his clothes and wipes his face with his handkerchief then walks down the small lane to where the stone is set.

"I'd like to hear it," he says. "Read it out loud. Would you?"

He waves his hand, bidding my mother and me to join him. Clyde steps up to the lane to stand beside me. My mother squeezes my hand.

I step forward to read.

Buried here in unmarked graves are dozens of women and children who came to the Door of Hope seeking refuge and a safe haven.

May they rest easy knowing that they are remembered.

"And I will give her her vineyards from thence, and the valley of A'chor for a door of hope: and she shall sing there, as in the days of her youth, and as in the day when she came up out of the land of Egypt." Hosea 2:15

THIRTY-SEVEN

Clyde and I have settled into our seats on the train heading for Chicago. My mother is standing on the platform waving, throwing kisses. I lean against the window, throw a kiss back. Give her a smile.

The train lurches forward. She remains on the platform, waving. I wave back.

I blink and she is gone. I am gone from her. The train is moving down the track heading for Chicago. I wonder if we shouldn't be going to Florida, to fulfill my grandmother's wish to stand on the beach, feel the warmth of the sun, the gentle push of the ocean against her feet.

"He had to come back, didn't he," I say to Clyde.

"To be with her, with the three of them. Do you think he saw them, dreamed them the way you did?"

"If he did, he never told me," I say.

"I never told my mother about my father. About dreaming him. Seeing him that time in my room. Hoping to see him in the shadows. Wishing there was something left of him for me to hold onto. Is that crazy?"

"You could feel the babies? The women?"

"Yes, and every time I walked into our garage alone, I could feel my father in the same way. It's like there was something left of him. Not trapped, but left. Waiting, I guess to be felt."

"They were waiting for us," I say.

"So, what are you going to do now that your three companions are gone?"

"They're gone, aren't they?"

"Resting easy, now, I hope. Now that the work here is done."

"Hmmm." I brush the back of my hand against the coolness of the window. I watch the trees tick by like notes on a score. "I'm going to miss the three of them."

"So, what are you going to do all alone in the world?" Clyde asks.

"Get a job at the Art Institute."

"Doing what?"

"I'm not sure, but there's something about the museum that feels right. Sometimes, in my dreams, I would feel myself standing by the window in the Studebaker Building looking out at the Art Institute. I didn't know why or what I was looking at or looking for. And then, that day when I first thought I saw her in the museum, I tried to catch her. But I couldn't. At first I thought I had been wrong and she wasn't there at all. Then I heard her whisper something."

"What?" Clyde asks.

"Promise you won't think I'm crazy."

"I promise. What was it?"

This is why I came to Chicago. I wanted to see everything beautiful there was to see in the world. Know everything. Be here. Be here. Be here with you.

THIS BOOK IS DEDICATED TO

SUSAN (SUSIE) BROWN KNOWLES

Mother Knowles | Matron of the Door of Hope

PAUL KNOWLES

My father

and

MY FATHER'S BIRTH MOTHER

and all the other women who came to
The Door of Hope seeking refuge
and a safe haven

ACKNOWLEDGMENTS

I need to thank Trevor Moore for inviting me to participate in a special exhibition at the Brisbane Institute of Arts in 2017 in Brisbane, Australia. The name of the show was: *The Inevitable Past.*

I was initially flattered, then quite challenged by his notion that each of us in the show, all "dual" artists, should create new work bringing the various elements of our artwork together in order to address the idea that the past is, indeed, inevitable in our lives.

His challenge forced me to confront the story of my father's mother, my paternal grandmother, who has haunted me my whole life.

All I had to go on was the one story our father knew and told us about her. That she was a young woman who was found beaten and unconscious on the train station platform in Macon, Georgia. The woman had no identification on her and no one knew who she was. The police realized she was pregnant and took her to the Door of Hope. She remained unconscious. The doctor determined she was dying and decided to try to save the baby. The baby was my father.

I have always wondered what of her is part of me.

She is my inevitable past.

I am indebted to the amazing staff at the Genealogical Archives of the Washington Library in Macon, Georgia. Their expertise brought to life the history of the Door of Hope and the matron there, Mrs. Susan Knowles, who adopted and raised my father. I also want to thank Laurin Mauldin of Historic Macon who helped me find Mrs. Knowles' gravesite.

I need to thank Gene Hayworth, my publisher at Owl Canyon Press, for once again believing my writing deserves to have an audience. Thank you, Gene!

I want thank Peggy Payne, my good friend, fellow writer, and office mate, who read the book and pushed me to polish its rough edges.

My beautiful friends: Helen Ling, Sharon Lee, Jennifer Hamilton and Susan Gibson who read various drafts and sent their love and approval.

A loud shout out to my husband, Jeff Leiter, and our children, Neil, Hedy and Cole, who have always whole-heartedly supported my work as a writer.

And, last, but far from least, a big thank you to my amazing siblings:

Chuck Knowles, my younger brother, who was a stellar research assistant on this project. I couldn't have done it without you. Thank you.

My sister, Lolly Mindel, who, after reading the first draft, called to thank me for giving her a grandmother.

And, to my older brother, Gary Knowles, who told me that our father was the most amazing person he had ever known.

CPSIA information can be obtained
at www.ICGtesting.com
Printed in the USA
LVHW031302191121
703773LV00001B/52